Paterson's Plains

Lee Boehm

ISBN: 978-0-6459063-0-1
Paperback

Facebook: Lee Boehm – Author
Instagram: Lee_Boehm_Author

A catalogue record for this
book is available from the
NATIONAL
LIBRARY   National Library of Australia
OF AUSTRALIA

To Ann Clark, Alexander McKenzie,

Mary McKenzie, Thomas Beswick

and Jane Beswick.

This book is dedicated to you.

Thank you for making my children and I who we are today.

To my husband, Christopher, who listened to countless 'interesting' things as I discovered them and probably now knows as much about colonial Australia as I do and is and will be my faithful companion as I visit all the places that I write about to research my stories. Thankyou darling.

Thank you to all my beautiful friends, who, over the years have accepted me, validated me and loved me, and allowed me to be who I am, warts and all. You are my brothers and sisters of the heart.

Australian history is almost always picturesque.

indeed, it is so curious and strange,

that it is itself the chiefest novelty the country has to offer,

and so, it pushes the other novelties into second and third place.

It does not read like history,

but like the most beautiful lies.

And all of a fresh sort, no moldy old stale ones.

It is full of surprises and adventures,

an incongruity's, and contradictions, and incredibility's

but they are all truth,

they all happened.

The Wayward Tourist: Mark Twain's Adventures in Australia, originally published in 1897

Table of Contents

Chapter 1

Sydney, 1810

*A*nn Clark clambered awkwardly from the small boat and onto the shore at Sydney town. John, the young officer who had helped her to stay safe during the journey gave her a steadying hand that was a little firmer than would normally be expected, for this would be the last time that he would touch Ann, and he wanted it to last.

Ann could smell odd scents in the air. The smell of wood fire was familiar, but the groups of natives standing around the small fires along the shores as they came into the harbour, were not. The scent of human and animal excrement was very familiar. She had recently spent time at Newgate prison, and her hometown of Liverpool smelt similar, but there was another odd scent that she didn't know. It smelt a bit like wood, but also slightly sweet and astringent in quite a delicious manner. The scent wafted to her nostrils on the slight breeze and as she contemplated what it was, a leaf floated overhead and landed on her shoulder before falling to the ground. She bent to pick it up, made increasingly difficult by the bulk of the child inside her, and held it to her nose as the sweet, tangy new smell invaded her senses.

Ann had had plenty of time to think about her life to date while sailing on that wretched ship, the *Canada*, although the ship had been a relative dream compared to Newgate. It was almost six months since she had left England's shores at the end of March 1810.

"Right, you lot, stand over there to be counted, the surgeon needs to inspect you all." After several days of sitting in the harbour and watching all the preparations for disembarkation, Ann was herded with the other women to an area off the side of the shore, where a rather grand settlement was beginning to take shape. There were several buildings, some rather substantial, and she could see what looked like barracks, and row upon row of neat single storey whitewashed dwellings, their entries decorated with pots of red geraniums. Closer to the docks there were also many tents and hut type structures that seemed to be made from trees and mud.

"Right line up, if you're lucky you'll get outta here and off to ya new homes today."

John had warned Ann that on arrival the female convicts were paraded for inspection by the inhabitants of Sydney who, if they liked what they saw, would sign to take them on for the duration of their sentence, as maids, cooks, or free labour, and often as wives. There were still very few women in the colony and lots of men. The outcomes for the women were varied, with horror stories relayed by the sailors, but also stories of happy new lives.

While on the *Canada,* Ann had sat through many lessons from the ladies and gentlemen of the Missionary Society who were also travelling with them, and took it upon themselves to make sure that the women convicts were well versed in the Lord's bible and in moral fortitude, and what to expect in Sydney town.

John, a midshipman, and the 8th son of a Viscount from Cornwall had been able to keep Ann safe and healthy due to his position on the ship. Other women on the ship also formed similar relationships that guaranteed them the best berths, clothing, food, and companionship on the long voyage. While the senior officers and the Missionary Society members frowned on this behaviour, they all seemed to understand the transactional and positive results brought about by these friendships. Ann was even able to leave the ship twice on working parties to help collect supplies. Both times they were docked in warm, exotic places with sights and smells that Ann had never imagined in her wildest dreams. She saw the most wonderful animals with little faces that were almost humanlike and that happily ran alongside their owners, and people with dark skin and amazing colourful clothing. The colour in their clothing was only dampened by the blueness of the sky and the warmth in the air. In Liverpool she would occasionally see people such as these, who were doing business in the town after arriving in foreign ships, but mostly these lands were so very different to cold, dark England. She even got to taste a banana; a long yellow fruit encased in a thick skin that easily peeled off. The taste was like heaven.

While their relationship started as one of mutual benefit, Ann and John had grown to care for each other and it was with sadness that they parted ways in Sydney, particularly now that Ann was noticeably with child. While John patted her stomach and talked to his 'boy', they both knew that the child could also be a result of the many rapes that she had endured in her last few months at Newgate, after her money ran out, and then so did her luck and almost her life.

How she had managed to keep herself alive in Newgate was a miracle. For most of her time there Ann had financial help from her sister Mary and the friends who she had met during her short crime spree in Liverpool. But after a while this stopped coming. In Newgate, money talked, and while Ann had money, she was able to have some space to sleep and move, clothes and blankets to stay warm, clean water and enough food to survive. And protection from those in the prison who took their entertainment from harming other people, especially the young women. But once the money ran out her body was a free-for-all for every unsavoury character needing a lustful fix, prisoners, and guards alike. Any attempts to prevent the attacks were met with violence, and she had seen many girls die after those attacks, their bodies left to rot in a corner, sometimes for days, until a guard yelled for them to remove the offending mass. Funds which she thought might come from her father had not, and she realised that to him she was as good as dead now, after the troubles she had put him through.

"Surgeon Sir, this one is no good, no one is going to want to take on a lass with a new bairn," one of the soldiers who was supervising the 'exchange' of women noticed her bump and quickly caught the attention of the Ship's surgeon.

"Corporal, I assure you that Miss Clark would be found to be a very suitable servant for any of the settlers in this fine colony," said the Ships surgeon who had kept an eye out for Ann during the journey once it was discovered that she was with child. Although his concern was not all altruistic as his payment depended on the health of the passengers at the end of the journey.

"Aye, she's a pretty one, but no use as a maid with a bairn. Lass, go to the end of the line and join the crones and poorly lasses down there."

Ann gave a shy and sad wave to John who was now getting back onto the ship to continue his duties. She walked to the end of the line were several of the older women, pregnant women and a couple who were noticeably sick, were waiting. She knew that several of the other women on the ship were with child, but none were showing as she was, so could get away with it. As she watched, the women were picked off one by one and taken to a table to have their new assignments recorded before being taken off to God knew where with these strangers.

John had told her that it would be best for her if she could attract the attentions of a soldier as even the Private soldiers were greatly privileged in the new colony. Maybe not as well as the previous bunch who had got totally out of hand with corruption under the previous Governor, but they had all been sacked before Governor Macquarie arrived with his own impressive Regiment of Scottish Highlanders. Now Sydney town was full of the sounds of their rolling vowels and musical vocal expressions.

And it appeared to be true, as the soldiers were given first pick of the new women, followed by any free settlers and then convicts. Convicts nearing the end of their term were allowed to choose their own convict labourers in preparation of receiving their own land grants once they had Tickets-of-leave. Once they became TOL holders they were free to go about the town and earn a living as they wished, and with free land grants and convicts provided to work the land, many were becoming successful farmers, selling produce back to the government and quickly contributing to the growing population and success of the colony.

But this was not to be for Ann who was herded with the other 'rejects' to a boat which was much smaller than the ship she had been on but much larger than the boat that had brought her to shore. Ann was not too happy about another boat. Her whole body was wracked with an odd rolling sensation every time that she tried to stand still on the land, and she had been this way ever since she started her voyage in March. She imagined that this had something to do with being on the ship as others complained of the same ailment. The sailors had laughed at the unfortunates who spent the early part of the journey, and some poor wretches the whole journey, being violently ill off the side of the ship. She had a small amount of this early in the journey but had been told later by the older women that it could also have been the child inside her causing the sickness.

The rejected women spent the night huddled on the boat's deck. They were given ragged blankets for warmth; some had their own in trunks they had bought on the journey, and they were given bread and some kind of salty gruel to eat. In the morning the ferrymen loaded up any spare room on the deck with supplies and a few travellers also embarked, along with a few soldiers. The journey, which took them up a huge river, was long and took half of the day, but they finally arrived at their destination.

Their destination and their new home was the Parramatta Gaol, set amongst green rolling pastures, the top floor of which had been converted into a factory, and the women were put to work spinning and looming wool and cotton, and sewing items of clothing for the soldiers and convicts. At night they slept on the floor. Little was provided by way of clothing, blankets, cooking facilities or food, and Ann soon found that many of the women stayed at the nearby barracks and soldier's dwellings, where new 'transactional' relationships were formed, and in this way, the gaol didn't have to worry about housing or feeding them.

One afternoon Ann was outside the factory hanging clothes when she noticed a broad, chestnut haired and very handsome soldier sitting off to the side on a low stone wall. He was all alone and quietly whittling away at a piece of wood.

"Hello sir," she said shyly. It was hit or miss whether the soldiers would be civil and friendly to the women or if they would yell at them and be unkind.

"Well hallo lassie, and how are you this fine day then," he said with a half-smile and a twinkle in his eye.

"Oh well I guess I'm as good as I can be, Sir," said Ann. Which was truthful, as she had eaten a decent breakfast and had meat the night before, and good and bad days were marked by whether one had eaten well that day.

"The sun is shining, and my bones are warm," she added, smiling.

"And so-for your bairn will be warm too, Lassie. Not long to go then?"

This was a rather personal remark for a man to make, but The Factory Over the Gaol, as it was known, was not a place for airs and graces. Somehow Ann felt that she could trust this man, this soldier. She moved closer and confessed to him how scared she was for both hers and her baby's future, especially the birth. So many women and babies died in childbirth at the Factory that it was not unusual that she would be dwelling on her possible demise.

"Aye, you'll be fine lass, plenty of women before you have birthed wee bairns on their own, let alone with the help of widow Smales, the howdie in there," he nodded his head towards the factory.

Widow Smales was an older convict woman who had been a midwife in Scotland and carried on her calling in the Factory in exchange for extra privileges. Howdies, as they were known in Scotland, not only helped to bring forth healthy babes but took care of the traditions needed to bring good luck upon the babe. Sandy felt the women were in good hands with widow Smales.

Ann was about to contradict him as tears threatened to well up in her eyes just with the mere thought of childbirth, when he rose from his seating and, towering well above her, handed her the piece of wood that he'd been working on.

"My name's Sandy lass, Private Alexander McKenzie of the 73rd Regiment at your service', he gave her a mock bow. "Here lass, I've been seeing you around and watching your progress. I thought it must have been near your time. This is for the bairn and to give you good luck in the birthing."

Ann took the strange object proffered by her new acquaintance. It was an odd, shaped round object polished to precision and with a kind of belt carved around the middle of it with the words VINCERE AUT MORI.

"Tis a charm lass, for good luck with the birth."

"What do the words mean?" asked Ann.

"Ah lass they mean: to conquer or to die," when he saw the look of horror on her face he quickly added "but you will conquer of course, not the other."

Suddenly feeling embarrassed Sandy told her that he had to return to his lodgings as he had to report for duty soon.

"Well thank you, Sir."

"Sandy" he reminded her with a wink.

At that Ann blushed bright red, she could feel the heat rising from her chest through her neck and into her cheeks. This man was kind. But not only that he was tall and broad and unnervingly handsome. And she, Ann Clark, was only a poor pregnant female convict, one of many poor wretches in the Factory.

But, she thought, her gender was a prize in the colony, where men vastly outnumbered the women. Women were valued for not only the obvious comfort they could provide to a man, but to cook, clean and care for the domestic tasks a man needed done, and to provide the kind of soft comfort and companionship that only a woman could. And of course, to increase the population of the colony, which, the women in the Factory had told her, Governor Macquarie was much interested in.

After Sandy left, Ann sat in contemplation for a few minutes, the sweet smell of the trees tantalising her senses, as for the very first time she thought to herself that maybe, just maybe, this place might not be as bad as she thought it was going to be. The squawks from a flock of white cockatoo's overhead brought her out of her reverie and she quickly gathered her basket and headed back to the laundry.

Chapter 2

Parramatta, 1810

*I*t was the 6th of December 1810, and the spasms of pain came in
sudden then long-drawn-out waves, making Ann's mind draw into
itself and the surrounding world disappear. Oh Lord, how did any
woman survive such torture, how were any babies born afterwards.
Surely once one had endured this kind of pain you would never,
ever go back to do it again. But then this baby was not exactly
planned.

Widow Smales and some of the other women who were helping the
widow ran a wet cloth over her forehead between the waves of
agony and coo-ed soft, encouraging words to her. Still, she couldn't
shake the terrifying feeling that these might be her last hours on
earth, in unbearable pain, tossing and turning, moaning, and
howling like an animal.

Since she had been at The Factory she had helped to carry the
bodies of the women who hadn't made it through their child births,
usually along with the tiny scraps of humanity they had brought
forth who also died. The unmarked graves out the back of the goal
were numerous.

She had helped to rock and sooth the motherless babes who lived
their early years in the two rooms in the Factory where children
were kept, while the highly sought after wet nurses fed them. The
title wet nurse was a stretch, as they were just other convict women
who had either lost their babies or they were weaned, and they
received larger rations for their 'work'. With their large bosoms

some of these women made extra rations and supplies selling their charms to the local soldiers and settlers, as many of the other women also did. These extra rations usually included supplies of rum, which also helped to make the babies sleep well.

In between the agonising spasms Ann began to think back across her life so far and how she had come to be where she was, living in The Factory at Parramatta, so very far away from her home.

Ann had brought so much hope and promise into the lives of her parents when she was born two days after Christmas in 1792. Her parents, Thomas and Ann, were natives of Liverpool, Lancashire and were both aged 21 when Ann was born. Liverpool was a huge city built around one of the biggest shipping ports in the world. The city had a large population which included people from many different countries and cultures, either living or passing through with the ships, with many different accents and clothing styles to be seen and heard daily. When Ann was born the town was bustling with newly built houses of brick and stone, very similar to London's newer areas. The streets were well paved and on any given day there was an abundance of people going about their business or leisure, those who were well dressed and fashionable, merchants, bankers and seamen, and those inhabitants who were not so fortunate.

As with all of England, the poor of Liverpool lived in dreadful conditions. Their houses were overcrowded, and the streets were filthy with no sewers, only cesspits. The worst were the cellar dwellings where the poorest people lived in cellars under buildings. Often, they slept on piles of straw because they couldn't afford beds.

While Ann and her parents were not 'cellar dwellers' they were not living on the fashionable streets either. Both had worked in the

11

factories looming and weaving cotton into cloth, since they were children.

One morning, when Ann was about six years old, her mother would not wake when Ann went to her bed for a cuddle after she had woken. Her mother's skin was burning hot and her lips dry and cracked. That, thought Ann, is one of the only memories that she still had of her mother.

Somehow, Ann must have alerted the neighbours and been taken in for the day while others sent for her father, who was already at work. From then on Mother was gone and it was just her, her father, and her little sister Mary, born the year after she was. During the day, Father paid the old ladies in the street to watch the girls while he worked. He was gone before daylight and home well after the sun went down. The old ladies made sure that the girls had at least one meal per day but that was the main extent of their care. On Sundays the girls and their father would attend church and afterwards would stroll down to the river, or attend the markets to purchase supplies, or on the best days they would take a picnic and eat and play in the park. On those days Father smiled and joined in on their make-believe games, pretending to be the fashionable ladies who they saw in carriages or strolling the city promenades with their beaus on their arms. Those were the best days.

Life was hard and there were few privileges in Ann's life. Cotton workers were considered well off if they could house, clothe, and feed themselves, and on only one wage, Ann's father struggled to provide for his little family. As soon as she turned 13, Ann joined her father at the factory. She also learned a little tailoring from the older workers and became quite skilled at sewing basic garments. Ann's sister Mary soon joined her and the two would spend their evenings at home doing private tailoring work to supplement the family income.

One day when Ann was 16 and Mary 15, their father became ill and was bedridden for many weeks. There were doctor's bills to pay, medicines to procure, and rent and food to pay for, all without Thomas' income, and the girl's income alone did not cover the payments that needed to be made. It was at this time that one of their workmates suggested a way to boost their income while their father was sick. It was a risky proposition but could be a way to get them out of their debt and to stop their poor father worrying himself into his grave. All that Ann and Mary had to do was take just a little extra cloth when they were cutting the lengths for their tailoring work. By this time the girls were well trusted by the foremen and as their father was well respected so were they. So, this they did. It was easy to skim off an extra yard which was not even missed, no one having any suspicion to look for it. Piece by piece the lengths of cloth paid off what was owing and then allowed the girls to purchase the remedies that the doctor said could help Father. In time, Father rallied and returned to work. But the new 'hobby' acquired by the girls was too good to give up. They explained away their news dresses and pretty things as being the spoils of their tailoring, or gifts from admirers.

Their luck ran out in June 1808 when the girls were caught selling cloth to a police officer working undercover to catch thieves, particularly those selling stolen cloth, which was something of an epidemic in Liverpool. By this time, they were also procuring and selling small sewing items such as needles, thread, and scissors. On 26 July 1808, the sisters were convicted at the Liverpool sessions, with Mary sentenced to three months and Ann to six months in prison, Mary got less time as the haul that she was caught with did not include a pair of expensive brass scissors which Ann had been caught with.

Ann and Mary were sent to Preston prison, a new prison in Lancashire and a new concept. Preston took mostly first-time thieves, beggars, and petty criminals into their 'House of Corrections' with the aim of turning their lives around to re-enter society as valuable citizens. Most prisoners had been sentenced to less than two years. While at Preston the girls spent long days looming and weaving, which was no hardship for them as they had been used to that in their workplace. They shared a cell together, while Mary was there, and the food while basic, was more than they'd had while Father was ill.

Ann arrived back home after her incarceration to find both Father and Mary much aggrieved at her, blaming her for the state of things. While Father retained his job he had been demoted and had less money coming in. Mary had been unable to find a job anywhere. Their situation had become dire, with debts building up. Unable to find work herself, Ann fell in with a group of people in similar circumstances who were surviving by buying cloth from the workers at the factories who had stolen it, and then on-selling it. This provided far less risk to the workers. Ann initially borrowed money for her first purchase but was able to pay it back quickly as she sold the product at a profit. This went swimmingly for a month or so, but her luck soon ran out again in March 1809 when, along with her new friend Elizabeth McCallum she was convicted of stealing two pieces of printed cotton and sentenced to be transported for 7 years. Her partner in crime was sent to prison for two years. Others on the same day with similar offences got only three or six months, but this was not Ann's first offence.

And so ended the crime spree of Ann Clark.

Ann reflected on all of this in between the agonising contractions as her babe made his way into the world. Widow Smales was all smiles as she smacked the tiny creature on the bottom as he emerged, howling, and flailing his arms around as if trying to grab the air for stability.

"Aye lassie, you've a bonnie laddie, with a very loud expression I'll say" laughed the widow, while checking with an eagle eye to ensure that no-one had closed any windows or doors while she was busy. Any evil spirits must have easy passage away from the babe.

Ann looked up from her laying position, the site of her agonies, to see her new son carried to her and placed on her chest. His crying stopped and like a little old man who had just woken from a long nap he screwed his eyes up against the offending light while searching her face and staring intently at her. His lips made tiny motions as he tried out his muscles, and he then settled into a quiet contemplation of his mother and his near surrounds.

Ann's first thought was "Oh, how extraordinary. I'm still alive." Her next instinct was to reveal her bosom to feed the new babe. John (how else could he be named) settled in hungrily for his first meal and with the women fussing around her and bringing her tea and bread, Ann settled in to a relaxed and contented rest.

Over the next few weeks John thrived, and when it was found that Ann had a talent for tailoring, she was quickly put to work teaching the other women. Garment making skills were in huge demand in the colony where everything had to be made 9,000 miles from England. Replacements for the soldier's uniforms were always needed, as was clothing for the convicts, most of which were made at The Factory.

Parramatta, 1811

It was after Christmas before Ann was able to take in a short stroll outside of the main building with little John, at a time when Sandy McKenzie was out looking eagerly for her, as he had been since their last meeting.

She saw him almost hop, skip, and jump across the yard towards her with a smile on his face that softened his strong features.

"Aye lassie, it's me Sandy," he beamed as he galumphed over to her.

Ann giggled "I know who you are," she said shyly.

"Well, look who we have here a wee young un, newly hatched," he laughed and tickled John under the chin. John stared at him with big blue eyes, interested in this new, deep voiced person.

"Well," said Sandy, "I've been looking for ye ever since that last time we met, and I've been praying to the Lord every night for your safe delivery. I spoke to some of the other girls who said you was doing well which made me happy, but I've been waiting to see you in person to make sure," he said enthusiastically.

This was not the talk of a man only 'interested' in a convict, this was the talk of a man who was enamoured.

Ann self-consciously ran her hand down her skirt, smoothing the fabric across her now flat stomach.

"May I?" asked Sandy, gesturing to little John, who was staring at him and coo-ing happily.

"Oh yes," said Ann "please. John seems quite taken with you."

"Aye, he's a bonnie lad, eyes like the sea." Sandy tickled John under his chin again and coo-ed gently as he held him in his strong arms.

"Do you have children of your own Sir, ummm Sandy?" asked Ann. While Sandy was well built and fine featured, she could tell that he was not in the first flush of youth, and probably not much younger than her own father.

"Nay lass, family life was not for me sadly. I chose the life of a soldier, and that life has taken my youth, and I never thought it fair to take a wife while doing the soldiering, it's not an easy life to be a soldier's wife." Sandy was quiet after he told her this information, contemplating what might have been.

Ann looked up coyly from under her lashes which was not difficult as Sandy towered a good foot above her "Well," she said "You're not dead yet. There's still time you know."

Sandy stopped rocking the babe and stared at Ann as if she had come out with some huge revelation that he had never even considered. In the same instance that he was taken aback, he was also drawn forward by the very idea that he, Sandy McKenzie, career soldier, could actually have a family. Could have a woman who loved him. Not just a woman, he'd had plenty of them over the years in ports all over the world. But a companion, a friend to live his life with. He had always thought that was beyond him.

Softy he said, "What are you saying lassie?" as he held his breathe waiting for her reply.

"I'm saying Sir, Sandy! That we are both here and I know that I am lonely, and I hazard a guess that you are too, and maybe we could help each other to not feel so lonely."

Sandy stared as her for a moment, shocked at her forthrightness. But also, more enamoured by the minute. This girl, who he had noticed in her bland convict garb, heavily pregnant and struggling over laundry, was more beautiful that any woman he had ever seen, and he, the big, tough, war hardened Sandy McKenzie of Fodderty was, for the first time in his 39 years, in love.

"Well lassie, that is quite a proposition, but I don't even know your name," Sandy laughed.

"Ann. My name is Ann Clark. I was born in Liverpool on 27 December 1792, and I stole some cloth and that is why I am here. I can weave and loom cloth and I can also make garments. That's what I'm doing at the Factory, teaching other girls to make clothing." This all came out in a quick outburst and Ann realised that she was maybe trying too hard to sell herself to this fine man who she had barely met.

"Well then Ann" said Sandy handing young John back to his mother, "let me take a little time to think on this idea of yours," Ann suddenly felt glum and worried that she had overstepped.

"And before I forget," Sandy reached into his pocket a withdrew a small item and pressed it into John's tiny palm, which closed over the object.

"What is that?" asked Ann concerned.

"Aye it's an Indian rupee, a coin, not even silver, but I thought it might do for here in the colony, where coins are rare to find."

"But why," said Ann.

"Well lassie, it's a Scottish tradition. It's meant to ensure that young John here has a long and prosperous life," he said moving slightly closer, "And if he's going to be my son, then I certainly hope that is what his future will bring." He winked at her, waved, and then broke into a happy trot as he left to return to his barracks.

Ann's stomach did a flip and her heartbeat faster. This man was certainly fine, and fun. Her fortunes seemed to be turning and in such a lovely way.

Chapter 3

$\mathcal{T}$he Parramatta Barracks were poorly built in 1790 and by 1810 were in such disrepair that they were starting to fall apart. Convicts spent a large part of 1810 trying to repair the damage, but it became apparent that it was irreparable. Governor Macquarie declared that he would be approving a complete rebuild of the barracks but until such time as that was possible soldiers were to find their own accommodations near the barracks.

This worked well for Sandy and Ann who moved into their dwelling soon after the declaration, in early 1811. Their two room, dirt floor dwelling was close to both The Factory and the barracks. Governor Macquarie approved Sandy to be assigned Ann and by the end of 1811, having proven herself a capable tailor and tutor and able to support herself financially, she was given an unconditional pardon and made a free woman.

This turn of fortune was only possible because, as one of his priorities, Governor Macquarie, who like Sandy was also a Scotsman, wanted the colony to be quickly self-sufficient and that meant families and children to explore, develop and expand the British interests. He encouraged relationships between the arriving women, who were mostly convicts; and the men in the settlement, be they soldiers, free men, tradesmen, or convicts. He was happy to grant pardons to women who entered into partnerships with the men of the colony. However, in 1812 the governor's ability to grant pardons was removed. Ann had been very lucky.

Ann continued her work at The Factory, tutoring the women in tailoring skills, but for a small wage, and she was able to take John along with her. John sat amongst the women or crawled around the fabric while they went about their work. Everyone loved bouncing blue eyed Johnny, and he was never without a lap to cuddle on.

The relationship between Ann and Sandy grew by the day. Sandy had turned 40 on 26 June and was completely in love with his darling 'wife' and his lovely 'son'. He was enjoying having a home of his own to come to after a hard day at work overseeing convict work gangs, sitting on the porch enjoying a meal and a cup of tea and talking about his day, and her day, with Ann. He enjoyed dandling Johnny on his knee and singing him old songs from Scotland that he remembered from his childhood. John had started to laugh and wave his arms in delight when he was amused by something and this in turn made both Sandy and Ann laugh. Life was good.

Ann, at 18, was glad to have a place to call home and a protector for her and her son. Sandy was a solid, stable, and loyal 'husband', and surprisingly given his size and profession, a tender lover, who always made her feel cherished and wanted. She knew how lucky she was, many women who came to the colony when she did were still at The Factory and might be for years and years unless they somehow found an escape route like she had. She had also heard stories of some of the girls from the *Canada* who had initially been assigned to men and who had been badly abused. Some had been re-convicted of crimes and some had died.

Towards the end of 1811 Sandy came home with the news that he was being moved back to Sydney, and he was allowed to take Ann and John, who now both carried the McKenzie surname, with him.

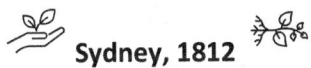

Sydney, 1812

They arrived in Sydney at a time of much activity. Governor Macquarie was determined to turn the town into a 'city' rather than a prison and had embarked on many and varied public works. The entire city plan was changed from narrow, winding alleys and laneways to wide streets and roads set out on a grid pattern. The roads that had previously been named for their inhabitants or landmarks where renamed; Sergeant Majors Row became George Street, Governors Row became Bridge Street, Stream Row became Pitt Street. Large well-built government buildings went up in record time, and extravagant buildings owned by merchants and traders, as their places of business and their homes, were going up on every corner. Ann was delighted to see the beautiful Hyde Park which had only been completed in 1811 and was already a popular location for horse racing, weekend picnics and other entertainments.

Ann's reputation as a tailor preceded her, and on her arrival, she was tracked down to the small abode that she and Sandy had been assigned, by the owner of a tailoring business who asked if she would come and work for him at his shop in Macquarie Place. As the shop was still close to the barracks it was considered a good idea for the couple.

Ann was excited to find out that she would be paid in the new currency, that had only just started circulation in the colony. To quell the rise in rum being used as currency, and the associated corruption that it had brought the colony, the British Government has sent ten thousand pounds worth of Spanish dollars to be used as currency. To make them stretch further and to make them unique to the colony, Governor Macquarie had arranged for a convict forger to cut out the centre of each coin making the outer ring worth the original five shillings and the inner circle worth fifteen pence. Ann would now be able to put away her pay and start a nest egg for herself.

Having only seen uniforms, calico, and plain cottons since her arrival in the colony, Ann marvelled at what was available in Sydney. Mr Smith's tailor shop was not far from Lord's store. The giant warehouse was owned by Simeon Lord, an ex-convict who, once freed, had made a fortune using his superior business talents. Ann stood with her mouth agape at the goods on display. There were tablecloths, silk handkerchiefs, ribbons, combs, pins, needles, thread, buttons, jewellery, shoes, and everything else that one could need. But Ann was most excited at the exquisite range of ready-made dresses for ladies, straight from Bond Street in London.

In High Street stood the glamorous store owned by Edward and Sarah Wills which also sold an array or amazing products and clothing. Edward had been a convict and Sarah was one of the few wives who had accompanied her husband to the colony. On arrival Edward had been assigned to Sarah, a free settler. This caused problems because a wife was not able to own land or sign contracts, and neither could a convict. To get around this, the Government treated such wives as single women and as such, they had the same rights as the male settlers in the colony. The Wills had then set about creating a retail dynasty for themselves.

Within six months, Ann had employed several other young men and women and was left with only the most complicated tasks and the management of the employees. Her employer, Mr Smith, was so happy with what she had done for his business he allowed the rooms above the shop to be part of her employment package and the young family moved from their meagre barracks dwelling into the much nicer rooms above the shop, although Ann said she was sad to be leaving her friend Mary Taylor. Mary had also come out on the *Canada*, and arrived very unwell, joining the other 'rejects' at

Parramatta. She had been lucky enough to catch the eye of Sandy's Sergeant, Donald Sutherland, and had moved to Sydney with him at the same time as the McKenzie's. Ann had gone to tell Mary the news when Mary flung herself into Ann's arms crying. Donald was being sent to Port Dalrymple, the new area being settled in Van Diemen's Land, and a primitive and remote outpost with little in the way of facilities. Ann commiserated with her and was glad that so far Sandy had got to stay here in Sydney.

Sandy's work involved supervising convict construction gangs and policing the Sydney town area. His days were long and tiring but he was allowed Sunday's off and on those days the family made good use of the new public facilities around the town. The Regiment had started organising horse races and that became a regular day out for the family and the rest of Sydney, along with picnics by the water to watch the ships in the harbour.

1812 went by quietly and steadily for Sandy, Ann, and little John. Sandy was still enthralled by his beautiful, young bride and set out at every chance to show her how much he loved her and how much she meant to him. Ann, in turn, grew in confidence and felt at peace with her life and her choices. What, she thought with a giggle, would life have been like if she hadn't stolen that cloth? Years and years of 13-hour days slaving over the looms in a dark and dingy factory, to go home in cold and dreary weather to an equally dark and dingy hovel. And one illness could be the death of you. Not for her. She may have arrived in an odd and challenging way, but the warmth and openness, the friendships, and the fresh air in the colony was the most beautiful thing she had so far experienced in her young life.

One Sunday evening the little family were sitting in Hyde Park as the sun went down, watching Johnny running around laughing and playing with other children. There was warmth still in the air, but a gentle breeze wafted through the trees and the stars sparkled overhead in the clear sky. The night was further enhanced by the scent of the newly planted flowers and bushes, and the far away but still audible drumming and clapping from the natives' camps as they carried out their ceremonies along the beaches.

"Lassie," said Sandy, "I may be wrong, but I imagine this is what heaven must be like."

Ann reached for his strong hand and held it to her lips as she gazed into his eyes, and she too imagined that this was what it must be like.

Little Johnny had not long turned two and was now running around the house and shop and babbling questions in his baby language when Ann felt that something was again very different in her body. It was not long after the end of year celebrations, which for the first year of her life, had included a Christmas feast that she though was fit for a Queen, courtesy of her employer and now friends Mr Smith and his wife Emily. The Smith's welcomed the McKenzie's into their home and other acquaintances had also attended. It was a joyous day and Ann felt she was fit to burst after the delicious meal that included real beef and not kangaroo stew for once, real ham from England and a huge plum pudding with custard.

And then once Christmas was over, the Hogmanay celebrations started. Ann was interested to know that in Scotland, Christmas was not celebrated and hadn't been since the 17th century, being considered a Catholic holiday and a reminder of atrocities carried out by the Catholic church.

And considering that the Governor and most of his men were all Scottish, Hogmanay was celebrated with great gusto in the fledgling new colony where any excuse for a party was welcome amongst the citizens, of all backgrounds. The native people seemed to enjoy the fairs and other celebrations as much as the colonists, seeming to be a people who revelled in regular ceremonies and celebrations in their own culture and were happy to participate in the colonist celebrations when they were invited.

On the day there were many traditions to be carried out, which Ann watched with interest. The holiday was traditionally a celebration of rebirth, as the old year ends and the new year begins. Sandy emptied the hearth and insisted that they clean the house from top to bottom.

A fair was held during the day at Hyde Park with poets and singers, puppeteers and contortionists all providing a colourful array of fun.

That evening, those not invited to the Governor's ball partook in progressive feasts from house to house, where gifts were exchanged and at least one bottle of whiskey was drunk at each stop. At midnight when the Scotsmen and women were all rolling drunk the town erupted with renditions of Robert Burns' famous Auld Lang Syne, sung in many different pitches and tunes.

It was not long after the new year's celebrations that Ann had the same queasy feeling that she had when she was pregnant with Johnny, and her breasts were so tender, she squealed if someone accidentally brushed past her, or Johnny lunged at her for a cuddle. Having been together now for two years with no signs of a baby, both Sandy and Ann had concluded that God was not going to bless them with their own. And it certainly wasn't for want of trying, as both Sandy and Ann had discovered that they took great enjoyment from the physical side of their 'marriage'. There were many nights when young Johnny was shuffled off to bed early so that his parents could indulge in their lovemaking as the sun went down and until the moon was high in the sky.

Sandy leapt into a strange Scottish jig when Ann told him the news.

"My own bairn," he said over and over "My own bairn. Lassie, you have made me the happiest man alive, I thank God every day that he put you and I in that same God forsaken place at the same time." He went around with a grin on his face for months.

Ann had an easy pregnancy, working and tutoring right up until a few weeks before the midwife deemed that she was due to birth the baby. Although she was huge and cumbersome, the weeks before the birth were boring for Ann. She was still only 21 and full of the energy of youth, and having been busy all her life, was loathe to sit around doing nothing.

For the past year Mr Smith's spinster sister had, for a small wage, been watching Johnny so that Ann could carry out her work in peace without a toddler getting in the way all the time. Miss Smith had decided to join her brother and sister-in-law in the colony after their parents died but had an unfortunate accident onboard the ship. A bucket of hot tar had accidentally spilled over a higher deck and onto where Miss Smith was standing admiring the ocean view. Sadly, the left side of her face had been badly scarred from the burn, and she had resolved herself to a life of spinsterhood. Luckily children are not so harsh in their judgement as adults, and after Johnny had asked in a matter-of-fact way why her face was 'angry', he was satisfied with her answer and loved her just as much as he would any other carer. Miss Smith usually wore a scarf across her head to partially cover her scars but if Johnny caught another child staring, he would hug her tight and kiss her scarred cheek.

Mary Ann McKenzie was born on 23 August 1813 just as the sun was rising and after an interesting night. Sandy was awoken from his slumber with an urgent request to 'Go get the midwife' and a kick on his butt as Ann writhed in bed. Once the midwife arrived Sandy was unceremoniously evicted from his house with little Johnny and sat in the shop until Mr Smith and Miss Smith arrived around 7am.

Their arrival coincided with Mary's first lusty cry which they all heard from downstairs and celebrated joyously with cups of tea (with a little rum for the new father and Mr Smith).

Four weeks later little Mary, named for her mother's beloved sister, was baptised at St John's Church of England at Parramatta. The little family travelled out by coach for the day and along with the Smith's and several of Ann and the Smith's customers held a small garden party in the grounds of the church. St John's was chosen, rather than the newer St Phillips in Sydney, because it was in the grounds of St John's that Sandy first saw and fell in love with Ann. Ann had no recollection of this. Not being a particularly religious woman, she had only felt the relief on Sunday's of being allowed outside of The Factory.

On the day, Sandy had his formal uniform on and Ann a beautiful dress that she had made for herself with fabric gifted her by Emily. This was a frequent occurrence as it was good for business for customers to see the fabrics and styles that could be created for them at Smith's. Ann, and some of the other employee's gifted with suitable figures, were nor only their tailors and seamstress' but also their models. And little Mary was dressed in the most adorable baptism dress in the colony. The dress was on loan from the business and was made with the finest French lace. Mr Smith had procured the expensive and scarce material over the past year for just such a garment, to showcase to the mothers of the colony the kind of work that his business could achieve for their little darling's special day.

Life settled into domestic bliss for the little family, and all seemed well. Sandy and Ann's relationship had moved into a more mature phase. The first flush of lust had moved into more of a deep love for Sandy and a warm affection by Ann, who felt she was still too young to understand what real love was, and too busy to think much about it. They certainly enjoyed each other's company and all that a marriage involved, and Sandy was a good and kind husband and an attentive father to both Mary and little John. Ann had adopted the name McKenzie for both her and her son since moving from Parramatta, and Sandy entered the family's details on the yearly census as McKenzie's. Reverend Marsden and the other clergy were far too busy with all the other activities that their jobs entailed to be constantly marrying all the new couples in the colony, and it was usual for common law marriages to be established and accepted.

Unfortunately, Sandy's Regiment had fallen out of favour with Governor Macquarie. Several of the officers, including Sandy's favourite Lieutenant David Rose, who he had served with over several campaigns, had been accused of being involved in gaining a financial advantage because of their status in the colony. Major Gordon had sunken into drunken debility which saw him hospitalised, and Lieutenant Rose was one of several officers who performed his duties while he was incapacitated.

One evening Sandy and Ann were enjoying a cup of tea by the fire when they heard a sharp knock at the door. This was not unusual because Smith's had gained a reputation of being able to handle even the most urgent and desperate tailoring needs at all hours of the day or night, thanks to Ann being on site. However, after Sandy went down to check, Ann heard the low rumbles of Scottish male voices travelling up the stairs.

"Ann, my sweet love, it's Lieutenant David, do we have some pudding to spare for the likes of him?" he called up the stairs.

"Of course, we do my love," said Ann. David was one of her favourites who always had a kind word for her and made the children laugh with his funny antics. Lieutenant Rose was about 10 years older than Sandy and had provided him with sound brotherly advice for all the years that they had soldiered together, and a warm friendship had developed between them.

The three of them settled into the cosy armchairs by the fire as Ann served warm apricot pudding with custard and real Scottish whisky in real glasses for the men. Reverend Marsden warned of the evils of alcohol and Major Gordon was surely a perfect example of that, but Scotsmen (and the women too) didn't seem capable of discussions without a small dram.

"Sandy, I've come here to warn ye," said David. "Macquarie is about to announce that he is over with the 73rd and they are soon to be sent from the colony."

"Aye Sir," said Sandy "I've been hearing word amongst the men, and I can't say I am surprised."

"No," said David "and enough of that Sir with ye too, I am no longer Lieutenant Rose but plain David Rose, I took my discharge last month."

"Aye ye never," said Sandy smacking David on the shoulder. "Well lad ye'll be on the next ship out of this place then, and back to England?"

"Well Sandy, I will be on the next ship out of this godforsaken Sydney town but only as far as Hobart. I've been granted land in the new settlement of Port Dalrymple to the north, and Sandy, this is what I've come to tell ye, you should come with me. Your time has got to be up with the Regiment and you have this beautiful wee family now. Take ye discharge and follow me to Port Dalrymple and we can start farming together."

Sandy laughed a great long guffaw and slapped his knee, eliciting an amused but annoyed 'Shoosh!" from Ann as she heard the baby stir in the next room. She had only put tiny Mary down after her last feed and the last thing they all needed was a tired screaming baby at this hour that was generally filled with peace and quiet after their busy days.

"And woot lad, do ye know aboot farming?', Sandy laughed. "I know ye know everything there is to know aboot soldiering and fighting and leading men, but I don't think you, or I for that matter, know the first thing aboot farming. For gawds sakes man, I doubt ye'd know the feeding end of a cow from the..."

"And that's about enough," said Ann with a giggle. "We all know which end of a cow does what."

"Aye Sandy, but that's the beauty of it, the land is given free for us soldiers and we are given convicts to help settle and farm. Convicts 'on stores' Sandy, we don't even have to pay for their keep. It's an opportunity man. I'll no go back to England, lad, or Scotland. There's nothing for either of us there anymore. Nothing but hunger and cold, disease and death." David rubbed the side of his temple as if just thinking of returning to England was painful.

"Aye, that much I know" said Sandy slowly.

"Sutherland is already there, well he has been, and he says it's just like Scotland, Sandy. Ye can ask him yerself as he's on his way back here now having been recalled for the next lot of duties, whatever they be."

The men sat in quiet contemplation for a few moments.

"But" said Ann tentatively "what happens now if you don't go to Hobart with David?"

"Lass, I owe the Regiment two more years before I can leave," he said softly.

"So," she said again more insistently "What does that mean for us Sandy."

"What it means lass," said David passionately "is that you will all be moved with the Regiment to whatever new godforsaken hell hole that the King decrees we need to conquer," He turned to Sandy and quietly said "more death Sandy, more hardship."

Ann drew a sharp breath.

"I don't have a choice, David." Sandy spat the words, forgetting the Sir in his sorrow.

"Ye do man," said David softly, "I can get ye out of your contract tomorrow, I can get ye out of those two years and you and I, and Ann," he said nodding towards a very concerned looking Ann, "can start a whole new life in a whole new land. Paid for by the King! Finally, we can reap the fruits of our labours. God knows we have earned it after all the years that we have loyally served him."

Sandy took a deep breath. "You know man I canna do that."

"Why not?" said Ann, by this time quite agitated with concern for their future.

"Murtagh," said David.

"Murtagh" said Sandy.

They looked at each other and nodded.

"Who in damnation is Murtagh, and what has he got to do with our lives Sandy?" said Ann getting more and more upset by the minute.

What was this all about. What was Sandy saying. She knew that eventually they may have to return to England with his Regiment, and she had settled herself to this notion. With her skills and references from some of the best people of Sydney she would be able to possibly buy herself a small shop back in England and her children would never need to work in the factories like she had to do.

But this new option of staying in the colony, in a new settlement, sounded like moving to the moon. Another upheaval as bad as her move to the colony in the first place. Now that she had a taste of a decent life, life in a town where there were people and parks and shops and doctors available, she had no intention of ever leaving that again to venture to some wild unsettled land across more oceans.

She had heard horrific stories of journeys to Hobart and to the Norfolk Island settlement, places much more primitive than Sydney was when she arrived. Her work involved making beautiful garments for the gentry of Sydney. How would she do that in a new settlement? And in Sydney her children could attend schools and play with and grow up with other children, good children from good families. Who would they grow up with in this new land, the natives?

"Eh lass, Murtagh was like a brother. We joined the Regiment together from Dumfries in the Highlands. Murtagh took care of me, and we fought in some fierce battles together. He always looked out for me and made sure I was safe. He talked often about when we discharged and how we would settle back in the Highlands together and raise bairns and farm the land."

"What happened to him?" asked Ann softly.

"He died." He said matter-of-factly, and with a sad expression. "He died in my arms at Maratha in 1804. He made me promise that I would fulfil my time with the Regiment as he would have done. And, so, I must fulfil his dying wish lass."

"Oh," said Ann, not knowing what else to say.

"Aye, I understand lad," said David, standing now. "But when you do leave, then come looking for me. I'll write you lad. I'll tell you how I'm doing."

The two men shook hands and looked searchingly into each other's eyes.

"Aye, do that David," said Sandy.

David stepped across and grasped Ann's hand, warmly and securely.

"You take care, lass. This man will do you right."

"Thank you" said Ann, not sure if that was the case.

Sandy walked David down the stairs and out into the night. He took a while to come back to the room where Ann sat confused and worried.

"What does this mean for us Sandy?" she asked as he sat back down.

"I dinna know yet lass, I dinna know. But once I do you will be the first to know." He walked over and kissed her gently on the forehead and indicated to the bed. They were both feeling troubled so melting into the safety and security of each other's arms was exactly what they needed.

Chapter 4

Ceylon, 1814

*S*andy was chosen for the advance party that was to depart for

Ceylon in January 1814.

There were many discussions held between Sandy and Ann in the months beforehand. Almost all the wives and children of the Regiment's soldiers had decided to go with their men to Ceylon, including Mary with Donald Sutherland, newly arrived back from Port Dalrymple with their own little John born in October the year before.

It was common practice for families to accompany the soldiers, but it was highly dangerous for all. While their journey would be better provisioned and they would be much better treated than on their original journey to New South Wales, the dangers of life at sea would be the same. Long, long, never ending days with heat, discomfort, and sickness. Ann had been told that Ceylon had the same climate as some of the places they had stopped on her journey out, and while the heat had been soothing for a day or two, the sticky climate would be unbearable if you were stuck there for unknown periods. And all that with a newborn and a toddler.

But what else could she do?

She knew that she didn't need Sandy's money to survive. The money that she got from the Smith's and from some private arrangements in her own time, meant there was plenty for her and the children to have a decent life. So why should she go with him? The Smiths were happy for her to stay and continue her arrangement with them. They didn't need her to have a husband to be an asset to them and their business, and a friend. Miss Smith expressed with many tears, how her life would not be worth living without her little Johnny and little Mary to care for.

Even Sandy started to talk to her about the perils of following a soldier to the battlefield. If she and the children survived the journey (as many died of typhoid, an ever-present peril at sea), they would be living in a foreign land, under tentage or worse and would barely see Sandy, if at all.

So, it was decided. Ann and the children would stay. She would continue working for the Smith's and as soon as Sandy had fulfilled the term he was obligated to serve, he would return to Sydney, and they would resume their lives together.

Christmas 1813 was a joyous affair in Sydney town, although sad and subdued for the McKenzie's. Due to the extremely warm weather, it was decided to celebrate the day with a picnic at the park and several other families agreed. Oh, how different it all was from an English Christmas, all snow and cold.

Tables and chairs were carried from houses and businesses near Hyde Park, and food was transported from multiple kitchens so that an amazing spread was laid out for all the attendees. For so many people so far from extended families, their new friends had become their family in the colony. The children played their games together on the lawn and the men played informal games of cricket to pass the time in the afternoon. The women, who had mostly cooked the amazing spread that everyone was enjoying, sat talking quietly, worked on their tapestries, reading, or napping if left alone for long enough to succumb.

Sandy departed Sydney on 24 January 1814, aboard the ship *Earl Spencer*. Lieutenant Colonel (formerly the hospitalised Major) George Gordon had rallied from his previous incapacity to command the Regiment again and travelled with the advance party of 350 souls.

The eight-week journey was uneventful for Sandy, who, like the other lads, spent their days attending to their kit and cleaning their weapons, helping with the manual labour onboard the ship and trying to keep out of the sweltering heat. As Sandy had feared, the fever broke out onboard the ship during the journey. One soldier and two wives died and several of the children. Sandy felt relieved that his family were safely back in Sydney.

On arrival, the advance party were put to work getting the primitive barracks in Colombo ready for the rest of the Regiment who would arrive in 5 ships over the next 12 months. There were not enough rooms to house the 350 troops and families who had already arrived, let alone the 1000 or so more expected over the next year.

Sandy and some of the men were put to work building new accommodations. This became their main task, apart from the usual jobs that were needed when the Regiment arrived on a new campaign, such as the much-hated latrine digging and supply positioning. Thankfully this time there was no fighting necessary, although after four years of policing and supervising work in Sydney the men would have welcomed the opportunity to train and practice their profession again.

The climate was stifling. Both the days and the nights were warm and humid, and the men would strip down as often as possible to their underclothes as their thick woollen uniforms were meant for a much cooler climate. Whenever they left the camp, they had to don their full accoutrements, the bright red of their jackets providing a visible British presence to the native people.

Every so often the sky would erupt with monsoonal rains, so heavy that the areas by the ports became unreachable as the roads and tracks flooded. But, as soon as it had started it was often quickly over, leaving everything waterlogged and sodden but also leaving the air fresh and clean. And then the snakes, so many snakes, came slithering out of their hiding places searching for the rats and small creatures displaced by the rain. One had to remain constantly vigilant for the snakes who invaded every dwelling, not just the barracks, and had already taken the lives of a few soldiers and one of the children.

One balmy evening Sandy sat on the veranda outside of the barracks quietly polishing his boots while other men read books or wrote letters to their loved ones. There was a soft breeze moving the heavy air gently and the delicate songs made by unseen, exotic bird seemed to float on the air, and in and around the bright orange flowers that adorned the heavy leafed plants surrounding the building. Palm trees swayed gently nearby. Further out Sandy could still make out the shapes of buffalo traipsing through the rice fields that seemed to carpet every bit of land that was flat.

This place was so different from the Scottish Highlands where he had grown up, so different from cold, dark England and so different even from the dry and dusty air in Sydney. Sandy found himself reminiscing about his life. He was no longer a young man having just had his forty third birthday. He had seen things in his life that could have destroyed a man, and he had seen many men destroyed from the work. He had seen and held so many men as they lay dying. He had thought that his destiny was to be one of them.

But all of that had changed when he got to Sydney and met his beloved Ann. Just a slip of a girl she was still only twenty-two and she loved him; Alexander McKenzie, grizzled old soldier from the Scottish Highlands. To him she was the most delightful thing he had ever seen and every moment in her presence or with their bairns, were the best moments of his life. At times he swore to himself that his Scottish brain made him so pig headed that he hadn't taken up David Rose's offer to get him an early discharge, so that he could have stayed and made a new life for them all together in the new colony in Van Diemen's Land. Some of the soldiers who had been stationed there during their time in the colony said that the climate was very similar to Scotland, which further warmed his heart towards it. While most of the soldiers seemed to enjoy the warmer climates, even the stifling heat here in Ceylon, Sandy did not enjoy it at all and longed for a chill in the air.

Ah, the Highlands. The thought of his land made Sandy smile at the memories. Sandy had lived in his parent's home right up until he joined the Army aged 28. He was born on 26 Jun 1771 in Fodderty, a parish, in the county of Ross and Cromarty, two miles from the town of Dingwall from where his mother's family got their surname. Every second person in the area was a McKenzie, as Sandy was born right in the middle of ancient McKenzie clan lands.

As a child, young Alexander was taught all the usual McKenzie folklore which he and all the other little McKenzie's lapped up. The story of the Brahan Seer was a favourite one. A man who had once been a labourer at the Earl of Seaforth's Brahan Castle near Dingwall, the Seer had apparently foreseen the fate of the McKenzie clan over a hundred years before the fated Battle of Culloden where the Jacobite McKenzie's became the first defeated clan who were forced to surrender and be ruled by the English. Brahan Castle, which was the seat of the McKenzie clans, although now abandoned, stood as a reminder of the McKenzie's previous status and reputation as fierce highland warriors.

The people in the area where Sandy grew up were divided, as the old-timers still remembered which McKenzie's had supported the

Jacobite cause (to have Scotland ruled by their chosen Charles Stuart or Bonnie Prince Charlie as he was known) and those who supported the English King. After the defeat of the Jacobite's, all Highland clans were banned from wearing tartan, carrying weapons, or playing the bagpipes. However, if they joined the English Army in one of the Highland Regiment's, they not only got to do all those things amongst other men of Highland descent, but also got to practice the profession of war and soldiering, for which the highlanders had been renowned for hundreds of years.

Sandy remained in his home village until he was way past the age when he should have been married or out making his own way in the world. Sandy had just turned 20 and was getting ready to leave home and make his way in the world, when his mother, Isobel, died of the fever, leaving his young siblings Donald aged four and Mary aged two. Isobel didn't think that she could have more children after Alexander was born, but God had other plans and 16 years after Alexander was born along came little Donald, very unexpectedly, followed not long after by Mary.

With his father needing to bring in food and money for the family to survive, Sandy stayed at home and took care of the house and the children. And being a man of no means at all, he was certainly no great catch for any of the village ladies, who gave him a wide berth. Alexander was a dashing young man in looks, but those were meagre times in Fodderty, and a woman needed a man who could provide for her.

Eight years later, though, when young Mary was 10 it was time for him to leave. Sandy had seen many men leave home to join the Highland Regiments and they had come home with exciting stories of adventure and wearing the coveted Highland tartan. Sandy joined the infamous 78th Regiment in 1799, and soon left for India where the Regiment was busy with the Fourth Anglo-Mysore War. This was a time of great adventure for the young Sandy, and he found that he had a talent for soldiering, and that he enjoyed the camaraderie of being among the men and the banter and routine in the camps.

Sandy had been in India for several years getting used to the tempo of military life, with tasks in barracks and skirmishes every now and then, at which his Regiment excelled. Early in 1803 they were sent to Poona under the command of Major General Wellesley where they joined a force that included the 74th Regiment, the 19th Light Dragoons and several Indian units fighting for King George III. Later that year, a fierce battle was fought near the village of Assaye, where the enemy front line on the British left was broken by the 78th Highlanders. In his dreams, Sandy could often still hear the howls and screams as the majestic highlander giants, in kilts and feathered bonnets ran directly into the enemy forces that far outnumbered them.

The battle, which lasted for three hours, was a victory, but nearly a quarter of Wellesley's troops, around 1,600 men, were killed or wounded. This was the first time that Sandy had seen such bloodshed and heard the screams and cries of wounded men on such a level. It crushed him to his core. Many of the men cried for their mothers and there was nothing he could do to ease their pain other than hold their hand and coo gently to them in Gaelic as they passed into the next life.

Years later when one of his fellow soldiers turned melancholy and got that far away look in their eye it was common for one or the other to just say 'Assaye' and that would explain it all.

The Regiment returned to England in 1806 and Sandy and some of his fellow soldiers spent time with the Dumfries militia recruiting for the 78th at Inverness, the Regiment having lost so many soldiers in India. Being close to his home allowed Sandy to spend some time with his father, brother and beloved little sister Mary who was then

17 and had blossomed into a beautiful young lady, much admired by the village beau's. Donald was busy working the land with his father but was enthralled by Sandy's tales of his time with the 78th.

It was not long though before he was recalled back to England. At the time, having lost so many men in India and having trouble recruiting, the Regiment lost its highland status, and therefore the privilege to wear the tartan. The newly formed 73rd Regiment all became 'red coats' like the rest of the British Army.

Sandy was just getting used to life in barracks again when the Regiment was told that they had been chosen to replace the current troops in the far-off colony of New South Wales, and their commanding officer was to be the next Governor.

And that was how Sandy came to be in New South Wales at the same time as convict girl Ann Clark.

But that was then, and for now he was bored and sweaty and stuck in another foreign land, but with no Ann this time to brighten his days.

In Ceylon the days marched on, long and tiring and long and boring. There was not much soldiering to be done by the 73rd. Other companies were sent to different areas around the island, but Sandy spent most of his time in Colombo with the main barracks.

Boring times are not good for soldiers. Around mid-year a young soldier by the name of John Stevenson got himself into mischief at another of the bases that the 73rd had been sent to. He was charged with mutiny for trying to organise a group of men to take over the stores depot and abandon their post. Perhaps he felt that a better life might be had in the mountains with the natives and their very friendly womenfolk. Whatever the reason, young Stevenson was brought back to Colombo and executed by firing squad on Galle Face Esplanade with as many of the Regiment as possible bearing witness. The British Army could not afford to have dissention in the ranks.

The months went by, and Sandy spent many long nights writing to Ann about life in Colombo and many pages about his love for her and his hopes for their future, but by Christmas 1814 he had received but one letter in reply. It was a trite letter that told him only that she and the children were doing well, and that business was doing well, who had won the latest horse races, and that was about it. He began to think that his pig-headedness may have ruined his chance at happiness, but quickly brushed that aside, as soldiers must, as there was nothing that he could do about it.

Early the next year word came that the King of Kandy, who the British had come to depose, had surrendered without so much as a shot fired. The King was a much-hated man amongst the country's gentry due to his empathy towards the middle and lower classes and their treatment. He loudly advocated for their fair treatment, which made him an enemy of those who had a vested interest in keeping the lower classes down. However, when one of them would step too far out of line the King was swift in his reprisals, and beheading, mutilations and impalements were common punishments. The British soldiers were shocked at seeing these punishments, but Sandy thought a quick death like that might be kinder than the British way of keeping petty thieves in hulks to starve or die of illness, and then transport them to the ends of the earth.

The people were not surprised that their King had given up. The might of the British Empire was too hard to fight, and some thought that under British rule their lives could be improved. So, from then on, any chance of real soldiering was gone for the 73rd who fell into policing duties and tasks set to establish King George III as the ruler of Ceylon.

Many of the older soldiers had started submitted their requests to discharge and were thinking of going back to Britain to reunite with loved ones. Some were even thinking of going back to New South Wales. Governor Macquarie was happily giving out land grants for ex-soldiers, as well as ex-convicts and free settlers who were starting to trickle into the colony.

Deaths were common in the Regiment, it was a weekly occurrence for someone to be taken down with the fever, especially the children. Snakebite was an ever-present problem, and lions and leopards would find an occasional victim. Then there were the usual illnesses brought about from accidents and wounds that failed to heal, a soldier's enemy. However, one occurrence that happened in mid-1815 cemented Sandy's newly formed idea to leave the Army for good. Many of the officers and even some of the soldiers, had started to send their families back to Britain, the campaign in Ceylon nearing its inevitable end. Colonel Geils had sent his four eldest sons, the eldest being 13, on to England with a nanny, to meet up with their grandparents and wait for their parent's arrival later in the year. In an absolute tragedy for the Regiment, their ship, the *Arniston,* that also carried many wounded or ill soldiers, was wrecked off the Cape of Good Hope. The children were amongst the 372 passengers and crew who were drowned. There were only six survivors. Sandy began to feel the fragility of life and the importance of spending as much time as he could with those he loved, and those he loved were Ann, John, and Mary.

Sandy had begun to get more and more concerned with the lack of communications from Ann and was by then desperate to return to her and the children to find out what their future together held. Not long after the mourning for those lost on the *Arniston* finished, Sandy submitted his discharge after 16 years of service to the King.

Sandy wrote to his friend David to tell him of the latest development and before Sandy left Ceylon in December 1815, he received word back that David had already started the process of getting a land grant for Sandy near his own land near Launceston at Port Dalrymple. Not only that, but Donald Sutherland, with Mary and their son John were already in Sydney, having left Ceylon earlier that year, and would soon make their way to Van Diemen's Land where David had also acquired land for them near his own grant.

Sandy then began his journey back to the colony, back to Ann.

Chapter 5

Sydney, 1814

*A*nn had had a busy couple of years in Sydney. After her

workdays ended, she had started to take on private work for the wealthy ladies of the colony and had quickly gained a reputation for her beautiful work, creating exquisite one-off pieces for the formal dinners and galas that had started being a regular occurrence in Sydney amongst the well to do.

Sydney was such an interesting place. So different to England, where only the landed gentry, and some senior military officers, indulged in such pursuits. Here in the new colony, it was not only the few titled members who had found their way across the sea, who graced the tables of Governor Macquarie's events, but they were also joined by men who had left the military, merchants and traders, foreign travellers, free settlers and explorers. This group called themselves the 'exclusives' and held themselves above the emancipists (ex-convicts). Shockingly to the exclusives, the Governor also invited emancipists, those who had become successful merchants, farmers and others who had done well and were often wealthier than those who had come free. The Governor's events were also graced by the presence of some of the prominent natives of the area, who the Governor had befriended. All these people were forming a new nation and would eventually make it a plentiful and prosperous land to live in. And the men had wives and children, all of whom wanted to dress in the latest outfits from England and Paris, the hubs of world fashion.

There was great delight and rejoicing in Sydney in April when it was announced that Mrs Macquarie had delivered a healthy, live son. The poor woman had been plagued with miscarriages and stillbirths, and this was her ninth pregnancy. It seemed that everyone in the colony, Ann included, left gifts and flowers at the entrance to Government house for the ecstatic new parents. Ann left a beautiful bonnet and dress for the new baby, lovingly embroidered with wattle and gum leaves by Miss Smith; and within a week, orders poured in for the same outfit from all the pregnant or wishing to be pregnant wives.

As news of her work spread, ladies would arrive with lengths of the most superb fabric, lace and notions and trust Ann to turn them into wearable delights. Miss Smith became a research whizz and along with the magazines that Mr Smith ordered, she would find snippets in the newspapers or pictures from books brought from overseas of the latest dresses, which helped Ann to ensure that her ladies were always looking up-to-the-minute in the clothes that she made them. At night, after the children were in bed, Ann and Miss Smith would sit by the hearth and sew together. Ann would sew the fabric into the structure that it needed to form the garment and Miss Smith would use the talents that she had grown up learning in her genteel family, to embroider delightful motifs into the fabric or the lace. Ann's pieces were truly extraordinary.

In this way Ann grew to know the 'good' people of Sydney and they in turn grew to look at Ann as, if not one of them, certainly as a trusted friend, and not just an ex-convict. However, as much as Governor Macquarie extolled the importance of the emancipists, who would be the main group to develop and make the colony successful, the exclusives still held themselves above the emancipists and did not quite approve of mixing in the same circles as them and could make them feel quite uncomfortable.

Being a pretty, young woman, Ann was invited to most of the town's galas and events but most of the time she preferred to stay at home and do her work or play with the children. Rather than spend her precious free time making small talk with people who had little of substance in their lives, she preferred to busy herself with small tasks for Mrs Macquarie and the Reverend Marsden, who organised many activities to help and support the female convicts and those who found themselves free but stuck in the colony, being unable to pay their fare back to England.

There was much excitement towards the end of May when many explosions were heard from the harbour. Fearing that a foreign ship was attacking, the colonists came out of their houses and places of business to see what was going on. There in the middle of the harbour sat the ship *Three Bees*, which had arrived three weeks earlier with a large group of mostly sick convicts. Smoke billowed from the ship and the guns were exploding and shooting cannon balls all over the harbour, most landing safely in the water, but some that made their way to the town. Ann later heard that one had gone right through a window of Captain Piper's extravagant new home on the water's edge. Finally, the ship exploded, and bits of ship and cargo slowly floated to the shore. The ship had been fully stocked for its return journey to England, so the flotsam and jetsam was extensive. The fire burned throughout the night casting an eery glow over Sydney town.

Over the next few months two more ships arrived with very sick convicts who needed immediate care after a typhus outbreak onboard that had killed a great number of them. When the *Surrey* arrived all but one of the ship's officers had died, including the Master.

Then in August the town erupted into mass celebration when a Russian ship arrived with news that Napolean had been defeated and was imprisoned by the Russians, which meant that the great war with France, that had been going since 1793, would now be over. Celebrations went on for three weeks with every tavern full of the shouts and songs of the Russian marines along with the same from the British colonists. Candles were lit in the windows of every home, Ann's included, while the wealthier homes hung coloured paper lanterns. Sadly, the colony learnt a few months later that Napolean had escaped to continue his war.

1815

After a while Ann had put aside enough money to be able to afford a small house of her own and with sadness but excitement, she and the children moved to their small but cosy home in mid- 1815. It was set amongst the other small, neat, white-washed cottages with roofs made of she-oak shingles, which resembled slate and gave them an air of elegance. Ann decorated the doorway with pots of red geranium like most of the other houses. With them came Miss Smith who welcomed the opportunity to leave her brothers' home and have some independence and still be with her two small charges who she loved with all her heart. Ann was eternally grateful for this wonderful woman who had come into her life and had been the real reason that Ann was in the enviable situation that she had found herself in.

Every now and then Ann thought about Sandy. She enjoyed receiving his regular letters with their beautifully detailed descriptions of life in Ceylon. His heavy use of endearments and hopes and dreams for their future made her nervous. Ann did not know if she loved Sandy in the way that a wife should love a husband. He had been there when she needed him at Parramatta to get her out of a bad situation, he had stuck by her in Sydney and had given her gorgeous little Mary. But when Ann thought of Sandy it was with the kind of fond thoughts one might have for a beloved uncle or a respected family friend. He did not make her stomach flip or her cheeks flush, as she had heard some of the ladies say.

Later that year Ann had decided that her side business was taking up so much of her time, and she had trained so many staff for Mr Smith who were all now quite competent to help run his business, that it was time to go out on her own. Mr and Mrs Smith had by then become like family and they happily saw Ann move on to this new phase of her life with their blessing. Miss Smith was also glad to have Ann around the house more because the two women found each other's company a joy.

In November both women received interesting but jolting information. Ann received a letter from Sandy saying that he was leaving the Army and was taking up the grant in Van Diemen's land that David Rose had told them about, and he wanted Ann and the children to go with him.

Miss Smith received news from her brother that he was bringing out an old friend from England, a fellow businessman who hoped to start a business in Sydney and had already purchased a warehouse. He was also coming out to marry Miss Smith.

Miss Smith was incredibly taken aback by this news. She had not even thought about men in such a way since her accident onboard the ship that had stolen half of her face. While she was now able to sit uncovered with Ann at the hearth she would only do so if her damaged side was facing away from Ann so as not to repulse her. Ann had told her a hundred times that her face did not repulse her and that she and the children loved her as she was, but Miss Smith would have none of that. She was a monster and must stay covered and in the shadows. What sort of man would want to marry a monster?

Ann later discovered from Emily that Mr Smith had agreed to pay this young man a hefty amount of money, enough to start his business and pay his way for a year or more, to take Miss Smith as his bride. He had made sure that the man in question, Avery Stodges, knew about Miss Smith's affliction and had even commissioned an artist in private to draw an image of Miss Smith, with the damage to her face, to send to Mr Stodges, so that he could better decide on the contract.

It would make Mr Smith the happiest man alive to see his darling sister married with a husband and a home of her own, maybe children of her own to light her life. God knew she loved the McKenzie children so well.

The two women spent many nights pondering this new phase of their lives and prophesising about how things might turn out.

Both of their lives were quite blissful in Sydney, and they realised with gratitude how much better their lives were than if they went back to England. For Ann and her children, life would certainly be a lot harder as there were many, many seamstresses in England, and all much better than her. She would also have the 'convict stain' to deal with, being forever tainted because of her conviction. It would be far harder to make a living. For Miss Smith it would mean hiding alone in her bedroom, unable to face the world where the genteel people of her world were so much crueller and less accepting than here in Sydney, where, although she was still an outcast, there were others who bore scars but were still out and about in society.

Only one small annoyance tainted their lives. Charlotte Prendergast.

Charlotte was the wife of one of the Lieutenant's under Colonel Whyte, serving in the 46th Regiment who had taken over after the 73rd had left. While the men of the 73rd were mainly rough and ready Scotsmen from the highlands, the men of the 46th were mainly from Devonshire, and particularly the officers, held themselves far above the inhabitants of Sydney. Ann had only met Lieutenant Prendergast once, at Mr Smith's offices, and he had appeared aloof and indifferent even to Mr Smith, with whom he meant to do Government business. Charlotte, however, was just plain rude.

Mrs Prendergast had commissioned two outfits from Ann immediately upon her arrival in the colony. On receiving them she had been extremely critical and vehement with her discontent of Ann's work. She had tried to extort a refund and then a discount, while also, of course, keeping the garments that had been made. Ann and Miss Smith then heard that Mrs Prendergast had been trying to sully her name around the town. Luckily for Ann she was one of only a handful of seamstresses in the colony and with so many women relying on her and always happy with her work, Charlotte Prendergast's complaints soon fell on deaf ears.

Over tea one afternoon Ann and Miss Smith reminisced over how much they appreciated their friendship and their time together. The formal Miss Smith title was now mostly reserved to when other people were around, and Ann addressed her friend by her first name of Margaret. A plan was formulated to hold a weekly morning tea, as a way for Ann and her customers to get to know each other better. Also, while there were plenty of public houses and men's clubs to entertain the men, there were few places that ladies could gather to discuss, well, lady's matters. The only other places where women could get together was at church or when involved in charitable activities. And while most of Ann's clients attended both of those, it was at Ann's weekly morning teas that they had the most fun. Ann's parlour was a place where they could entertain themselves with the extravagance of fashion and the triviality of gossip with no expectation to be pious or to work.

Ann's parlour became a central meeting place for many of the women who she did business with, to gather and discuss womanly things. And a lot of the time it was the men that they were gossiping and giggling about. The young ones about potential beau's and the older ones about potential sons-in-law.

Ann would busy herself brewing multiple pots of tea and Margaret would whip up some of her delicious biscuits the night before with whatever ingredients were plentiful at the time. The women had a wonderful time and the ladies found out about all sorts of interesting goings on in the town, things that their husbands didn't tell them, thinking they were irrelevant to womenfolk. It enabled them all to be better informed of their neighbours and their town. And for most of the time, it was a happy and jovial atmosphere. The most popular topic of late had been two novels which had mysteriously been written by an unidentified woman, the books noting only that they had been written by 'a lady'. The novels, *Sense and Sensibility* and *Pride and Prejudice*, where full of romance and intrigue and the ladies in Sydney lapped the stories up. Every now and then one of the ladies would have on their airs and graces, as Ann said, and cause some displeasure, but this was few and far between. Until Charlotte Prendergast arrived.

Charlotte arrived in a buggy accompanied by one of the other Lieutenant's wives. This was unusual because there were not many people who travelled by buggy within the town, being such short distances between everything. And Mrs Prendergast was certainly not impaired physically. She was an average woman of ample bosom, who came dressed in the latest fashion and adorned with jewels that most women would keep under lock and key for special occasions. She burst into the parlour as if she owned the place. There were half a dozen ladies, along with Ann and Margaret, already enjoying their morning when Mrs Prendergast arrived. After stepping through the door, she looked each woman over, sizing up her status amongst them. Determining her superiority, she looked down her nose at a slight lady closest to the tea table.

"Mrs Jamieson isn't it?" she snapped.

"Yes Mrs Prendergast," said Agatha Jamieson shyly, looking down at the floor.

"Sergeant Jamieson's wife am I correct," barked Charlotte.

"Yes, ummm, ma'am," said Agatha, then quickly "would you like a seat ma'am?" as she quickly stood and moved across the room.

"Oh, but you shouldn't have dear" smirked Charlotte, but quickly took up residence in the vacant chair. Her companion gave a similar look to one of the other junior ladies who also deferred and went to stand next to Agatha.

"So, Mrs McKenzie, I hear this is the place to be in Sydney" said Charlotte, addressing herself to Ann in a most superior manner.

"Well, I am honoured you have heard that Mrs Prendergast," said Ann humbly, looking at the clock and wondering just how long she would have to endure this woman.

After the initial bristling the ladies all settled into small talk and the next hour was, if not totally relaxing, not as uncomfortable as Ann feared it might be.

From then on Charlotte Prendergast was a regular visitor to the parlour, and the other ladies had grown to understand to leave a seat for her or to quickly move if she arrived and there were no chairs left. To displease Charlotte Prendergast might mean that her husband took it out on their husbands.

The most interesting thing, though, was that while Charlotte was openly unfriendly to Ann, she made it noticeable that she was trying to befriend Margaret. While she was usually critical and condescending to Ann, she was sweet and complimentary to Margaret. She even invited Margaret to one of her own tea parties. Margaret would normally never go anywhere without Ann or her brother but in this instance, Ann urged her to go, just to see what she could find out about this strange woman who was so belligerent towards Ann.

Later that afternoon Ann and Margaret sat in the parlour, "Well," said Margaret, "it was most strange. It was only Mrs Prendergast, Mrs Simson, the one who is always with her, and I."

"What did you talk about?" asked Ann intrigued.

"Well, the strangest thing is that all they wanted to talk about was you."

"Oh," said Ann "That is odd. I am not that interesting a person to be talked about by those two, surely."

"Well," said Margaret, "They think so. They wanted to know all about you. Where you are from, how you came to the colony, all about Sandy."

"What did you tell them?" asked Ann.

"Just that you are my dearest friend in the world and no matter where you came from or what you did, I only know you as the sweet, kind talented woman that you are, and the best mother and the best friend anyone could ever want."

Tears sprang to Ann's eyes, and she got up and gave Margaret a big hug.

"Whatever those women are cooking up Ann, I don't like it. We need to keep a close eye on them."

Ann agreed. It was all very strange.

The following week Alexander McKenzie arrived back in Sydney.

Chapter 6

Sydney, 1816

*I*t was strange for Ann to see Sandy dressed all the time now in

his day clothes, being so used to seeing him dressed in his red-coat and uniform previously. He had changed little in the two years since she had seen him last, although his skin was a deeper brown and there were a few more wrinkles and few more grey hairs around his temples. His chest and back were still as broad as she remembered and his hands as large and calloused as they were when they met. He looked strong and handsome.

Sandy's physical presence was a stark contrast to Ann's slight figure. In the two years since he had been gone Sandy noticed that Ann had blossomed into not just a lovely girl but into a beautiful woman. After two children, the young girl's body had been replaced with one of womanly curves, although still in all the right proportions. Her chestnut hair fell to her waist when not tied up for the day, and at 23, her fresh complexion was still clear and bright despite the ravages of the hot sun in the colony. Having an indoor job certainly helped with that. Sandy had seen women younger than Ann with skin like leathered old boots from labouring under the sun all day.

Ann always maintained a demeanour of kindest and peace and was always friendly and warm to friends and customers alike. Still, there was a part of Ann that was also shrewd and protective of herself and her children. She had lived in circumstances where being kind and quiet were not helpful to survival. So, while outwardly she let the world go on around her with an air of quiet observation only, inside she was always thinking of ways to protect her family, financially and physically.

Sandy had spent the eight-week journey back to the colony remembering with passionate longing the nights when he and Ann had put the children to bed early and spent the night in each other's embrace. How he longed for those nights again. But their first meeting was anything, but passion filled. Ann met him at the dock along with Miss Smith and the children. Johnny was now five and stood up to Sandy's waist. After two years he was shy and reluctant at first to embrace this big bear of a man who he vaguely remembered as his father.

"Good morning, Sir, ummmm, father," the young boy mumbled awkwardly putting his hand out for Sandy to shake.

Sandy obligingly shook the small hand after crouching down to John's level.

"Hallo, wee lad," he said, "My but you've grown into a man since I've been gone," he said tousling Johnny's hair.

Sandy stood again and turned to Ann who was holding young Mary, who at two and a half was the spitting image of her mother with chestnut hair and large bright blue eyes.

"And who have we got here?" said Sandy with a grin, "wee Mary McKenzie if I'm correct," he reached out to take her from Ann, but Mary cried out and turned her head into her mother's neck.

"She's just shy," said Ann, "she doesn't know you," and that's your fault she thought to herself.

After Sandy had left Sydney Ann had heard through her networks that almost 50 soldiers from the 73rd had decided to take their discharge or stay in the colony and transfer to the 46th Regiment before Sandy left for Ceylon. He could have done that as well and they would have had the past two years together. But now they were like strangers. Old friends who were just meeting to catch up on old times. But Ann could tell that Sandy was keen to resume their former relationship with all that entailed.

Ann had her new house. A house that she had purchased by herself and decorated the way that she wanted it. It was a female house, only filled with the sights and sounds of womenfolk, John being the only male who had ever been in the house. Even the house cat who they called Molly the Mouser, was female.

Sensing the distance between them, Sandy said "I have taken the liberty to arrange a room with my old friend James Morrissey for a while. I thought it might be strange for you having me back so I thought a settling in period might be a good idea."

"Yes," said Ann quickly "That would be a good idea. The children need to get to know you again before you think about moving into my house." The 'my' was especially pronounced.

"Aye," said Sandy warily. "And have ye given any thought to moving with me to Van Diemen's land then lass?"

"Well," said Ann, "There's a lot to think about. I have my business here and all my customers, and my house and Margaret........" Her words drifted off and she turned to touch Margaret's arm, who had been standing off to the side feeling extremely awkward.

"Right, well I dinna want to hurry you but I need to take up that land by mid-year for the offer to stand. David is eagerly waiting for our arrival'.

"Yes, right." said Ann flustered "Well, let's see how things go shall we." She turned to leave with John and Margaret following and

Sandy bringing up the rear noting that Ann fully intended on leaving on her own. At the end of the dock, they went their separate ways, leaving Sandy sad and confused.

A week after Sandy arrived back in Sydney the town was again thrown into rejoicing when a visiting ship delivered the news that this time Napolean had really been defeated, the previous June, in the hugest battle in living memory at a place called Waterloo. A Grand Ball was held by the Governor, with so many guests that the venue had to be moved from Government house to the newly built hospital. Many of Ann's gowns were on display, and in the following weeks orders poured in.

The months flew by. Ann was just as busy as usual with her work and her weekly parlour morning teas. The children were growing, and John had now started attending the new free school with many of the other young children from the area. He came home with funny little stories of his antics with the other children and could almost word for word tell her the stories that the teacher had read to them that day. Mary was flitting in and out of the workroom and parlour, making mischief and being cute as a button, finding new words to express herself every day. Sandy would come over for tea or dinner several times each week and play with the children and tell them his own stories of Ceylon and Scotland. Sadly, Sandy's romantic intentions towards Ann had so far remained that, intentions.

Sandy busied himself with arranging and gathering supplies that David said he would need in Van Diemen's Land. There was no trade of any substance yet in Port Dalrymple and everything had to be brought in by ship. From David's accounts, the land was wild and mostly unsettled. Natives roamed randomly through the hills and coastline, and they were not always friendly. On the most part, a good relationship had developed between the Sydney natives and the white settlers who would trade amongst themselves. Some white homes had black women working as maids or cooks, and some black men worked for the white settlers on their new farms.

The settlers had benefitted greatly from the knowledge of the native women about the local plants that could be used as medicines, and how they could be used to supplement the produce that the English were madly trying to make thrive far away from England. Sadly, for the natives, the diseases that the English brought with them seemed to affect them a lot more than they did the white people, with some family groups and whole tribes regularly and quickly wiped out by a common cold, or the dreaded fevers. They didn't have any bush medicine to cure these new illnesses.

Sandy had heard the tales of violent clashes with native tribes that had happened before he arrived in the colony, but once their leader was killed the natives around Sydney melted back into the bush or decided to live with the white people's presence. Those who lived near Sydney town seemed to enjoy the new trade and activities that the white men brought. Oyster shells, collected by the coastal natives who lived close to Sydney, were a particularly needed commodity due to the lime they contained that could be used to make the mortar needed to lay the bricks for new buildings. These were traded for tools, utensils, warm clothing, and blankets. It was quite a sight to see a muscular black man stride into the town wearing nothing, but a cloth wrapped around his nether regions, and a black top hat.

There were still regular violent clashes between native groups outside of the town, reminding the town folk that the natives seemed in essence to be of a warlike nature. The screams and howls could be heard on the breeze. The ceremonies that the natives indulged in with huge bonfires, long, hollow logs that they breathed into and that emitted a deep booming sound and wooden sticks that they clapped together, could be heard most nights coming from the coastal areas.

However further out from Sydney, where Governor Macquarie was trying to establish settlements and expand pasturelands, there was regular attacks against settlers. It was said by some that the attacks were brought on by similarly cruel treatment of the natives by the settlers. In Van Diemen's Land, David spoke of phantoms who appeared in the night and murdered settlers in their beds, then faded away before authorities arrived. The areas where the settlers lived were all quite remote from each other so it could be days or even weeks before the heinous crimes were discovered. There was also the problem of bushrangers. Usually escaped convicts or prisoners who formed gangs and terrorised and stole from the settlers and natives alike.

But Governor Macquarie had a mandate to expand the colony. So, in April 1816 he effectively declared war on any 'hostile natives who do not submit to colonial rule', and from then on, the relations between the blacks and whites became increasingly dangerous outside of Sydney town. Much of the 46th Regiment began being sent away to wage war on the native populations and there was increasingly more work in the town for ex-soldiers and freed convicts in the overseeing of public works and other government activities. Sandy wondered if he would just be better off staying in Sydney to stay close to Ann and the children who seemed so happy and settled. He had only recently started again to have a more friendly relationship with young Johnny. He had whittled a toy boat for the boy and together they would go and sail it at the park. Johnny would regale him with tales that he had heard at school of animals with sharp teeth who could rip you to shreds, and valiant battles fought by soldiers. Sandy didn't tell him that he had seen such animals and fought in such battles.

Margaret's fiancé Avery Stodges arrived in the colony not long after Sandy. While Margaret was terrified of their first meeting, she needn't have been as Avery was the epitome of good manners. For Margaret, the next few months were spent promenading with Avery around Hyde Park or attending dinners with Avery and her family so that they could all get to know each other better. Avery did not even flinch when he saw Margaret's scars for the first time, preferring to bend and kiss her hand tenderly and tell her that he was sorry that she had had to go through the pain that had caused her injury. He told her that since Waterloo it seemed that every second man was scarred in some way with either burns or missing limbs, and it was not such a big thing.

Convicts had started to arrive who had been at the Battle of Waterloo, a battle that saw so many English and French die together and so many return to England, maimed, ill, and unable to work. Many then turned to petty crime to survive, and before long found their way to the colony to fill the chain gangs building the roads and towns for Governor Macquarie's vision. Many were tainted with burns or even missing ears or noses.

Avery was busy putting his business together and arranging a beautiful new home for him and his new wife. The date was set for the wedding, May 1816, when the air would be cool like an English summer. And after they wed Margaret would still spend her days with Ann and the children for as long as she was needed or until her own family came along.

Life moved along, and the only blight on their lives was Charlotte Prendergast.

The woman would regularly attend Ann's morning teas, although thankfully not every week, but each time she would cause some kind of bad feelings in the room. She would hone in on one poor woman at a time as her victim for the day to belittle and criticise.

Every week she would say or do something to try to belittle Ann. Charlotte had taken to having her garments made by someone else, so Ann and Margaret were at a loss as to why she kept coming to Ann's parlour, except for the obvious, to be mean.

A difficult situation occurred not long after Sandy had arrived back in the colony. Ann had noticed that when she was taking her regular walks with Margaret and the children through Hyde Park they would often come across Lieutenant Prendergast. Sometimes he was with other officers, but often he was alone. He would make a habit of approaching Ann and trying to make small talk. Ann was always polite and friendly to him, but Margaret said that he made her feel frightened in her stomach. She was not sure what the feeling meant, only that Lieutenant Prendergast had the means to cause chaos in their peaceful lives.

"What on earth do you mean Margaret?" said Ann when Margaret voiced her concerns.

"I've seen the way he looks at you Ann," said Margaret carefully, "He does not have good intentions towards you."

"Oh fiddle-dee," said Ann brushing it off. "The lieutenant is a married man, what would he want with a seamstress, an ex-convict?"

"You're a woman Ann, and a beautiful one at that. I tell you now the sooner that I marry, and Sandy moves into this house the better. At present there are men in the colony who think that you are ripe for the picking with no man to protect you."

"But I do have a man," countered Ann.

"Do you though," said Margaret, "Unless I've missed something you have not taken Sandy to your bed since he got back, and he is still living with that friend of his. And as far as I know he still intends to leave for Van Diemen's Land soon and you have not yet decided or told him one way or another about if you are or are going to accompany him or not."

Had Ann missed something. Was the reason for Mrs Prendergast's open hostility because she had been told of the regular attention that her husband paid to her, in a public place! Ann was mortified. But the lieutenant appearing from nowhere while she was out and about was a recent thing, and Charlotte had been mean for months.

Ann tried to put the unpleasantness to the back of her mind and get on with her busy daily life. Not only were there commissions to be made, but she had almost finished Margaret's wedding dress, with the most exquisite materials that a wealthy Sydney merchant could buy for his beloved sister. Ann was deeply happy for Margaret, who seemed to have gotten over her initial reluctance and had warmed to Mr Stodges. And even though Ann knew the real reason that Avery was in the colony, she could not help but notice how well he treated her friend.

She still hadn't made up her mind about going to Van Diemen's Land. She was happy with her comfortable life here in Sydney with all the creature comforts available to her. In Van Diemen's Land she had heard that there was nowhere to buy provisions, and everything had to be grown or shipped in. And she was guessing that there would be little need for her seamstress skills other than to mend worn out farm clothes. The small settlement in Launceston, that Sandy's land grant was near, was not much more that a military barracks and government offices, with very few women, either convicts or wives. But since Margaret's revelation about Lieutenant Prendergast, Ann had started thinking that she had very much enjoyed having the protection of such a large, strong, and kind man that Sandy was.

May came around quickly and the day of Margaret and Avery's wedding. It was a beautiful sunny day in Sydney and the Reverend Marsden had come down from Parramatta specially to preside over the nuptials. Margaret was beautiful in the dress made for her by Ann, of yellow silk with a lace overskirt sewn with silver threads from the empire line bodice to the floor. Her bonnet had a veil that was made from a pattern that Ann had created just for her with a simple yellow covering that framed her face and covered the scars to the side of her face. This too was covered in the most exquisite lace that her brother could import, which also flowed behind her to the ground. Johnny, Mary and several of the Smith's nieces and nephews formed a mini tribe of attendants all dressed in the most adorable white outfits and carrying yellow flowers. The wedding was attended by all the best people of Sydney including all of Ann's and the Smith's customers.

Sandy came to the wedding to accompany Ann and help to keep the children under control. His time with them since he arrived home had been fruitful and he and Johnny now enjoyed many good times fishing or exploring together, building forts in the back of the shop, or quietly sitting by the hearth for stories. Mary would climb up onto her father's lap and rub his collar as he told them stories of fairies and sometimes trolls, of which Mary was not fond, and of monkeys and tigers and the other creatures he had seen on his adventures.

He was still staying with his friend but is seemed more and more likely that Ann would say yes to going with him to Van Diemen's Land. Ann was still having a terrible time with Mrs Prendergast and had mentioned several times that she would welcome a chance to be rid of her. He hoped that meant by leaving Sydney. With him.

Life got back to normal after the wedding, and Margaret moved into her lovely new home with Mr Stodges whose business was already very successful. She would arrive at Ann's each morning to take care of Mary and walk Johnny to the school so that Ann could get on with her work. Even though they were no longer living under the same roof, their friendship was as strong as ever.

Ann was so grateful to Margaret for her friendship and everything that she had done for her in the colony, that she had been thinking hard of something that she could do to thank her. She finally settled on a perfect plan, a beautiful quilt in the yellow and pink that Margaret loved. She had been working on it for months, for longer than she had worked on the wedding dress. She couldn't work on the quilt during the day while Margaret was there so her work time was restricted to after the children had gone to bed and by candlelight. Sandy had said to her often that she would end up with a squint in her eye from doing such fine work in the dark.

Finally, it was finished. Ann knew that Avery worked at his house on Tuesdays and Thursdays, time away from the shop allowed him to do so much more, he said. So, one Tuesday she made an excuse to Margaret and bundled the quilt up and arranged for a carriage to take her to the Stodge's residence.

The street where Margaret and Avery lived was very central to the town and was very busy during the day with foot traffic, coaches, carriages, and horses travelling both ways. Ann alighted from the carriage and walked quickly up the steps to the front porch of the beautiful new home. It was then that she heard a raised voice, a woman arguing. She stopped in her tracks and listened closer. It was that awful Mrs Prendergast! She would know her screechy voice anywhere.

"Avery, Avery, you know you can't stop this feeling between us," she wailed.

"Mrs Prendergast, now stop this right now I have told you I am married, and I love my wife."

"Oh, but Avery how could you have relations with a monster, look Avery look at my clear complexion, my round bosom, look, look, come closer, you know you want to."

Ann realised that Mrs Prendergast was throwing herself at Avery. She didn't need to hear anymore. She burst through the front door that was already slightly ajar. Just in time to see the awful Charlotte Prendergast with her top buttons undone and her breasts spilling out of her bodice, grabbing Avery, and trying to kiss him, on the lips. Avery had turned his head to one side and was trying to push her away.

"Charlotte," yelled Ann. Charlotte, shocked, spun around to confront Ann, her breasts still falling grossly out of her clothing.

"What?" she yelled back at Ann, "Well of course it's you, of course it is. Always trying to ruin my life aren't you."

"What are you talking about Charlotte?" said Ann.

"That's Mrs Prendergast to you, you pathetic convict whore." said Charlotte "Not happy are we unless you have every married man in the colony. Not happy just to be a whore for your soldier, you must steal my man as well. You've come here now for Mr Stodges as well, have you?"

"What on earth are you talking about?" said Ann shocked.

"Don't give me that innocent face," said Charlotte "I know that you have been meeting my husband regularly. The other women say that all their husbands talk about you, and my John has called your name in his sleep," she spat, "he has obviously been in bed with you!" she poked her finger at Ann as she struggled to restrain her breasts back into her bodice. "And don't look at me like that, I'm only helping Mr Stodges here. He lives with a monster, your monster friend, I was just offering what you have been giving out to all the men in the colony."

Ann had to stop herself from hitting this abominable woman right in her mouth.

Charlotte gathered up her clothes and her belongings "You haven't heard the last of this Ann Clark, I'll show you that you can't go around stealing other women's husbands." She then rushed out of the door and disappeared into the town.

Poor Avery had by then fallen into a chair as shocked and as disgusted as Ann was.

"Avery, how did this happen?"

"I have no idea Ann. She has been visiting the shop with that Simson woman and making small talk but only infrequently, and I never imagined that this was what she had in mind."

"Hmmm," said Ann "I think both you and I are the unsuspecting victims of those vile Prendergast's." The words turned sour in her mouth as she realised just how unclean the whole situation had made her feel. Avery expressed similar sentiments and assured Ann that although he had come to Sydney and married Margaret as a business deal, he had come to love her dearly and would never, ever think of doing anything with another woman, especially the vile Charlotte Prendergast.

They eventually had a cup of tea and spoke of gentler things. They took the new quilt to Margaret's room and Ann helped Avery to lay it on the bed, so that Margaret would see it when she arrived home. Ann lay a folded letter on the quilt which expressed her appreciation and love to Margaret.

Then Ann left for home. The town was busy and noisy. But her mind was closed to anything other than awful thoughts that would not leave her. Avery had said that they both had to be careful of the Prendergast's and Ann knew this was true.

Chapter 7

A week of so went by and Ann received a note from Mrs Prendergast. The note was delivered by a servant boy, strangely enough. Ann knew that Charlotte's husband's status in the colony afforded them a lifestyle that most envied, and as well as having their own carriage and horses, they had several house staff, including a maid, cook, errand boy and Lieutenant Prendergast's batman. Ann had heard on the grapevine that Charlotte Prendergast's family were minor gentry back in England, however she had yet to find out what family she was attached to. After the incident at Margaret's house, Ann had tried to think of Charlotte Prendergast as little as possible.

The note, handwritten on paper with a small flower motif, appeared to be a kind of apology. Charlotte wrote that she regretted the incident and invited Ann to come alone to her home for morning tea and to personally provide her some advice on her new wardrobe for the next season.

Winter was creeping in, and Ann knew that an order for a full winter wardrobe would ensure that the family were well off through the winter months when traditionally the dress making business died off. There was not much call for beautiful gowns in winter, but demand resumed as spring instilled its warmth back into the colony, and weddings, balls and other entertainments returned, that required beautiful new outfits.

As much as Ann dreaded the thought of time alone with Charlotte, she also knew that being enemies of Charlotte Prendergast in

Sydney town was not a good thing for her or her children. Sandy was ramping up the arrangements for his move the Van Diemen's Land and farming life, and Ann was less and less excited about the proposition of moving to an isolated wilderness. In the past month she had spent some romantic time with Sandy, more because of her own physical need to feel the touch of a man once again, than from a longing for Sandy himself. Ann decided that if business went well in the next few weeks she would stay.

The morning tea with Charlotte went remarkably well. She couldn't have been nicer to Ann. The maid served cucumber sandwiches and tiny jam filled cakes sprinkled with powdered sugar, and they chatted about pleasant topics, the latest fashion and Sydney events. Two topics off the agenda was anything to do with Charlotte's husband or Margaret's husband. Ann took Charlotte's personal measurements and discussed an order for several dresses, coats, and underwear. Then, after a polite period of time had elapsed, Ann left, with a friendly wave and a smile from Charlotte.

The next morning Charlotte's friend, Lieutenant Simson's wife, arrived unexpectedly as Ann was in the middle of a complex piece of sewing and Margaret was about to take Mary out for her morning stroll to the park.

Ann arose from her work to greet the visitor.

"Oh dear, please don't fuss yourself, sit, sit," said Mrs Simson, "I only came to have a chat with you about the excellent wardrobe that Mrs Prendergast had told me that you are creating for her. I thought maybe I could bother you for a few pieces also."

Ann saw the twinkle in Margaret's eye, followed by a small frown. She also knew how much a few key commissions would mean for Ann's little business, and she was so happy to see her friend succeeding, but could this woman be trusted?

"I'll pop out now shall I Ann and leave you and Mrs Simson in peace to discuss business," said Margaret.

Margaret left and Ann and Mrs Simson were alone.

"I hate to bother you, Mrs McKenzie, but could I trouble you for a cup of tea, I am quite parched after the stroll all the way across the park," said Mrs Simson, in a veiled insult that Ann's house was on the 'wrong' side of Hyde Park with her house was on the 'right' side where the colony's officers, dignitaries and noted citizens lived.

"Of course, Mrs Simson," said Ann, "I was just going to ask you that very same thing."

It wasn't morning tea week so there were no fresh biscuits made by Margaret, but Ann managed to find a couple left from the previous week that were still fresh. Once the tea had brewed, she prepared a tray with the tea, sugar, milk, and biscuits and carried it carefully into the foyer.

"Oh fiddle-dee," said Mrs Simson looking flushed and standing near the door, "I completely forgot that there is a meeting of the officer's wife's charitable society right this very morning and I must rush now if I am to get there on time. I shall visit you again soon Mrs McKenzie to discuss fashion."

And with that Mrs Simson rushed out the door, down the steps and out into the street, almost like a rabid dog was chasing her.

"Well, that was odd," said Ann to Margaret on her return.

"Very odd," agree Margaret. "I don't like those women at all."

"Yes, but if I can secure two commissions for winter there will be money for improvements to the workshop and I'll be able to afford to buy the newest fabric to expand my designs."

"Yes, I know, I just hate it that it has to be those two women."

Later, in the afternoon, all was quiet and peaceful. The noise from the crowds out in the street dulled at this time of day and it felt like the whole world was taking a siesta ready from the evening chores. A dog barked in the distance and the squark of the galah's could be heard every now and then as they made their presence known amongst the white intruders. Ann sat sewing a particularly ornate collar, Margaret creating a tapestry wall hanging, and little Mary played with her dolls quietly on the rug in front of them.

Suddenly there was a loud bang on the door. This turned into a loud thumping and a loud, "Open the door! Open the door now!"

Ann jumped up in fright and raced to the door to find out what was wrong. Immediately she thought that something had happened to Sandy.

Five soldiers burst through the door as Ann went to open it.

"Ann Clark?" said one.

"Yes," said Ann "yes, but I go by McKenzie here. Private, well ex Private Alexander McKenzie is my husband."

"I'm sure he is Clark, but we are here to see you, not him. I understand that you have recently been at the home of Lieutenant Prendergast?"

"Yes," said Ann, "I was there yesterday to discuss some garments that Mrs Prendergast wishes me to make for her for this winter season."

"And what else did you do while you were there Clark?" he said gesturing to the other soldiers who then started to search the house and look behind furniture and under couches.

"What, what do you mean?" said Ann, by now scared and angry.

"Sir, it's here," called one of the soldiers from the parlour, the room where Ann held her morning teas. He came into the front room holding a fob watch and an emerald necklace.

"Ah!" said the Corporal, "Once a thief always a thief hey Clark," he grabbed Ann roughly by the arm and turned her towards the door.

Ann was so shocked that she couldn't make a sound, allowing herself to be manoeuvred towards the door.

"Stop!', said Margaret, "Stop! Leave Mrs McKenzie alone, she is not a thief, she is an honest businesswoman. That woman has been trying to harm her for months. Stop, stop!" But her words fell on deaf ears. Little Mary started to howl in confusion.

"This woman," spat the corporal "should still be a convict, and now she is a prisoner, and will soon be back in gaol where she belongs. Stealing from the town's gentry is a most heinous crime madam."

In her haste and anger Margaret let her veil fall from her face and her scars were on full display. The soldiers looked in horror and grimaced, a thing that Margaret had not been exposed to in a long time. She quickly grabbed the fabric and tried to pin it back into her hair, while holding a screaming Mary. And then Ann was shuffled into a waiting cart and disappeared up the street.

Margaret fell to the floor clutching little Mary and they both dissolved into tears of despair. Margaret was blatantly aware that in the colony an ex-convict had little by the way of legal or human rights if they committed a further crime. And to steal from a member of the higher classes was the worst form of crime, when resources were so scarce and luxuries such a jewellery were so rare and precious.

It was a very bad day, thought Margaret, a very bad day indeed.

Chapter 8

Newcastle, 1817

*I*t was a very different Christmas for Ann at the end of 1816,

spent once again at the Parramatta Goal, where, after her conviction in July, she was again put to work at the loom, and then sewing garments for the soldiers and teaching others to sew. The very basic work was boring, and conditions were harsh.

Despite Sandy and Mr Smith trying every possible way to prove that Ann had not stolen from Lieutenant Prendergast's wife, along with eyewitness reports from Margaret and Avery Stodges about what Charlotte and her friend had been up to leading up to the 'incident', Ann was still convicted of larceny in July 1816 and sentenced to six months at Parramatta followed by seven years at the new prison in Newcastle.

Sandy tried in vain to call in favours from the officers in the colony who he still knew. His friend, and former officer David Rose, now a prominent settler and landowner in Van Diemen's Land, appealed to Governor Macquarie, and even some of the wives in Sydney who relied on Ann's work for their beautiful dresses, appealed to the court, but all in vain. Ann's conviction stood. It was a small consolation that afterwards, Charlotte Prendergast was not welcome in most of the society homes in Sydney, being blamed for the loss of the lady's morning teas and of their favourite seamstress.

Following the conviction, knowing there was no use him staying in Sydney, Sandy left for Van Diemen's Land. Long discussions were held about whether he should take the children with him. It was debated about if it would be better for John and Mary to live free with Sandy, no matter what the isolation and primitive conditions in Van Diemen's Land were, than to be stuck with Ann in the prison. In seven years' time John would be almost 13 and during that time he would be able to help Sandy on the farm, one day even taking over from him, as Sandy had promised. It was decided that little Mary, not yet three, needed to be near her mother. But then Margaret and Avery stepped in and offered to take the children into their home for as long as was needed.

After Ann was arrested, Margaret was heartbroken. Ann and her children had been almost her entire life since she had arrived in the colony. She thanked God for Avery, who she had found to be a kind and pleasant man who treated her with true affection, and she thought, love, something that she thought she would never have for herself. Avery welcomed the children into the house and the transition was easy, as Margaret was, in effect, their second mother. Although every now and then Mary would ask Margaret longingly where 'Mumma' was. "Margie, Margie, where Mumma gone?" This broke Margaret's heart but what could any of them do.

In late 1816 after Ann had been at Parramatta for many months, she received word of the transfer to Newcastle. Governor Macquarie had decided not long after his arrival in Sydney that a separate prison was necessary for Ticket-of-leave convicts and free settlers who were convicted in the colony. It was not considered to be appropriate for them to be under the same conditions as arriving convicts who were living amongst the soldiers and settlers biding out their time until their own freedom and land grants. Plentiful amounts of both coal and timber were found near Newcastle as well as fertile farming lands. There was a high need for prison labour for both the mines and the lumber yards, as well as to help the settlers to get established and therefore the colony prosper.

A small prison was built around 1810 but was in the process of expansion when Ann arrived with John and Mary in January 1817 after a journey onboard the ship *Henrietta* from Sydney. On arrival, Ann and the other new prisoners were brought before the commandant of the prison, Captain Wallis, and allocated tasks as appropriate to their skills. The men were quickly sent off to the lumber yards or to the coal mines. While many of the women prisoners who arrived at Newcastle were sent straight to work for settlers, Ann was again sent to the fledgling gaol, which had a smaller version of the Parramatta Female Factory in its grounds that provided laundry and clothes making services. While allocated as servants and labourers the prisoners were classed as being 'on stores', which meant that the government provided for their needs such as clothing and tools if needed, and also provided their rations. If they were allocated, additional rations were sent to the settlers they were allocated to. Anyone with experience as a tailor or seamstress was highly sought after to produce all the clothing needed by the government.

John and Mary were sent to the 'nursery', which was basically a concrete quadrangle in the middle of the gaol, with two concrete floored rooms leading from it with an assortment of cribs and mattresses on the floor. Some of the women who were too elderly or otherwise disabled to work, were left to manage the children. Luckily for John and Mary, the clothing workshop was in the same building and Ann could visit them sometimes during the day and take them to sleep with her in her dormitory at night. This ensured that the children remained fed and stimulated with more than four concrete walls and the growls from the carers.

The days rolled on with Ann quickly moving on to teaching other women with little to no experience the art of seamstress work and providing quality checks of the garments before they went out for distribution. So long as the work was done at the rate expected the bored and lonely guards were happy to let the women prattle on amongst themselves and go off together on daily walks around the small town, including the beautiful beach. They were also happy to have the company of the women, rather than the exhausted and angry male convicts in the labouring camps. Once again, it was not uncommon for relationships to form between the prisoners and the soldiers, which was a quick way for the women for gain a pardon and a husband.

The colony's Principal Surgeon, D'arcy Wentworth, believed that fresh air and exercise helped the constitution and prevented all kinds of illnesses and injuries, so encouraged the female prisoners to get out and about for a daily walk. That, with a decent daily ration that always included a good portion of meat, some bread, and some vegetables, as well as a cup of milk every few days, ensured that Ann and the children remained fit and healthy during their incarceration.

One afternoon Commandant Wallis came down to the workshop and asked to speak with the 'Head woman'. Eliza Jones had been the head seamstress but had left the week before after being granted a pardon due to her good and loyal work over a period of two years. She had met an emancipist farmer and he had asked the commandant to seek a pardon for Eliza from Governor Macquarie so that as a couple they could continue to expand his farming interests. The other settlers in that area had also petitioned for someone with such experience as Eliza, so that they could more easily have their clothing and other work items repaired quickly rather than wait for the work to be done at Newcastle.

The next most experienced was Ann, and the other women quickly nominated her as their "Head Woman'. She meekly approached the Commandant, unsure of his intentions. He quietly took her to the office area of the gaol and asked her to sit, as did he. He then requested tea from one of the convicts working in the office. He then politely asked about conditions in the prison. Ann told him honestly that the conditions were quite good for the seamstresses, the rations were good and the freedom to enjoy the fresh air and the town were greatly welcomed. But the cleaners and the laundry woman, the women in the nursery and the scullery maids and cooks were not afforded the same good treatment. The children were also kept in quite appalling conditions unless their mothers were able to attend to them, as Ann was. Wallis listened attentively and promised that he would investigate the conditions of the other women and children straight away. It was his intention, he told Ann, to make Newcastle a thriving, successful and prosperous town, rivalled only by Sydney, and since his arrival in 1816 he had set to work, with Governor Macquarie's approval, building many necessary buildings and infrastructure in the town.

Ann was most intrigued as Wallis explained to her that he was an artist, and not such a bad one at that, he proclaimed. 'James' as Wallis introduced himself to Ann had been working with a convict called Joseph Lycett who had been a prominent artist in England before his conviction. Lycett was on the transport with Ensign Wallis when he came out to the Colony in 1814. Together the duo had been capturing on canvas, the natural sights, and their botanical and fauna finds, and the new urban developments in Newcastle, as a record for future generations. Lycett was also responsible for much of the town planning that Wallis had been engaged in since his arrival.

The reason for him wanting Ann's help, he said, was to ensure that he was able to have the very best canvas, cloth, and parchment available, for his art works. Thinking quickly Ann remembered that she had heard that a convict who she thought was also named James was operating the government paper making and printing workshop in the town and not far from the gaol. Ann could make sure that the looms could make cloth fine enough for the Commandant's needs, but the paper was another thing.

'Sir," she said "I am confident that I can ensure a supply of cloth to the quality that you require, but paper is not within my remit. However, I have heard that a fellow convict is supplying very good quality paper just down in the town."

"Ah yes," said Wallis "that would be Wells, James Wells, stout fellow. I placed him there in mid '16 when I first arrived. He had worked at a printing press in Kent before he found his way here to the colony."

"Well, if you allow me Sir, I can visit this man and see if I am able to secure the quality and quantity that you require."

"Yes, yes please Clark, that would be very suitable. And I shall tell the guards that you must be given special consideration in your work to have the time available to attend to this very important task that I need undertaken."

"Sir, if I might ask, I am most humbled by your consideration of me for this task, but if you could please look into the conditions for the women and children who I mentioned before I would be most grateful."

After a promise from Wallis to investigate conditions, and a time and place set for the first exchange of cloth and paper, Ann was released back to her work. There was much excitement and chatter when she returned to the workroom about what has transpired. The women looked forward to some improvements in the gaol.

Within a week Wallis had made good on his promise to Ann, and the older convict children, including John, started to be taken to the newly built school and were given better accommodations, even the orphan children. Some of the younger convict women were taken from the laundry and the scullery and were tasked with taking the children out in the afternoons for fresh air and a stroll along the foreshore. When the weather was warm, they were also allowed to frolic in the shallows and build sandcastles.

Ann had made her way into the town and tracked down the workshop of James Wells. It was a small cottage towards the centre of town with a wide veranda across the front where several men sat, waiting, she assumed, for products to take back to their appointed Masters. On entering the cottage Ann was confronted by a very brightly lit room on account of the huge windows across the back, facing the morning sun. She rang the tiny bell on the wide counter that spanned the length of the room. Within a few seconds a tall, burly young man burst in from the back room, his blonde hair flopping across his forehead and his bright blue eyes flashing as he gave Ann a cheeky grin.

"Whoah, to what do I owe this absolute pleasure on such a glorious day?"

Ann felt herself blush. This extraordinary looking young man was definitely not what she thought she would meet at this paper workshop.

James quickly jumped the counter, with the ease of youth, and introduced himself with a wink, a grin and a bow, then called for his young assistant to man the shop while he escorted Ann towards the back of the workshop. There, he skilfully made her a strong brew of bush tea and even offered her a jam biscuit which was unexpected "I have a deal with the closest farmer. His convict ladies bring me home cooked meals and the like. I'm hopeless at anything but paper making," he gave her another wink and a deep chuckle. Ann found herself feeling a flush rise from her chest.

Ann told him about what Commandant Wallis was after and why.

"I'm surprised the fellow has any time left for artistic pursuits with everything else that he has going on. Him and that Lycett fellow have been in here a lot and sometimes they just stay and lean over the counter and draw up rough maps and plans for the town right here on the counter. Why, since just last year he's had built that huge church that he preaches at, the hospital, the new gaol, and the barracks. And there's the house for the assistant surgeon, a new barracks and workshops going up all over. The school he built is already well attended."

"Yes," said Ann "the older children and orphans from the goal are now attending, including my son John."

"You have a child?" asked James. "He must be a good-looking chap then," and he winked again.

"Oh" flushed Ann, "I also have a young daughter, although she is not yet ready for school."

"Well then, I shall look forward to meeting these children of yours Mistress."

Ann was very flustered and kept looking at the ground too worried that if she looked into his eyes, it might betray the strange longing that she suddenly felt.

Finally, they got back to business and discussed what was needed and agreed to another time to meet to exchange the stock for the commandant. At first James said that he was happy to bring the stock to the gaol to save her the trip, but Ann quickly told him that trips outside of the gaol were things that she very much looked forward to, to break the monotony of prison life. James told her when the products would be ready, and she agreed that she would arrange her time to come and pick it up after that.

Ann went to bed that night with her thoughts in a quandary. Why had that short time with that young man left such an impression in her head. Such an impression, that she found it difficult to sleep and during the day to think of anything other than him, how he looked, how he sounded and even how he smelt, as she had caught a gentle waft of fresh, clean maleness as he rose from his chair after their discussions. She was intoxicated with it and was concerned that her own wits had left her.

On rationalising it though, Ann decided that her only experience with boys and men had been the dirty, half-starved waifs and youths of her childhood before her conviction in Liverpool, or drunken dirty old men who smelt like beer and stale sweat, who hung around the streets stalking young girls, and then even worse looking and smelling ones at Newgate. John from the journey to the colony. He had been kind and as clean as one could be when stuck on a ship for months on end, but no one could smell anything after a while on that ship. He had been a little older than her but was stocky and strong muscled with a face a little like a bull, or a bulldog, the type that the aristocracy liked to own. It was for this reason she was unsure of John's parentage, as he looked nothing like a little bulldog.

Then there had been Sandy, tall and strong muscled with a face that shone with kindness but also showed the hardships of the years that he had endured in the Army. To Ann, Sandy was like a kindly old uncle or a father who she would have liked to have had. While she had lain with him and enjoyed their romantic times together, he surely had never made Ann feel the way that she had meeting young James Wells. The fresh flush of youth still shone from James' clear complexion and his bright eyes, but age had developed his body into a long, lithe, and very well-proportioned stature, not yet afflicted with the ailments of age, and able to physically take on anything that the world could throw at him. His shiny golden hair appeared as a halo and his face and arms were bronze where they had been kissed by the warm Newcastle sun.

Ann wasted no time in organising her next visit to collect the supplies for Captain Wallis. The commandant was very happy with the stock that Ann supplied and ordered her to keep it coming. Therefore, over the next few months Ann and James saw each other frequently. Visits to collect stock turned into picnics behind the workshop, walks around the town and strolls along the foreshore, which got longer and longer each time. James met John and Mary and was an immediate hit seeing as how he had been able to procure some sticky taffies from his convict women suppliers. James was young and fit enough to be able to run and kick a ball with John and have a play wrestle on the grass, with young Mary jumping in for good measure and 'winning' the fight.

Christmas again came around and by then Ann had been having the odd sleep over in the comfortable quarters behind the printing workshop. Captain Wallis fully encouraged these relationships which Governor Macquarie said were vital to the growth and prosperity of the colony in the long run. Ann revelled in the newfound physicality and desire that she found in James' arms, and when they were apart, he was never far from her thoughts.

1818

As nature intended, it was not long after Christmas that Ann found that her courses had not appeared for several months, and she felt considerably queasy when the smell from the fatty joints of meat wafted into the workroom.

James was ecstatic when he found out. He immediately applied for his own quarters, which due to both his and Ann's good standing with Captain Wallis was granted straight away. A small abode was found close to both the printing workshop and the gaol so that both Ann and James were close to their workplace. The cottage was small, with just two rooms, but it was sturdily built and kept out the wind and rain. James had acquired furnishings over the years he had been at Newcastle and any other pieces that they needed was gifted by members of the community who all knew James and were getting to know Ann and the children.

Captain Wallis asked that Ann stay on at the gaol workshop and she was still able to utilise the nursery for little Mary until her confinement. Captain Wallis arranged for Ann to be given a full pardon after the baby was born, and for James to be given a Ticket-of Leave, a plot of fertile land near the town, as well as a small stipend if he agreed to stay on to train other convicts in his printing and paper making skills. James knew most of the other settlers and many of the convicts from the area that Captain Wallis had suggested, as he often went over there to collect the wood pulp necessary for his trade.

James and Ann were gloriously, ecstatically in love. They both agreed that the small deprivations of colony life were nothing compared to the conditions that they had left in England, where starvation and disease was ever present and the wet drizzle and constant cold crept into bones and made people old before their time. Their days were filled with satisfying work and their nights were filled with love and passion. Their dreams were filled with visions of the future that just seemed to be fuller and happier as every day went by.

In May the new settlement was treated to a visit from Governor Macquarie who came to see what Captain Wallis had been doing and to officially open and lay a cornerstone that was to become a pier or causeway. He also named several areas after Wallis. There was much fanfare, as he brought his military band with him and his ceremonial guards. Refreshments were provided for all the inhabitants of the settlement, even the timber workers and miners were brought in for the day. During the official ceremony Governor Macquarie declared that the land mass known as New Holland would now be known as Australia. Everyone cheered for the new name, which abolished any perceived ownership by anyone other than Britain. At the end of the day fireworks were set off across the foreshore. James and Ann, wrapped up in their love bubble, greatly enjoyed the celebrations that ensued and revelled in their good fortune and love for each other.

Ann rarely thought of her sister or father anymore. The letters from them soon dwindled to nothing during her incarceration at Parramatta when she first arrived. She had sent them letters to let them know of John's birth to which her father had replied that she was a harlot and dead to him. The letters from Mary had stopped not long after Ann had arrived in Sydney, which meant that they had both most probably written her off as a criminal and a harlot as her father had said. She hoped they were both well and were thriving as well as two people of meagre means could do, stuck in dark, dreary Liverpool, with its constant rain and smog from the ships and factories.

Letters from Sandy were regular. He had been thriving in Van Diemen's Land with the help of David Rose. He described the area where he had settled as wonderous and fairy-like and very similar in geography and climate to the area where he had grown up in Scotland. He had managed to clear some land and had his own home garden plot that made him self-sufficient, along with the possums and kangaroo's that frequented land surrounding the cottage, which were a 'good feed' he wrote. He had a cow provided from the government stores, and several convicts that were busy clearing and planting crops. While the farm was being prepared, he supplemented his income by working as a convict overseer supervising the gangs who were busy building roads and government buildings between Launceston and other towns as they were settled.

Sandy's letters regularly pleaded for Ann and the children to join him in Van Diemen's Land as soon as she was able. He had heard from David's contacts that Ann had taken up with another convict and was being given a pardon, although not the reason why. Sandy lovingly and poetically extolled his love for her and the children, but Ann was completely besotted with James and after a cursory read she burned his letters. Her future and the future of her three children lay here in Newcastle with the handsome, popular, and successful James Wells.

Letters arrived almost weekly from Ann's beloved Margaret who, Ann was delighted to hear, had given birth to her own daughter, named Agnes Ann in early 1818. So far life in Sydney was doing them all well and Avery's business was thriving. The evil Prendergast's had left the colony much to Margaret's joy and she now felt she could breathe in her own town. Margaret was pleased to hear that Ann had met a nice man, and that a new babe was on the way, but reminded Ann that Sandy was willing to take care of her and John when she was all alone. This was not lost of Ann, who often had pangs of guilt, especially when Sandy's pleading letters arrived. But then she just had to glance over at her beautiful, golden young man and see his cheeky grin and his delicious laugh, and remember the feel of his warm, smooth, silky skin on hers, and Sandy quickly left her mind and disappeared into her past.

Baby William was born in the cottage in August on a very cold and windy day. Two women who Ann knew from the nursery came to assist in the birth, but little assistance was necessary as no sooner had Ann thought the baby was coming than he decided to slither his way easily into the world, with James, John and Mary all watching in fascination.

The women said that the laying in was very important for new mothers and if able to, a week in bed was encouraged to avoid the risk of childbed fever. This of course was not something that Ann wanted to do and hadn't done so with her other two babies. She was back in the workshop with tiny William strapped to her chest within two days. The matron of the hospital was quickly summoned to tell her that her services were no longer required by Captain Wallis and to return to her bed. Ann sadly obliged.

Two weeks later the Reverend Marsden was visiting the settlement unexpectedly as he was yet to see the magnificent new church that Captain Wallis had built. Captain Wallis sent word out that the Reverend wanted to christen as many of the new babies and young children as possible, so that their eternal souls would be saved and so that the colony could be assured of being populated by good God-fearing Protestants. James immediately signed up John, Mary, and William. He enquired about a marriage ceremony for he and Ann but was told that there was no time for approvals to be granted by Governor Macquarie. Captain Wallis told him that a civil marriage, arranged and blessed by him as the Commandant, was just as good in the colony as a marriage sanctioned by God.

However, on the day of the christenings, little Mary was very ill with the fever that had been getting around, so James diligently took John and William to the ceremony, with strict instructions that John be christened as John McKenzie to honour the man who took them under his wing when they had nothing.

The christening ceremony was one of the largest occasions held in Newcastle since its inception. It was held at the Church of Christ that Captain Wallis had built and had been lay preaching at every Sunday in between all his other activities and interests. It was highly unusual for Reverend Marsden to venture out of the Sydney or Parramatta area so there was as much pomp and ceremony as the Captain could create around his visit with every available soldier cleaned and pressed into their best uniforms and as many convicts and prisoners in their best attire, congregated along the street as the Reverend arrived by ship, and as he made his way to the church.

The ceremony went for most of the day with each tiny child given the attention deserving of their status as Newcastle pioneers. The orphans arrived looking angelic in white and were all christened along with the other children. This was followed by the singing of hymns, a long church service and refreshments on the lawn outside the church. By this time most of the newly christened protestants had fallen asleep in their parent's arms or under the pews.

By the time James and the boys returned home they found Ann in a desperate state. Mary's condition had much worsened during the day and her fever had turned into the bloody flux. She was unable to keep any water down and writhed in pain on her cot. Ann was distraught and yelled at James to leave and to keep the boys away. James and Ann had both seen enough children, and adults, die from the wicked disease that took people overnight.

James took the boys to the gaol nursery and was allowed to leave them when he explained the situation. A wet nurse was quickly found for newborn William and big brother John, now almost eight, cuddled him close and crooned the words to him that he had heard his mother sing with Mary and recently with little William.

For three days John carried and rocked tiny William in the orphan's nursery, taking the babe to the wet nurse when his cries changed to screams of hunger. For three nights he snuggled the babe to warm them both on the smelly mattress that he had been allotted. And he wondered and worried about where his mother was, where James was and how his beloved sister Mary was.

On day three he was pacing the concrete quadrangle, tiny William held close to his chest, when his mother quietly walked through the door and approached him with tears running down her face.

"Mary!" croaked John in a voice that betrayed his grief.

"No son, Mary is fine, she is recovering at home," Ann took a deep shuddering breathe, "it's your new Da, James has died." She fell to the ground next to John.

Eventually her grief subsided enough for her to talk. "That first night he spent going to and from the well for icy water and slept beside Mary all night dripping water into her parched mouth. We both took turns rubbing her belly and cleaning her cloths from the flux," Ann paused as a sob wrenched through her soul.

"But by noon the following day our beautiful, golden husband and father was taken by the flux and before the morning came, he was gone."

She dissolved into tears as several of the nursery women came to support her and the boys. Women from the church society came to collect them and ushered Ann back to their cottage where convicts had removed and burned all their bedding which had been replaced by new straw mattresses and bedding provided by the government stores. While a nursery maid attended to the children, Mrs Smyth, one of the officer's wives who had been running the new church aid society, talked to Ann about her next steps. Naturally now without James, the offer of land was invalid, however Ann was a free woman now and Captain Wallis would be pleased to have her stay in the settlement, and if she wished to, work for a small stipend and the use of the cottage at the clothing workshop. William could attend the nursery and John and Mary where already happy at the school. Mrs Smyth also told her that Captain Wallis had been sent money from Mr Avery Stodges from the sale of Ann's small cottage in

Sydney, which now as a free woman she was able to access. If she wished she could start a business in Newcastle, which would be the first of its kind.

After the elaborate funeral, which was attended by, it seemed, everybody in Newcastle and its surrounding area, it took several months for Ann to even leave the house, so deep and all-encompassing was her grief. The entire town shared her grief and a deep fear, because if the Lord could take such a fit, strong, handsome man as James Wells, who seemed godlike with his looks and physique and would surely be immune to the ailments of mortal men, well then everybody was at risk. The convict girls who had previously supplied James with food continued to do so, otherwise Ann would have faded away to the ghost that she wished she was. She continued to feed and nurse tiny William who, with his tiny fuzz of golden hair and his non-existent eyebrows, Ann just knew that he would grow to be the image of his father. The children, John almost eight, and Mary five, were collected each morning and taken to the school, so that they and their mother could survive, with Ann in an almost catatonic state.

Worse news was to come when she received a letter from Sandy in November to inform her that he had given up waiting for her and had been convinced to marry Elizabeth Murphy, the young ward of one of the neighbouring farmers. He had already sent a letter to Ann, signed by the magistrate, that legally appointed Mary as the heir to his estate, no matter if any other children, either sons or daughters were born to him. He had resolved himself to the fact that Ann did not love him, he wrote, and now his only wish in life was to see Mary again before he died.

In another surprise Ann discovered that despite her desperately sad situation and barely having eaten since James' death, she found herself again with child. At first, she thought that the pangs of nausea were all related to her depression and sadness, but then came the sore breasts and her small, starved stomach started to protrude of its own volition. To her horror she realised that she must have fallen pregnant again in the very days right after William's birth, when after having such an easy birth, and followed by several months of abstinence for the sake of the baby, James and Ann could not keep their hands off each other. With the children at school all day and Ann relegated to compulsory bed rest and home duties, James would race back to the cottage for morning tea, lunch and often afternoon tea as well, all little jaunts that could on any occasion have resulted in the creation of a new baby Wells. Ann had become so excited and accustomed to his visits in those two weeks before he died that she would make sure that the baby was sleeping, and she was divested of her undergarments at the times when he was expected home.

These two revelations were all that Ann, the survivor, needed, to pull herself out of the quagmire of grief that she had been living under, and decide that both she and her three, soon to be four, children would survive, and they would thrive, despite all that this godforsaken world had thrown up at her.

And the saviour of the day, would be none other than Alexander McKenzie.

With the help of the society women Ann arranged for her funds to be transferred to the island colony and then on November 26, Ann, along with John, seven, Mary, five, and 3-month-old William, boarded the *Prince Leopold* bound for Launceston.

Chapter 9

Launceston, 1816

*A*fter Ann was convicted in July 1816, Sandy appealed to Governor Macquarie himself and then through his friend Lieutenant David Rose. Although the general gossip in the town was that both Prendergast's were of dubious morals, neither of them had been convicted previously, as Ann had. While ex-convicts enjoyed many of the privileges of living in the new colony and had every opportunity to build their farms and businesses, they were still looked down on as second-class citizens by those who had come free, particularly by the military families who considered themselves to be above everyone else.

There was nothing that Sandy could do, except to visit Ann and take her whatever supplies that she needed while incarcerated in Sydney and then at Parramatta. At first, Sandy was fully accepting that he would take the two young ones with him to Van Diemen's Land, but tales from Lieutenant Rose told him that it was no place for children with no mother to care for them. Conditions were harsh and primitive with the ever-present threat from natives, wild dogs, and bushrangers. The climate, while perfect for two Scotsmen, might be difficult for two children used to the more temperate climate of New South Wales, especially until a suitable house could be built to accommodate them. Until then, Sandy would be living under canvas in the middle of winter, although he was welcome to stay with David while his house was being built.

When Margaret and Avery offered to care for them until Ann was able to have them again, it seemed the best thing for the children. However, leaving the children, and Ann, broke Sandy's heart. In the weeks leading up to his departure he busied himself going to and from the Stodges' warehouse for supplies and making sure that all the arrangements for his move were on track. David had sent him an extensive list of things that he would need to bring from Sydney, as well as what he could procure once he arrived. There was also a request via David from the Commandant, Major Gilbert Cimitiere, for a quantity of luxurious brocade cloth, in a French pattern, presumably to adorn the new Government house that Cimitiere was trying to have built; and Avery Stodges gifted the fabric to Sandy as a farewell gift. The funds from the Major would come in handy as Sandy set about building his own home. Avery threw in an extra length of similar fabric for Sandy's own use.

Since his arrival in Van Diemen's Land, David had busied himself setting up his farm, which he named Corra Lynn, at Paterson's Plains on the North Esk River and eight miles from Launceston. David had been initially appointed six convicts as servants who were 'on stores', and several cows by the government. This enabled him to establish a substantial house for himself and quarters for the servants, along with farm buildings and fences. When Sandy arrived in 1818, David, then 62, was proud that his farm was producing sufficient wheat and beef to sell to the government and to his fellow settlers, as well as producing bricks. Just before Sandy arrived, he had sold 3,000 to Major Cimitiere for the government stores.

David had named his property Corra Lynn after a beloved area in Scotland where he had grown up. At the edge of the northern boundary was a steep gorge with towering cliffs that guarded a waterhole with patches of sand, rapids, and rock falls. David found this to be a wonderful place to cool off in the summer or to contemplate life in the cooler months. From the gorge, heading east, the North Esk River formed a natural landmark, and with its steep sides and rocky outcrops made a natural barrier, as river crossings were perilous, and impossible for cattle or carriages. This was important for security as the whole area was prone to random attacks from both natives and the occasional bushranger. Luckily, the notorious Michael Howe, who had declared himself the Lieutenant Governor of the Woods, and had been terrorising Van Diemen's Land with his gang of thugs for a year, had recently been caught and killed.

The whole area, in both its climate, plains and rocky outcrops was so like Scotland that David just knew how much his fellow 73rd Regiment soldiers would love it. Therefore, it was to the south of the river and north-east of his property that David suggested the 100 acres for Sandy, and a bit further down the river another 100 acres for his previous Sergeant, Donald Sutherland, who had also decided to take up David's recommendation to settle in Van Diemen's Land.

As many ex-soldier's did, David took up a government position to supplement his income while his farm was getting established. He was appointed as the inspector of government herds and livestock at Port Dalrymple which encompassed the whole area surrounding Launceston to the coast, a position that made him both friends and enemies.

David's one regret in life was that he had never found himself a bride, spending all his life serving in the military. After a few years in Van Diemen's Land, he found himself with a decent house, a thriving farm, and no one to share it with. His evenings, after a hard day's work, were spent writing letters to all his many friends, all now so far away; and sometimes he would sneak down past his herd and listen to the music from the local natives.

While many settlers found the natives to be savage, David had not had that experience. Many of the settlers were also savages, having spent time in Her Majesty's prisons learning the dark side of man. Their treatment of the natives was far from neighbourly. David had also, of course, seen the dark side of humanity, but he was also intrigued enough to want to learn from these dark-skinned people who had lived on this harsh land for so many years, as his ancestors had learned to survive in Scotland. And so, David Rose's friendships with the local natives began early on. He learned from them, and they learned from him. It wasn't long before one of his friendships, with a native girl who he called 'Mary' became more than friendship and their lack of verbal communication was enhanced by their new physical way of communicating. Although unconventional, it was not unheard of for white men and black women to form relationships, there being a distinct lack of white women in the colony and the inability to form natural friendships due to the requirements of status and the problem of geographic distances.

As Mary began to understand and speak more English words, and David learned more or her words they were able to share stories of their lives more easily. Mary laughed as David described Scotland and England and the places he had been with the Army. Mary told him the dreamtime stories of how the earth came to be and how the hills and mountains and rivers and lakes were formed from serpents and dreamtime entities. David laughed at that. To each of them the other's stories seemed like fairytales.

Mary's father told David that they had had a white man living with them for over a year, but he had recently died from a wound while hunting. This man had taught some of the men in Mary's tribe how to read and write basic English words, with the help of a small book, called Truth without Treason, which Mary's father kept as a prized possession. Given the accent that Mary and the others spoke in, David figured that the man must have been Irish. Mary's father asked David to read to him some of the chapters of the book that he was stuck on, and David showed him his book collection at which the man marvelled. David opined that the man who had lived with the tribe had most probably been an escaped convict, as there were many stories of such men living amongst the natives, and amongst the tribes could be found little children with lighter coloured hair and skin that showed the extent of the white man's influence already on this ancient population. These children, said Mary's father, were not always the result of voluntary couplings and it was common for emancipists to capture native women to sate their lust and then throw them away when they were finished, or worse, kill them.

David and Mary's delightful little son, all caramel skinned with big brown eyes, was born in Aug 1815. Just before little John was born a tragedy befell Mary's family. An illness swept through the tribe and within two weeks everyone, except Mary who had been staying with David, were dead. Mary mournfully tried to explain the funeral rituals to David but having so many bodies to dispose of and only his own convict labourers willing to help, Mary agreed that a cremation would have to be performed. The happiness of little John's arrival was sadly tainted by tragedy on such a large scale. After the death of her family, Mary started to wear English clothes, speak English words more often and sleep in the bed with David. Every now and then, though, she would don her possum skin cloak and disappear into the hills for a few days. David understood. Men in Scotland would often do the same thing.

Many of the Scottish soldiers and the Irish emancipists had a great empathy for the natives, as the English had done the same to them, taken the land as their own and made the native populations change their customs and traditions to suit the English way of life. Like the natives in the colony, they had also suffered atrocities at the hands of the English and their families had also been starved, enslaved and murdered by the English Government.

Sandy arrived just in time to celebrate little John Rose's first birthday.

On arrival in Port Dalrymple, Sandy McKenzie found that Sergeant Donald Sutherland, who had been the loud and flamboyant Colour Sergeant during their time in Ceylon, had also been granted land near David's settlement of Corra Lynn and was also to be his neighbour, carrying on the brotherhood of Scottish loyalty, stoicism, and dark humour. Several other 73rd Regiment members took up land in the same area. Mary Sutherland was eager to know how Ann was and Sandy sadly told her the story.

Sandy was 45 years old and had never farmed before. However, with good advice from the older and more experienced Rose and Sutherland, Sandy began to develop the land while also working in Launceston as an overseer of convicts. His stern nature earned him the nickname of 'Sergeant McKenzie' among the convicts and settlers. He received a cow in 1817 as a grant from government stores and thanks to Donald's virile bull, he soon had a herd of 32 cattle and a 40-acre crop of wheat.

Sandy continued to write pleading letters to Ann requesting news of the children and asking her to again consider joining him as soon as she was able to. Sandy knew that with her skills, Ann would not be a prisoner for long. However apart from the rare letter with news of the children's growth and the weather, he received no other information.

Paterson's Plains, 1818

Almost two years after his arrival Sandy was visited by Samuel Porter, one of the other settlers. Samuel told him that he had an Irish woman working for him called Hannah Murphy. Hannah was an ex-convict and, with Private Michael Murphy of the NSW Veteran's Corps (that was stationed in Van Diemen's Land) had five daughters and a son. Murphy left Van Diemen's Land in early 1813 as part of the detachment to Norfolk Island for the evacuation, and it had become apparent over the next couple of years that he had abandoned his family. He was last heard of in New South Wales.

Hannah had skills as a governess and Samuel agreed to take her and her children on with Hannah working as governess for Samuel's four children who were around the same age as Hannah's. Things had been going along well and Hannah was a wonderful teacher for the children however there was a problem with Samuel's son John, who had gone sweet on Hannah's daughter Elizabeth. Samuel had higher hopes for his second eldest son, now 16, and needed a way to remove Elizabeth from the property. Luckily Elizabeth, aged 14, was still more interested in dolls than boys. However, Porter knew that Sandy could provide an excellent home for young Elizabeth and maybe have children of his own, as it was obvious that he was very lonely all alone on his large farm with only his convict labourers, the wombats, and the birds for company. It was not unusual for single settlers to form relationships with their assigned convicts, but both of Sandy's convict women were married to two of his convict men, and very happily. They had both recently been advised of their own land grants once they received their Tickets-of-leave in a couple of years, and Sandy was pleased that they were learning how to be successful farmers to his great benefit.

Sandy was certainly lonely and longing for his family, but marrying a child was not something that he was interested in. However, Porter convinced him that there was no harm in him meeting young Elizabeth. The following weekend Sandy attended the service at St John's in Launceston, with everyone else from the surrounding areas. The building in Cameron Street, doubled as a school during the week, as a dedicated church was yet to be built.

Sandy had to admit Elizabeth was a lovely young lady, and one day would make a fine wife. Her mother had already taught her her letters and she knew how to cook basic meals and sew basic garments. She had lovely manners and her glorious red hair shone in the sun like so many beautiful girls he had known in his childhood.

After the service Sandy and Elizabeth exchanged pleasantries over refreshments provided by the church committee, guided by Samuel with a touch of desperation. It was obvious that Porter had already discussed his idea with young Elizabeth and that after meeting Sandy, and learning of his large land holdings, she did not find the idea totally awful. There were a lot worse marriages that a young girl could make in Van Diemen's Land. Young John was suspiciously absent from the day's proceedings.

Sandy scratched his beard and thought into the future. At this time in his life and in the situation that he was living it was highly unlikely that he was going to meet any other ladies. He desperately longed for a family to fill the rooms of the comfortable house that he had built for Ann. He had even built four bedrooms in case one day his situation might change. This might be his last chance.

While he certainly didn't see himself bedding such a young girl, he could certainly take her into his home, make it a formal civil marriage to make the town happy and both he, Elizabeth and

Samuel Porter would all be better off. Maybe not poor John Porter, though.

"Right then," said Sandy "I'd better go and see the Major, and you with me Porter," he winked at Elizabeth, who blushed and looked at the ground "There's none to worry ya, lass, you can come and live with me and I have a room for you to stay in, only when you are ready will we become true husband and wife." Elizabeth looked back up at him and as he winked again, she gave him a smile that melted his heart.

Alexander McKenzie and Elizabeth Murphy were granted a civil marriage from the Major which was promulgated on 1 August 1818. A church service would not be possible as Van Diemen's Land was only visited by the Reverend Marsden on rare occasions and the new permanent Reverend, John Youl was yet to arrive in Launceston.

The following week Sandy brought his gig across to collect Elizabeth. There were tearful farewells from her mother and sisters, but they knew Elizabeth would not be far away and they could visit often. Porter had bestowed on Elizabeth a trunk full of items that she would need as the young wife of a successful settler.

When they arrived at Sandy's house, the housecat Timmy was standing guard on the porch. As Elizabeth climbed from the gig with the help of Sandy's steadying arm, Timmy came up to her rubbing himself all over her legs and lifting his head for a scratch as Elizabeth leaned down to pat him.

"I think he likes ye lass," said Sandy.

He led her into the house and showed her to the room that he had prepared for her, with a soft feather down mattress, a soft quilt made from pink and green fabric, and plump pillows. A dressing table sat next to the bed with a water pitcher and bowl in pink ceramic with a rose pattern. Sandy was grateful to the ladies of the church committee for helping him choose suitable items. A soft Turkish rug adorned the floor.

"I hope it's to your liking lass, I wasn't sure what ye may need, but no one has knocked back a feather mattress who I know of" Elizabeth giggled. Sandy then showed her the rest of the house, his room which was on the other side of the combined kitchen, dining, and front room. Two comfortable chairs sat before a hearth which had long windows on either side which looked out to the pastures below.

Sandy had prepared a joint of meat for their dinner with a thick gravy, potatoes and carrots from the garden and an apple pie (prepared by one of the servant girls). While Sandy now had eight convicts on government stores, he liked to prepare his own food for the main part, asking the two girls to make him his bread and puddings only. The four men were out all day tending the cattle and the wheat crops. The girls tidied and cleaned in the house and took care of the milk cow, chickens, and the vegetable garden. Timmy was the real 'man of the house', parading around all day, when he wasn't sleeping in a sunny spot, and demanding food and attention from the girls. To earn his keep he frequently presented assorted dead rodents and small lizards on the front doorstep for Sandy's approval. Of an evening Timmy sat on Sandy's lap in front of the fire while he read whichever book that he had been able to acquire, or the newspapers when they were available.

Now with Elizabeth in the house, Timmy had taken to sitting on her lap rather than Sandy's, and Sandy now had someone to talk to of an evening, something that he had missed so much after leaving Ann's house. Elizabeth told Sandy about her sisters and brother and the Porter children, and about what her mother had been teaching them lately. Hannah had been in the process of explaining about the monarchy and how King George III and Queen Charlotte came to the throne, as well as all about England and the different shires and counties. Elizabeth hoped one day to see London for herself, as it seemed to be like a fairy tale that places called city's existed and had so many people living in them. Sandy told Elizabeth all about Scotland and England, of Sydney and Ceylon and the other lands he had been to. Elizabeth listened wide eyed as if he was describing another planet, because to her these places where unimaginable and places that she would probably never see.

"I wish I could be a soldier and do all of those things," she said in awe. Sandy laughed "Not likely lass, but ye could find yeself a soldier's wife one day." Lizzie looked at him sharply "Nay, nay I don't want to get rid of ye, but I'm an old man lass, one day I will die, and you will still be young, there are plenty of lives that you could lead one day." Elizabeth seemed satisfied with this answer and snuggled Timmy again.

Over the next few months Sandy was able to spend more time at home on the farm as his government job was winding up now that the farm was beginning to produce enough to sell for a profit. He slowly told Elizabeth about Ann and about little John and his Mary. Elizabeth could feel his heart aching to be with the children. She wished she could do something to make him feel less sad.

One night as they were sitting having their evening chat, she suddenly looked at him with her chin raised "Mother told me about what husbands do with their wives, how babes are made. If you wish to, you can do that to me. I'll not cry. You've given me a home, and I can see that you are a good man and a good husband."

Sandy was shocked, but then laughed "Nay lass, how about ye just concentrate on learning how to wrangle that old rooster out there and get more milk in the pail than on the ground first." He laughed again and winked at her "Plenty of time for all of those wife things once ye're grown a bit more hey." Elizabeth looked relieved. Before he left them, she had heard her father grunting and huffing over her mother and every time another baby arrived not long after. She had also heard the screams and seen the blood every time a new babe was born. She was in no hurry for any of that.

The days rolled on. Now he had finished his work in Launceston, Sandy was free to spend his days working on the farm. He had started to clear more trees in preparation for a larger wheat crop. It was almost time for Christmas and Hogmanay and the Port of Dalrymple was about to welcome its first preacher, the Reverend John Youl who was visiting for three weeks to inspect his new parish. During his visit, the Reverend intended to marry as many couples as he could and baptise as many children as possible. Sandy had already put his name down to be wed formally to young Elizabeth. Donald Sutherland was also marrying Mary finally, after having three children and many adventures together.

One afternoon as Sandy was coming in from the back fields, he saw a plume of dust caused by a fine carriage coming up the road towards the house. The only person he knew with such a carriage was David Rose, whose land was not far from his. Sandy had invited David, Mary, and baby John to have Hogmanay with him and Elizabeth, knowing that while David would be welcomed at any home in the area, Mary and little John would not be. Sandy enjoyed the company of Mary who now knew quite a bit of English and what she didn't know, David instinctively understood and would interpret for her. Mary and Elizabeth were also able to converse in Mary's language, Elizabeth and the other children having learned from the local natives in what Hannah saw as an adjunct to their schooling. It was Mary who was mainly responsible for the success of the crops on the Rose, Sutherland, and McKenzie farms, with her ancient knowledge of the land and the climate.

Sandy started to jog towards the house so that he could have a wash in the outside tub before the carriage arrived. David would be here to discuss the Hogmanay and wedding arrangements, he thought.

The carriage pulled up out the front of the house and Sandy glanced up and squinted in the sun as he saw first David and then, oh no, it couldn't be, how could it be? Sandy's heart leapt in his chest with all kinds of strange emotions, because there in front of him stood Ann, his Ann, holding a very new baby, and behind her clambered down John, grown much taller in the two and a half years since he'd seen him, and then like a ray of light, a rainbow after a storm, came Mary, his little Mary.

Since he had last seen her, Mary had grown from a tiny toddler of three to a gorgeous five-year-old with huge blue eyes and dark curls rolling down her shoulders. She boldly marched up to him as he stood with his mouth open unable to form any words such was his shock.

"Good afternoon, Papa," she said and gave him the cutest curtsey. Finally, the spell was broken, and Sandy burst out laughing, scooping Mary up into his strong arms and shaking the hand of eight-year-old John who had thrust it out to him in greeting.

He then turned to Ann, who was standing next to David, rocking on the spot, with her finger jiggling in the mouth of the tiny babe who she held.

"Well lass," said Sandy, grinning, "ya better come inside, ye've got a wee bit of explaining to do," and he laughed again.

Chapter 10

Several hours and many cups of tea, and a few drams of whisky later, Ann had brought Sandy up to date with her life over the past few years. David had already heard the story on the long carriage ride from the boarding house in Launceston where he had been summoned to collect Ann and the children a couple of days after they arrived from Newcastle. Ann had needed a couple of days to make sure that her funds had made their way from Sydney, and to compose herself before she saw Sandy for the first time in two and a half years. She did not send him forward notice, unsure of the reception if she did, as she was aware that he had married around the same time as she had lost James.

On the journey to Sandy's farm David had told her that the area where they had their farms was known as Paterson's Plains, after Colonel William Paterson, who led the establishment of the settlement at Port Dalrymple. In 1818 his wife Elizabeth was the biggest landowner, holding 2000 acres near David's 800 acres, however the land was barely being used as the Paterson's had long left the colony, William dying at sea in 1810 and Elizabeth now living back in England. Ann was interested to know that Elizabeth Paterson was also a Liverpool girl.

Ann was also excited to know that Donald and Mary Sutherland were in Port Dalrymple and that Mary and little John had survived their time in Ceylon. Ann looked forward to hearing her tales. David told her that they now had three children, two boys and a girl, aged two, four and six.

Sandy good-naturedly appraised Ann of his own situation and introduced his wife Elizabeth, who had been hovering around with interest and busying herself with making the tea and playing with John and little Mary.

"I don't of course expect you to take me in as your wife again Sandy," said Ann sadly, "You have your home and your wife now, but if you'll acknowledge little Mary as your own and let her get to know you that would greatly warm my heart."

Elizabeth then jumped up and burst out "No, Miss Ann, it is most clear to me that Sandy here is very much in love with you and always has been. He was kind enough to propose to me at the time because he thought that you were lost to him. But now you are here I can clearly see how much you mean to each other. And no!" she said quickly "While we are husband and wife in name we are definitely NOT husband and wife in the ummmm" she struggled for the words "ummm in the ways of men and women. Like not in the ways of sheep and cows when they make lambs and other ummm babies."

Everyone stared at Elizabeth in shock and then a big smile came across first Ann's face and then the others, and then Elizabeth turned beetroot red and looked as if she was about to cry. Ann quickly jumped up and threw her arms around the girl and shepherded her out into the kitchen where they both had a little laugh and a little cry and talked a bit about the situation and how it could be made to work.

The men had had a few more drams of whisky when the ladies joined them again in the front room, after spending some time outside perusing Sandy's new additions to the house and yard and kicking a ball around with young John who was very lithe and quick, where David, in his 60's and Sandy now 47 were not.

Ann stood with her arm around young Elizabeth. "Right, it's settled then," she said.

"As you and Ann were already married" said Elizabeth to Sandy "We only need to go to the Major and have our marriage made null and void, which is a thing, Ann just told me."

"And" said Ann "If you will have us, the children and I would very much like to move in with you here Sandy and make this our home. Of course, Elizabeth is welcome to stay here for as long as she likes as well."

"Yes," said Elizabeth "I can teach the children their letters and some of the other lessons that my mother taught me." With that she grinned and hugged Ann.

The two men looked at each other, quite astounded at how well the situation had gone, considering everything. Sandy took a moment to find his words.

"Right then, it's decided."

"The children can sleep in the room next to me," said Elizabeth quickly, "Ann will need her rest with the baby and another on the way," Ann gave a noticeable cringe.

"And Ann," said Sandy, trying to take some authority "can sleep in the room next to mine. I shall get the women on to it now as the mattresses will need to be brought up from the store house and bedding found before it's dark."

Later that evening Sandy sat dandling tiny William on his knee as the babe gurgled and squealed in delight. "Aye, look at me lassie, I've still got the touch as I did with the other two when they were wee bairns."

"That you have Sandy," said Ann, feeling exhausted from the day.

Sandy's convict labourers had all been gathered at the homestead to meet Ann and the children as Sandy explained the unusual situation to them. Everyone then scurried off to ready the house for the new occupants and ensure that there were enough supplies in the home for the extra people who needed to be fed.

David said his farewells. Promising to bring Mary and little John over soon for a visit to meet the new members of Sandy's family. The children were fed, bathed, and taken to bed by Elizabeth who told them a fairy story as they drifted to sleep in their soft, warm feather beds. Sandy, Ann, and Elizabeth then enjoyed a delicious kangaroo stew prepared by Sadie, one of the convict women. A plum pie with clotted cream straight from the house cow followed. Elizabeth confessed that she was actually very glad of what had happened, because she thought of Sandy as a kind, old uncle, with an emphasis on the old, which made them all laugh.

"Dinna worry lass, ye can stay here for as long as you need to and when the time is right, we will find you a fine young husband, worthy of all of your beauty and kindness."

"Yes," said Ann "And until then I will be very, very grateful of your help with the children. Nursing one while growing another is a bit more tiring than I thought."

They all slept that night basking in the glow of love and happiness and so very grateful for their good fortunes.

Before they knew it, Christmas was upon the now extended McKenzie clan. Christmas had become the most celebrated holiday in Australia due to the Christian and mainly protestant influence on the colony, however Hogmanay was still celebrated with gusto by the Scots and had become New Years Eve to the rest, so the celebrations went for a week, with lots of preparation beforehand as well. Being mid-summer, the weather was perfect for outdoor parties which was very different to the cold, snowy holidays in Britain.

Both Ann and Elizabeth had taken to helping Sadie and the other convict woman, who they discovered was Sadie's sister Sarah, in the garden and the kitchen. Margaret had done most of the cooking for Ann, so she was keen to learn some more skills, and Elizabeth was also new to cooking, other than baking a few cupcakes as part of lessons that her mother ran with her and the other children.

On Christmas Eve the entire household gathered at the front of the house where the men had prepared a small bonfire, and toasted chestnuts. The adults drank eggnog heavily laced with Sandy's prize whisky, aged now for 2 years in the still in the store house. Christmas songs were sung, and a little dancing was enjoyed by all.

The day dawned with a warm glow in the sky and the aroma of eucalypt could be smelt throughout the house which had been decorated with red berries and gum leaves.

The Rose and Sutherland families arrived mid-morning with gifts for the children which they excitedly received and ran off to play with, Elizabeth in tow.

In the weeks before Christmas the children had been having fun chasing the fattened turkey around the home yard, but young Mary was inconsolable when she found out that the delicious looking roast that had been cooking all morning was the same fat old 'Turk' she had been chasing around. Although she refused to eat any of poor 'Turk' she made up for it with extra fruit mince pies and Yule log. Sadie and Sarah had never eaten let along cooked such treats, having grown up in the slums of London, but the ladies from the church had shared their Christmas recipes with the rest of the parishioners so that everyone could enjoy a proper Christian Christmas.

1819

Life went on for the McKenzie clan. Sadie and her husband John Clements announced that they were going to be parents before the following Christmas, another cause for excitement on the farm. The wheat crop was doing well and at David's recommendation, Sandy had started the men making mud bricks, which once they perfected the art, Sandy would be able to sell at a great profit to the government stores. In the meantime, they were used to build more substantial dwellings for the labourer families and make other improvements. The cattle were thriving, and the house animals were all doing well. The family ate extraordinarily well with a fat chicken most evenings and a joint of meat every Sunday. Ann and the others remembered their days growing up in England where a chicken bone with a tiny bit of flesh was a treat.

One afternoon as Mary Rose, Ann and Elizabeth were musing about what the baby would be like, Mary surprised them by stating that she had helped her grandmother to birth babies back in her tribe. She told them about the natives traditional birthing practices and their 'Grandmother's Law." "All de babies born healthy," she told them "None of the mothers get sick like here." She referred to the childbed fever that took so many of the young mothers in the colony. So far Ann had been lucky but there only had to be one time.

Mary offered to help Ann to birth the babe and was excited as she explained how she could show Sandy how to build a special birthing hut which she said was a necessary part of the ritual. Mary herself had run away into the bush when she knew it was time to birth her own little John, preferring to do it alone than have widow Jamieson, the only midwife in Port Dalrymple, other than one of the brothel Madam's in Launceston, attend her. David had thought she had run away for good and despaired for the whole day and night and was so relieved when she arrived back early the next day, smelling of smoke and eucalyptus, with a gorgeous chubby babe at her breast. She didn't have the words back then, she said, to tell him what she needed for the birth.

Sandy, under Mary's guidance, and the intrigued watchful gaze of the rest of the household, prepared a hut with bark walls, around a strong gum tree with the circumference of its trunk tested to ensure that Ann was able to get her hands around it to hang on. There was a shallow hole dug into the ground about a foot from the trunk and laden with soft hay and rabbit furs. Mary said the hole would usually be lined with gum leaves, but she had to admit the fur was much softer. A steel firepit was against one wall and Mary advised that this could be filled with hot coals when the time came, and with the bark hut sealed with the door flap, it would be toasty warm inside.

Young John begged Elizabeth to let him have afternoons off so he could go out with Sandy and watch while the men cut down the huge eucalypts. Sandy and the men showed John how to make fences with the posts they had cut from the felled trees, and John enjoyed nothing better than holding the posts like a man and sharing billy tea with his father and the others. Mary preferred to stay near the home with Ann and Elizabeth and play with little William, learn how to braid hair, listen to stories, or help in the kitchen. William, at almost nine months was a delightful baby with golden curls who happily sat playing with whatever objects he was given and laughing at the antics of his sister.

Having already delivered three babies Ann was not too concerned when she started feeling contractions in what she knew to be her ninth month, as the sun dawned on a cold morning in early May 1819. Sandy dispatched Sarah and her husband to go and collect Mary and if he was available David Rose. They arrived before lunch and Mary set about preparing the birthing hut. Sandy had started a large bonfire several days before and shovelled the hot coals into the fireplace that had been prepared in the hut.

Being so soon after her last birth and with the help of gravity from holding onto the tree trunk, swaying her hips from side to side and listening to the soothing rhythm of the birthing songs sung by Mary, the new babe was soon ready to be born. With Mary and Ann's approval, Elizabeth, Sadie, and Sarah sat quietly against the hut walls, joining in with the rhythmic chant of Mary's songs when they could, and feeling the magical emotions brought forth by the event. As the baby was born Mary gently helped it out and into the softly lined 'crib' directly under where Ann had been squatting, holding onto the trunk for dear life and groaning with unearthly sounds. The babe let out a hearty cry and Mary indicated to the other women to come and hold Ann by the arms while the afterbirth was delivered. The women were then guided to hold Ann over a bowl of smoking embers to which gum leaves had been added, to promote healing and prevent blood loss.

"It's a beautiful girl child Ann," said Mary as she gently massaged the tiny body and rubbed earth into the baby's soft skin "she's as golden as the boy."

Mary called out to the men who were waiting a decent distance from the hut "It's a wee girl child," she had picked up a few distinct Scottish words along with her slight Irish accent.

The women could hear the Scottish woots and howls of delight and knew that a new bottle of whisky would now be opened.

Ann fell into a relaxed slumber with the new babe in her arms and shortly after let the women gently guide her back to the house and into her bed, where toast and a cup of tea was waiting.

Ann looked at the tiny babe suckling at her breast, her golden fuzz, and transparent eyebrows a replica of her brother's and her father's. She allowed herself a tiny moment to feel the grief of the loss of her James, which would always be there. But she then buried it deep inside her heart because she knew that he was gone and her life, and the lives of her children belonged here now with a big-hearted Scotsman who had loved her since he first saw her in Parramatta.

Chapter 11

*W*inter was harsh that year, with rain, hail, driving wind and constant storms. Luckily Sandy and the others on the farm had built their houses to a sufficient standard to keep out the cold. And luckily, they had cut enough wood before the cold set in because even the wood of the trees became damp and frozen.

The womenfolk were kept busy with the babies. William, about to turn one and Margaret three months, were all chubby, pink cheeked, blue eyed and golden haired. Ann spent a great deal of her day nursing one or the other, although William had started taking some porridge and sucking on bread. Young Mary enjoyed spending her days playing with the babies, or helping in the kitchen, and would become a bit sullen when Elizabeth summoned her to work on her letters. John was happy if he could join the men in their tasks. A large barn had been built and the lambs and calves were mostly in there while it was so cold. This created a new job of mucking out the barn, a job that was never ending. That was not John's favourite job, but doing that task gave him the leverage to be allowed to spend more time with the men.

With the ground frozen, tending the herd, producing bricks, and making improvements to the farm, became the main tasks for the men during winter.

In August, every person in the colony had to register for the colonial records. Sandy diligently went and registered his little family. Alexander McKenzie aged 48, Ann McKenzie aged 26, John McKenzie aged eight, Mary McKenzie, six, William Wells McKenzie just turned one, Margaret McKenzie aged three months; and Elizabeth Murphy, aged 15.

The harsh chill started to leave the air around September and the McKenzie's and the other families on the farm, along with other settlers from the Port of Dalrymple area started to attend services again. Sadly, the fledgling church where Reverend Youl had carried out his mass marriage and baptism service at Christmas, had not progressed over the winter as Governor Macquarie had decided to move the seat of government from Launceston to George Town, near the coast. However, there were several settlers who acted as lay preachers and gave the townsfolk a reason to get together. Such activities were very important, as they gave everyone an opportunity to meet other farmers, merchants, traders, and businesspeople and develop relationships that would be advantageous in the future, either for personal or business reasons. Many marriages had their first introductions at these church gatherings and many land and trade transactions were first discussed there. On days when there were visiting officials, farmers or merchants from Hobart or the mainland, the town became almost festival like, with music and entertainments. And like Sydney, Launceston had quickly adopted horse racing as it's favourite sport, providing another reason to get together, and a source of entertainment.

Sandy, Donald, and David had started to enjoy the company of a group of Irish and English farmers living on land further south. They included men around the same age as the Scotsmen, including emancipist Irishmen Thomas Brennan and James Jordan who had come from Norfolk Island during the evacuations and had been farming for longer than David Rose had. There was much to learn from each other. Samuel Porter also lived down that way and the Scottish contingent would use young Elizabeth as an excuse for a get together when they could. While Elizabeth visited her mother and siblings the farmers would spend the day discussing farming business.

Sometimes the days turned into nights. If there was one thing that drew the men together other than farming, it was whisky. Both the Scottish and the Irishmen had a love of the spirit and there was as much competition over who had the best whisky as who had the best cattle or the best farm. One evening around a bonfire Sandy was discussing life with Thomas Brennan, a man a few years older than him. Thomas had spent his younger years in Ireland doing much the same as Sandy had, helping his father on the farm after his mother died. Desperate times called for desperate measures and Thomas and almost everyone he knew where only surviving by occasionally stealing food or items to sell to buy food. His luck ran out early, and he was convicted in Kildare when he was 24 years old and came out to the colony with the Second Fleet on the *Marquis Cornwallis*. He was sent to Norfolk Island and was soon given a Ticket-of-leave and a land grant to start farming so that the island could produce its own food. When it was decided to evacuate the island and send everyone to Van Diemen's Land, Thomas was given a Conditional Pardon and a grant of 30 acres at South Esk.

"That's when I had to start using one name," he laughed," I've been using different names all my life. I was born Doyle, have been Murphy, and came here as Brennan. I didn't want anyone to find me once, now I hope they do." He laughed again.

"And have ye no family Thomas?" asked Sandy.

"Well, there was a lass at Norfolk who lived with me for a long time. Her name was Mary, and she came out on the Second Fleet as well. We spent many years together making the farm work at Norfolk, but she died not long after we arrived here. And no," he said holding his hand up as Sandy was about to ask, "there were no children. Mary suffered some terrible injuries from her time in prison and on the ship, and no wee one's ever happened for us." He sadly shook his head.

"Aye man, that is a shame." said Sandy "Look at me now. For so many years I had no one then when I met Ann, I quickly had two bairns, and now four wee ones. Although with the din in the hoos sometimes I wish again for my peace and quiet." They both laughed. "There's still time ye know man, never fear that love has left ye go by, I thought that so many times, but now my life is so good I canna bear it sometimes, the feel of the love in my heart. If ye find someone worth having as ye wife, dinna stop until she says yes." He slapped his knee to emphasise his point. Thomas looked at him slowly, letting the words sink in. Maybe there was still time left to have it all.

There was more celebrating to be done when John and Sadie Clements added their own babe, James, to the McKenzie farm. Another smoking ceremony was held for the birth with Mary presiding, and the birth was easy and calm. Sadie and Ann enjoyed their time sitting by the hearth at the window overlooking the pastures while they nursed their babes together.

The days got warmer. Sandy and the men were once again out and about clearing the land for more pastures. This was dangerous work as some of the trees had trunks as broad as a house. Sandy now shared four bullocks with David and Donald, that he used to help pull the trees down once the men had cut into them enough to fell. The area where they were clearing was a good hour's ride from the house and John was vested with making sure that the men had enough water and food for the day. He was forever sweet-talking Sadie and Sarah to add extra slices of cake. Being so far away meant that if they encountered trouble, it was harder to get help.

One of the men had been bitten by a snake the month before and only intensive care-giving and native magic from Mary Rose had brought him out of the fever he had gone into after the wound festered. They often encountered groups of natives passing through and Sandy would always make sure to call out with the words that Mary had taught him and if they got closer to offer them something as a gift. After all, they were living on the native's land. Unlike some farmers, David, Donald, and Sandy did not begrudge the natives hunting on their farms. They were only interested in the lizards, possums, and kangaroos anyway and left the cattle alone. Every now and then Sandy would hang a slaughtered beast for them where he knew they would find it on their tracks, and would then find gifts in exchange, baskets and water bowls and sometimes interesting tools and weapons. Mary had told them that they were the Panninher and lived up around the area now called Ben Lomond.

Once, the men had come across what they thought were bushrangers camped near the river, and they prepared themselves with their rifles. However, it turned out to be a group of young boys who had run away, they said, from their cruel master. The stories that they told made Sandys' hair curl and he made a note of who the farmer was, so that David could mention him to the magistrate. Sandy and the men shared their rations with the boys and sent them on their way, telling them where they could find safe passage.

One afternoon the sun was high in the sky and beginning to make the men sweat as they laboured over their clearing work. One particular tree, a smaller one, was proving more difficult than usual to fell.

"I think there's a boulder or something stuck under it," said Sandy to John, "pass me that shovel and I'll see if I can budge it." John did as his father asked and watched as Sandy levered the shovel under a large boulder and strained to try and lift it. Suddenly there was a crack and the tree unexpectedly fell sideways, pushing Sandy to the ground and bouncing off his broad chest with a thud before rolling off to the side. It was a very quick incident but enough for Sandy to feel a crack in his chest and to feel a strong pain start creeping throughout his body. At first, he thought he'd been winded because it was suddenly very difficult to breathe.

The men rushed to his side, yelling, and talking all at once to try and figure out what to do. One of them went and got the bullock tray and harnessed two horses to it, and then the men gently lifted the gasping Sandy onto the back of the tray, one holding each side, while another balanced on the front to lead the horses as quickly as they could back to the house. John and the other man followed on horseback.

The women had seen the odd vehicle coming along the path at speed and raced out to see what the problem was.

"Quickly," said one of the men "Get the sulky and fresh horses, Mr McKenzie has had a tree fall on him."

Ann screamed at the news and ran to the tray where Sandy lay gasping for breath. "Oh, my love, my darling," she cried, running her hand over his brow. Sandy appeared to gather his strength to try and talk to his beloved "Dinna fash yeself woman," he said quietly but with a faint glimmer of a smile, "it's nothing and I'll be right soon." At this he coughed, and blood splattered across his shirt. "Move Mrs McKenzie," said one of the men. "We'll get him down to Lieutenant Rose; he'll know what to do." And with that three of the men took off at speed with Sandy lying across them in the sulky.

None of the women slept that night, and all the children sensing the solemn atmosphere were restless and unable to settle. Baby Margaret would nod off to sleep and wake within the hour inconsolable. The women took turns jiggling her around the house and making pots of strong tea. Mary Rose had made her way to the

McKenzie's and sat with the other women. Every now and then she would go outside and seemed to be chanting or singing something while looking up at the stars. She was "talking to the spirits," she said, trying to send good luck to Sandy. The women prayed to their own spirits for the same thing.

The following afternoon, which just happened to be young John's ninth birthday, they once again saw the dirt kicked up along the path that led to the house. Eventually they could tell that it was David's carriage along with the sulky and the other horses that had left the day before. "Thank God," thought Ann "David is bringing him home in comfort so that we can nurse him back to health here."

As the horses got closer everyone stood outside waiting. Finally, the carriage pulled up and David climbed down. His face was grim as he approached Ann with his hat in his hand and told her that Sandy, her big, broad, kind Scotsman had died. Ann collapsed onto the ground and the women gathered around, but they were all as inconsolable as Ann. Sandy had been a strong leader and protector for all of them. They all loved his capable and gentle ways, and he would be irreplaceable.

Alexander McKenzie, of Paterson's Plains, born in Fodderty, Scotland and previously with the 73rd Regiment, died on Thursday the 9th of December 1819 in Launceston, where David Rose had desperately begged the surgeon to save his life.

He had known adventure and he had known love. A life well lived.

Chapter 12

*T*he Reverend John Youl had arrived in Van Diemen's Land a few weeks before Sandy died. After a long delay and being told that neither his church nor his home had been built, he was eager to get back to his parishioners, so many of whom he had married and baptised the previous Christmas. So, at his own cost, he chartered the government brig *Prince Leopold* and arrived with his wife and children and thirty tons of freight at Launceston in November 1819 and moved into a government cottage.

Sadly, the first entry in the St John's church register was the death of Sandy McKenzie.

A funeral was held for Sandy in the makeshift church and Youl summoned the mourners with an iron drum. Mourners came from near and far as many members of the colony had grown to know and love the big Scottish 'Sergeant McKenzie" since his arrival in 1816.

David Rose arranged a wake to be held at his substantial home afterwards for close family and friends, but even then, at least 200 people showed up. Sadie, Sarah, Elizabeth, Ann, and Mary had kept their mind off their loss by baking for the wake and a huge spread was laid out. All the farmers who Sandy had his whisky 'competitions' with had donated several bottles of their finest which was being passed around the men, with the women also enjoying a dram or two in the kitchen.

Ann stood forlorn next to David as each mourner approached with their most sincere sentiments for her loss.

Back at the McKenzie farm everyone waited anxiously while David Rose investigated all the legalities of Sandy's estate. Eventually he was able to tell Ann that Sandy's wishes, that he had been so careful to have recorded back in 1816, would be made legal and young Mary was the sole inheritor of the farm and all of Sandy's monetary holdings, which had been accumulating from his wages, military pension, and proceeds from the farm. Ann, as her mother and now a single woman, would be given responsibility for the estate until Mary came of age, unless she married, in which case her husband would look after the estate. But everything would still belong to Mary unless she chose in the future to sell or gift any part of it.

Ann asked each of her workers if they would stay on to help her with the farm, and John Clements was made foreman. John and Sadie and Sarah and her husband Jeremiah Jones were due to receive their pardons and land grants within the next year so Ann felt lucky that she would have them at least until then. Three of the other four men had been wooing some of the women from around the area, so Ann was hoping that there would soon be more couples to stay on and help after the Clements and Jones' had left.

Once again Ann was a widow. Twice in less than two years. She felt that if she let the grief wash over her it would overwhelm her, and she would surely die from it. One morning she was listlessly nursing Margaret while Mary Rose kept her company and Elizabeth took care of the other children.

"Ann," said Mary quietly "no one has let him go yet. We need to have the ceremony." Ann looked at her with sad eyes as Mary explained that in her culture everyone who loved the person must get together and cry together and let their grief out. "Will you allow me to do this for you?"

"Yes," said Ann.

Two evenings later, out of the bush like ghosts, came a contingent of people from the local tribes. These were people who Sandy and the other men had formed relationships with while working out in the bush. Ann wondered if the group made up the entirety of the native population from the area, because Mary had told her that so many of them had already died of illnesses that they blamed the white men for or been killed in battles with the settlers. Mary told her that before the white man came her people had never known such illnesses and for the ones that they did know, they had treatments or even cures. The local natives did not like to come near Paterson's Plains because in recent years when a group of them were travelling to Launceston, they were set upon by some of the settlers and the whole group was murdered. Ann felt very grateful that they had come to honour 'Sergeant McKenzie' and to help her.

The men had painted their faces with red ochre and white ash and the women were bare chested. They set a large fire a short walk away from the house, and they started singing. The music and the songs sounded sad and mournful, even though the words were mostly unknown to the farmers. David and Mary arrived in their carriage, along with Donald and Mary Sutherland. The British settlers made their way to the ceremonial ground, Sadie staying in the house with the children and babies. The natives encouraged the settlers to take part in the chanting and the strange, slow dances that they were carrying out. Time seemed to stand still as the stars in the sky, the rhythmic chanting of the songs and the whirling of their bodies as they danced, gave way to an outpouring of grief as each person found the feelings that they had kept locked in their hearts and let the sadness that they felt at Sandy's loss take over them. It seemed like hours that they all swayed by the fire, flailed their arms around, crying and wailing, and then, suddenly, it was over. The clapping of the sticks, the rhythm of the didgeridoo stopped, and the natives, slowly faded into the bush, their job done. The settlers all looked at each other's tear-streaked faces and settled into humble contemplation by the fire. Though the participants never talked about the ceremony with anyone else, they all agreed in private that they all felt much better after it, as if they had sung and wailed Sandy into heaven.

The McKenzie farm did not celebrate Christmas or Hogmanay in 1819, although they did all attend the Reverend Youl's service on Christmas Eve. There was still too much sadness to celebrate anything, even Jesus' birth.

1820

The McKenzie household settled into a new rhythm, different to what they had been used to with the burly Sandy and his comings and goings. Now the house took on a more feminine feel, with Ann and the babies, young James, Sadie's baby, who spent the days in the house with the McKenzie two, and Elizabeth tutoring and caring for Mary and John. John Clements came down each day and informed Ann of what work had been done that day, to which Ann listlessly nodded. When asked what he should concentrate on next, Ann just waved her hand being ignorant of farming needs and at that time uncaring of it either. Luckily the farm was already set up well enough that the cattle thrived, and the wheat grew without too much help. The men were now expert at brick making and David Rose had gained a contract for Ann to supply them to the government stores.

Although the others went into the town for Sunday services Ann stayed away, not ready for the prying eyes of the other settlers and townsfolk. Elizabeth went, to see her mother and siblings, and the labourers went as well, the Clements' and Jones' to meet other farmers and form friendships that might help them once they got their land grants, and the other men went to meet girls.

One afternoon while she waited for the others to get back from services Ann was busy getting some food ready for the older children, when she heard a loud neighing out the front of the house. She hurried out to see two men on horseback carrying pistols. They screamed at Ann to stay outside as they ran into the house. The children began to scream as the men started to ransack the house. Ann heard John yelling at them to stop, followed by a loud whacking sound and then silence. She ran inside to see John on the ground and the men grabbing their belongings and shoving them into bags. She screamed and ran to John and was kicked by one of the men as he ran back out the door. Then no sooner had they arrived than they were gone again, galloping up towards the back paddocks.

Little John recovered quickly with just a bruise on his head and wounded pride, but Ann shook like a leaf until the others arrived back from church and she fell into Sadie's arms. Thankfully the bushrangers must have been in a hurry as apart from some items from the house, and the rifles from the stables, they didn't take anything or demand anything more.

David Rose arrived the next day. Over a cup of tea, he told Ann that he felt that it was too unsafe for her to be living without a husband. She was just prey waiting for every vulture and evil doer to swoop down on her. He could tell that she did not have a passion for farming and in her grief no inclination to develop one. David had an idea and told Ann just to hear him out. He knew that she was still grieving, and that romance was not on her agenda. But there was a farmer, a man who both he and Sandy trusted and liked, who lived not far from Samuel Porter. His name was Thomas Brennan.

"I know him," said Ann slowly "We have stopped at his house on the way home from visiting Elizabeth's mother Hannah."

"Yes, that's him." Said David. "Listen Ann, Thomas is not a young man, he is 54, and he has never married. He did have a common law wife in Norfolk Island, but they never had children and she died not long after they arrived here in 1813. He's a lonely man, Ann, and he's a good man. His farm is thriving, and he has six convicts also. He could help you to keep the farm and protect Mary's inheritance. That meant a lot to Sandy."

After David left Ann once again sunk into melancholy. Nursing her two babies while grieving two husbands had depleted every drop of energy that she had to think about the future. It would be nice to hand over responsibility for everything to someone else, and just be able to concentrate on her children. Maybe she could even start doing a little dress making again. Port Dalrymple was growing every day and there would be ladies arriving who would want to have beautiful dresses made for them, and there would soon be events for them to wear them at.

Mary Sutherland and Hannah Murphy came for morning tea the next week, to check on Ann and make sure that she was not pining away to nothing. They found her in higher spirits than they imagined she would be, but still with a grey pallor and shadows under her eyes from grieving and a lack of sleep. Margaret was teething and Ann would often be up for most of the night soothing her.

Ann told them about David's idea and they both agreed that Thomas Brennan was a good man. His house, if not pretty, was large and substantial and his workers said only good things about him. He donated much of the profits from his farm to the church and the orphanage to go towards those less fortunate.

Thomas Brennan married Ann McKenzie at St John's, Launceston on 28 June 1820, in a small but pretty ceremony presided over by Reverend Youl, who told Ann how happy he was for both her and for Thomas, who had longed for a family for many years. They also took the opportunity to baptise little Margaret who was baptised as Margaret Brennan, and Mary who was then seven and had missed out on being baptised in Newcastle due to her illness. She was baptised as Mary McKenzie.

When Ann first met Thomas, she was shy and embarrassed and a little ashamed, expecting a man who was kind enough to take her and the children 'under his wing', in an act of welfare. But the man who she met was very much like Sandy. Thomas was a large man, like Sandy, but with auburn hair and a beard that made him look like a large troll, she thought giggling to herself. But his emerald eyes had such a twinkle that if he was a troll, he was definitely a good troll. At their first meeting he had her giggling within the first half hour with his good nature and sense of humour.

When he met the children, he was equally as happy and entertaining, and they all took to him straight away. He may have been an older man, but he was nimble on his feet and within the hour he was wrestling on the floor with John and Mary and letting the babies crawl and drool all over him.

"I like him Ann," said Elizabeth who was now Ann's ward.

And Ann liked him too.

They decided for the least disruption for the children that Thomas would move into the house with Ann, as everything was already set up there for them, and Thomas needed to quickly get his head around the McKenzie holdings so that he could start making decisions for their future. Thomas moved into the room that Ann had slept in when she first arrived from Newcastle, but within a few weeks Ann and Thomas were sharing a bed. His rough warm arms reminded her of Sandy, and the warmth was greatly appreciated as the winter of 1820 was another cold one.

It was with immense sadness that the Brennan/McKenzie household found out over winter that their beautiful friend Mary Rose had died from a chest infection. She was fine and hearty as always and then one day was struck with a cough and congestion and was dead with the week. It was well known that the natives did not tolerate the illnesses that the British seemed to be able to recover from quite easily. A mild cough to one of the settlers could kill a native within days. And that is what happened to poor Mary.

David had already had a terrible year when his ethics and honour were called into question, along with the Commandant, Lieutenant-Colonel Cimitiere, by government examiners who questioned their honesty in their government dealings. The charges were finally dropped but left David feeling depressed, and he resigned his position, to concentrate on his farming interests.

After Mary died, David in his grief, found it hard to care for his son John, who was then five years old. John started to spend more time with the convict workers wives, and he started to prefer to sleep in their quarters rather than go back to the house and his drunken, crying father. David eventually sent for one of the girls from a neighbouring farm to care for John, who like the other children who were half white and half black in the colony, were half accepted, and half outcast by the society into which they were born. In the 'better' houses, like David's, it was not the 'done' thing to have a 'darkie' around, a fact that had upset David for the whole time that he was with his beloved Mary.

David, his life falling apart, and at the urging of Donald Sutherland, sent to England for his brother Alexander to come to the colony to help him. Alexander had also been a Lieutenant in the 73rd Regiment and had served with Donald and Sandy in Ceylon. Instead, Alexander sent his son Alexander Jnr, who thankfully took immediate responsibility for the property and provided a great support for David, although David was never the same again.

Margaret had just started to be confident enough to go outside and run around with her older siblings when Ann found she was again with child. It was not unexpected, as Ann had realised that God had obviously gifted her with superior fertility. The extreme tiredness that Ann had felt since Sandy's death had started to creep out of her body, as it was replaced with feelings of hope and joy with her new husband who had her smiling and laughing every day. She would be tending the yard when he would seemingly appear from nowhere with a flower behind his ear which he handed to her with a pat on her bottom and a gurgle in his throat. That always made her laugh. At night he would pretend to be a troll and get on the floor and crawl around chasing the children, making troll noises as they shrieked with delight.

 **1821**

There was much excitement in the colony when it was announced that Governor Macquarie and Mrs Macquarie were to visit Port Dalrymple mid-year, for the first time since 1811 which was not long after the first convicts had started to be sent there. The town of Launceston spent months preparing with painting and whitewashing, and tending the gardens to make sure that everything looked its very best for the Governor. The main seat of government for Port Dalrymple was at George Town near the coast, so any events for the Governor were being held there, much to the disgust of the citizens of Launceston, which was a much larger and more developed town.

With both William and Margaret now weaned and spending more time with Elizabeth and the older children, Ann had started to do a little dressmaking and found time to make a beautiful dress for one of the merchant's wives with cloth that had been purchased from Mr Avery Stodges and shipped to the colony. When Ann had appraised Thomas of her previous occupation and her old friends in Sydney, he had arranged for Avery to send a selection of fabrics and notions so that Ann could start her work again, as just a hobby if she wanted to, but also as a distraction from her grief, and from her pregnancy, which seemed to trouble her a lot more than her others had.

On their way from Hobart to George Town the Macquarie's stopped to visit their old friend David Rose. Macquarie wrote in his diary:

> "We travelled over Gordon Plains, passed the Sugarloaf, through Camden Valley and Paterson's Plains to Mr Rose's farm where we halted for half an hour to see our old friend and view the beautiful and picturesque Corri-Lynn on the North Esk River."

It was to be one of Macquarie's last duties as Governor as he was replaced by another Scotsman, Major General Sir Thomas Brisbane in December of 1821.

Little Thomas Brennan Junior was born on 21 May 1821. Without dear Mary to conduct her ceremony (something that Thomas did not quite approve of anyway), Ann was ably assisted by Elizabeth, Sadie and Sarah who had by then seen quite a few births. The sisters had been supporting several of the other local convict women through their births.

But little Thomas was not as healthy and strong as his brothers and sisters had been. He fussed and refused to nurse, and he barely slept between screaming fits. Ann was beside herself trying to coax the boy into nursing as he grew paler and scrawnier. Thomas took him for long walks to try and calm him, both rugged up, so that Thomas Snr really did look troll-like, at which the other children giggled.

Another event was brewing in the family as well. Young John Porter had never given up his quest for Elizabeth's love, and if there was any chance to see her, he would be there. As Elizabeth approached her 18th birthday, she finally realised that she did love the handsome boy who she had grown up with after her father had left. Her siblings only said good things about him, and he had already been given a land grant, near his father's farm and near Thomas Brennan's original farm. Although Elizabeth was very happy and comfortable where she was with Ann, at 18 she was rather old to be unmarried and she knew that eventually she would have to do so. She told John that so long as he built her a house that was as comfortable as the McKenzie house (as it was still known), she would marry him in the summer.

Tiny Thomas Brennan died as the spring lambs began to be born. It was once again such a sad time. The children had never known anyone to die but Sandy, who to them was very old, and they found it hard to understand how a baby could die, when he had only just arrived. The Reverend had made a visit to the farm to christen the babe when he continued to fail to thrive, so he was allowed to be buried in the church cemetery next to Sandy. Ann sadly folded and put away the baby clothes and items that had been so lovingly made ready just months before.

It was time for Ann to prepare herself for the fact that Elizabeth would soon be leaving. John was nearly 11, Mary 8, William 3, and Margaret 2. With no babe to care for, her time would be free to spend with her children. She had learned some of the lessons that Elizabeth had been working on with them and Elizabeth's mother

Hannah would give her more ideas, so that the McKenzie/Brennan children knew their letters and other things about the world as well. The older two would be able to go to school now and Ann was keen for this because after her recent sojourn back into dress making, she was eager to make use of the haul of fabrics that Thomas had bought for her. Maybe she could start teaching young Mary and some of the farm women, of which there were now four. Catherine and Martha had joined two of the convict men and were starting to become part of the household, as Sadie and Sarah were. Sadie and Sarah's husbands had now received their land grants and were spending their Sundays and any other time that they could building their own houses in preparation for getting their Ticket's-of-leave and their own grant of convict labour.

With time on her hands and to still the sadness in her heart, Ann set about making Elizabeth the most beautiful wedding dress that the Port of Dalrymple had ever seen. For the first time Ann was making a dress with a tight waistline, where the natural waistline sat, as the former fashion of the skirt falling from just under the bust line was well and truly gone in fashionable circles. But as Ann had not sewn such a dress before she sent for patterns from Sydney to make sure that she got it right. Margaret in Sydney was put in charge of finding the best pattern, cut from thin kangaroo hide rather than paper, as the pattern would last forever and not fall apart after a few uses. And choosing the perfect fabric, lace, and notions. As the wedding was to be at the height of summer a large leghorn bonnet was purchased decorated with extravagant ruched silk and satin in cream with a wide pink ribbon. Tiny cream and yellow silk flowers completed the look. The dress itself was made from cream satin and over that was a sheer pink pelisse decorated with the same cream and yellow silk flowers. To complete the ensemble Ann made a set of silk pantaloons for Elizabeth to wear under her dress, the height of luxury.

Of course, all the children were part of the wedding party and they all needed new outfits as well, so Ann was kept extremely busy throughout the second half of 1821, which thankfully kept her mind off other more sadder things.

1822

Elizabeth and John Porter were married on 4 Feb 1822 at St John's church, another happy occasion for the Reverend Youl, who at the time was being pulled between Launceston and George Town, where Governor Macquarie had insisted that the main town would be. Unfortunately, he had not listened to the people or to the Commandant who knew that most settlers wanted to be around Launceston where the water supply and land was better for farming. So Youl was obliged to hold services at George Town but also needed to attend to his main flock, in Launceston.

Elizabeth moved into the comfortable house that John had built for her and was pleased to see that everything she needed was already there, except her beloved children and the company of other women that she had come to love. John and his father Samuel were busy sorting out the newly arrived convicts and working out priorities for John's farm. But not busy enough to neglect his new wife which soon became apparent as Elizabeth was quite pregnant a few months later. She still spent a lot of time at the McKenzie/Brennan farm but had started to befriend the young convict girls who they had been allocated, two shy and unworldly girls in need of guidance, finding themselves on the other side of the world from everything they had ever known. Elizabeth immediately became more of a tutor than a Mistress.

Things at the McKenzie Brennan farm moved along well. Thomas was now expert at managing both farms and overseeing all the convict labour. He had started getting young John to spend more time with him, learning the business of overseeing, rather than staying at home with the women and children. After losing his longed-for son, Thomas had decided that rather than dwell of what could have been to concentrate on what he did have, and he did have a gaggle of children and a beautiful wife.

Elizabeth's first child, little Richard Porter was born on 28 September, a little earlier than expected but still hale and hearty with a yell that would awaken the dead. Elizabeth was ably assisted by Sadie and Sarah and her mother, who had all come in from their various farms as soon as they got word that she needed them. Ann visited in the days that followed with only Mary, then nine; the others staying at home with Catherine and Martha so as not to create any chaos at Elizabeth's house. Ann was able to tell Elizabeth that she was also expecting again. She longed for another babe after losing little Thomas, but she was also scared that maybe there was something in Thomas' blood that made his babies weak. She could not bear losing another tiny one.

Chapter 13

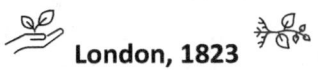 **London, 1823**

*T*homas Beswick, aged 17, lived above The Exeter Arms, in

Burleigh St, off The Strand in London, where his father, also Thomas, was the publican. He had a sister, Margaret, four years older and already married, and two younger siblings, Martha 15, and Samuel 10. Thomas's father was born and grew up in the centre of London, although his mother came from Hampshire and longed again for the country air. However, like his father before him, Thomas' father found good fortune in the publican business at Seven Dials, where he was never short of customers.

The greatest number of convicts transported to Australia came from Seven Dials and its surrounding areas. The area was fraught with poverty and was notorious for its population who were resistant to authority and hostile to lawful society. Seven Dials, and the people who lived there among chaos and squalor is best described by the great author Charles Dickens, who was fascinated by the miasma of life in the area. Pick pockets and fences, prostitutes and chimney sweeps, and all types of inhabitants all vied for space in the narrow alleys and tenements, where raw sewage was flung from windows to the slimy, stinking cobblestones below. Drinking, swearing, fighting, and stealing were the main activities of a population whose main source of nutrition was usually gin. Cockfights and puppet shows vied for attention along with pantomimes, orators and poets on every corner.

Thomas' family were well off in comparison to most in the area and Thomas' father was keen for his son to join him in the business, promising to help him into his own establishment if he showed an affinity for the work. For the most part Thomas went along with his father's wishes. He was a good and compliant boy, but the area was full of bad influences and Thomas was not immune to peer group pressure.

Thomas was frequently the butt of jokes and bullied by the boys from his local area. And being 17, like every other boy, he wanted to fit in. As much as his parents told him not to associate with the local boys, who else was he to 'associate' with?

So it was, that on Christmas Eve 1822 Thomas found himself 'associating' with a group of local lads, messing around as teenagers do.

"Hey" said one "Tommy toffy nose I bet ya can't grab that nice watch in the window there?" They were outside Thomas Walker's watch making shop in Eastcastle Street near Oxford Square.

"Why would I want to?" said Thomas defiantly.

"Because we know you won't do it Tommy too good, Tommy toffy nose." The boys started chanting and teasing him.

"I can too!" said Thomas suddenly angry and ashamed of how they saw him, and with that he grabbed a loose brick and smashed the front window of the shop, grabbing the watch, but only getting the case in his haste to run off. A customer who had been in the shop talking with Walker ran out and started yelling "Stop Thief', a common cry in the area.

Thomas quickly wrapped the watch case in his handkerchief and shoved it into his pocket as he ran into Wells Street. William Zietter, a citizen of the area, saw Thomas running towards him and heard the cry from Walker's customer, a Mr Brown, and side-stepped Thomas catching him squarely and throwing him to the ground. Brown soon arrived and told Zietter "That's him, that's the thief." Thomas looked around but none of his 'friends' were anywhere to be seen.

Thomas was tried at The Old Bailey on 16 January charged with `burglariously breaking and entering the dwelling-house of Thomas Walker, about the hour of six, on the night of the 24th of December, at St. Marylebone, with intent to steal, and stealing therein one watchcase, value 5s., and one watch hook, value 2d.' Thomas was found guilty and sentenced to death. He gave his age as 15, hoping to gain some mercy from the Court. He was in luck because his death sentence was later changed to transportation for life, given his age, his character, and the fact that it was his first offence.

Thomas spent the first half of 1823 on a prison hulk on the Thames River. After a morning wash, a breakfast of bread and cocoa and time spent washing down the decks and cleaning the ship, Thomas and his fellow convicts were ferried across to the dockyards where they spent the day unloading ballast and timber from ships. They moved cables, dredged channels, and shifted rubble. The men were required to always wear a heavy chain on one or both ankles. If they misbehaved, the weight of their leg irons would be increased. After they were rowed back to their hulks the convicts were free to engage in a range of activities. Thomas learned to read and write far better on the hulk than he had at school, and he also learned the basics of the trade of cordwainer, making shoes from leather. A group of men were engaged in learning this trade with other groups learning other skills. He fell into bed every night exhausted.

Thomas was transported on *The Sir Godfrey Webster*, which left Gravesend, not far downstream from the hulks at Woolwich, on 21 July 1823, first moving to Sheerness at the mouth of the river, leaving there on 8 August, and finally after sailing Westward in the English Channel departing England from Falmouth on 4 September. There were 180 male convicts on board. They called at the Canary Islands for supplies, left Teneriffe on 28 September and sailed for three months around the Cape and direct to Hobart, arriving there on 27 December 1823, just a year after Thomas was arrested.

A great adventure was about to start for Thomas.

Chapter 14

Paterson's Plains, 1823

*I*n January 1823 Lieutenant Colonel Charles Cameron had arrived at Port Dalrymple with his wife and children to replace Lieutenant Colonel Cimitiere as Commandant of the settlement. After appraising himself of the situation he was dismayed to see that George Town remained devoid of settlers, but grand new government buildings were going up everywhere. The town of Launceston was a thriving hub of trade, worship, and community, but much of its buildings and infrastructure was falling into disrepair. He immediately petitioned Governor Brisbane to move the seat of government back to Launceston which was obviously the preferred destination of the people. Brisbane appraised himself of the situation and agreed and ordered Cameron to start the task of moving the main seat of government back to Launceston.

To everyone's joy little Elizabeth Brennan was born on 17 Apr 1823. Ann was spooked by what happened to little Thomas two years prior and thought that it might have been because they didn't have a traditional ceremony like Mary Rose had shown them. This time the women who remembered how, set up a form of bark hut like Mary Rose had done, and tried as best they could to carry out a birthing ceremony. They had been unable to find any natives to consult as they had all been missing from the area for over a year now, which greatly saddened Ann, but was celebrated by many of the other settlers. There was so much that could have been learned from the natives. However, there were still violent skirmishes going on further out from Paterson's Plains in the mountains around Ben Lomond.

Thomas was unable to stay around for the birth, being too full of fear and anxiety. He spent the time with his friend James Jordan, a fellow Irishman who he had been on Norfolk Island with and came to Port Dalrymple with. James was a single man; his wife having died on Norfolk Island not long before they were to leave in 1813. James had been busy raising their five children, the youngest of whom was only four when they arrived and hadn't had time to find another wife. His three sons, Richard, James and Thomas, and stepson William Saltmarsh (his wife's first son born on the journey from England) had recently been granted their own land in the area. Another young man who received his land grant around the same time and was known to them from Norfolk Island was William Renton Kerr. James' daughter Catherine was married to James Davey, another local farmer. James Jordan's youngest son John was just a year older than John McKenzie, and the boys got along famously, plotting what they would do once they had their own farms.

Thomas was overjoyed when he heard of the safe arrival of his daughter and hurried back to the farm and to Ann. Ann was happily sitting up in bed with the new babe when he arrived home, being tended to by Catherine and Martha, who were taking turns being Ann's nurse and nanny to the other McKenzie children, although John at 13 and Mary at 10 were quite capable or looking after little William, five and Margaret, four, when needed. And now with Elizabeth living at her own house with her own baby they were expected to help more around the home. Both John and Mary attended school at Launceston during the week when the weather allowed, making the trek each morning and afternoon as far as Corra Lynn, where an open cart collected all the local children. Ann had been unable to find a replacement for Elizabeth as tutor, but the little ones were still too young for schooling anyway and Ann and the girls had fun playing with them and teaching them the basics of life, doing their chores, helping in the garden and the kitchen, and now helping with the baby. Margaret was ecstatic to have a little sister and was eager for her to start playing dolls with her, although baby Elizabeth just coo 'ed and giggled at her big sister.

Thomas had been very busy expanding the farm interests and building more substantial infrastructure on the farm. He was also acutely aware that the farm that they were all living on would be passed on to Mary and Mary's husband one day when she wed. He mentioned to Ann that now that the McKenzie farm was doing so well it might be time for them to move down to his own farm near Breadalbane and get it working just as well. Thomas' farm had fallen into a bit of disrepair in the three years he had been concentrating on the McKenzie farm and all his convicts, as well as Sandy McKenzie's convicts who came with the farm, were working the McKenzie land. The McKenzie farm had become quite a village with so many people living there. But both Thomas and Ann loved having so many people around, who they mostly thought of as family.

Mary Sutherland was often a visitor at the house. She had just had her fifth child, a son Adam, in 1822. Although Donald was a friend of Sandy's, he easily took to the burly and kind Thomas Brennan and when the families got together the 10 children had a wonderful time.

Chapter 15

Launceston, 1824

*B*eing summer, it was decided to march the convicts destined

for Port Dalrymple, and camp along the way. Thomas Beswick was in a group of 60 convicts who made the journey using the track that was opened up for Governor Macquarie's visit in 1821. The journey took about four weeks to complete. After leaving Hobart, they saw only remote scattered farms along the way, until approaching Port Dalrymple. After crossing the South Esk River they came across the settlements that included the McKenzie, Brennan, Porter, and Rose farms as well as many more. There they saw pastures of richness and beauty, with ponds and creeks and immense herds of cattle and sheep. The convicts marvelled at the sight of the falls at Corra Lynn.

The surveyor Evans had written in 1820:

> *The North Esk, flowing from its source, falls violently over fifteen or twenty ranges of large rocks, rising nearly as many feet in height from their base. Through the reach, which is nearly a mile in length, the water rushes rapidly, and with such noise, that it is impossible, while standing near it to hold a conversation. The overhanging rocks, and the apparently pendant trees nodding over the passage, fill the mind of the traveller with sentiments of awe and admiration. From this place to Launceston, a distance of about nine miles, a tolerable road leads through some*

cultivated land, particularly that situated on Paterson's
Plains.

Thomas spent some time at the new gaol at Launceston but was soon assigned as a servant to a young landowner called Anthony Cotterell.

Cotterell was an enterprising young man, aged only 17 to Thomas' 18, having come to Van Diemen's Land two years previously with his parents he petitioned for his own land grant and interestingly it was given. Cotterell was granted 650 acres at Cox's Creek, Morven on the Nile River, a tributary of South Esk. The grant made young Cotterell one of the biggest landowners in the Port Dalrymple area.

The land ran along the Nile River and the banks had been cleared with fire sticks by the natives for hunting purposes. Further from the banks the land was hilly and rocky and suitable for sheep but not crops, explaining in some part why his grant was so large for such a young, inexperienced man.

Thomas was one of his first convict labourers.

"Right lads" said Cotterell to his new group of assigned convicts "I intend to make a success of this farming, and I hope that you will help me to do so. I promise I will be a good, kind, and generous master if you do the same by me and put in an honest day's work every day."

The new workers all nodded and muttered. Three of them had already been assigned to other masters and one was soon to get his Ticket-of -leave. They knew that a lot of masters said a lot of things that they would do but didn't always do so in practice. Most of the men were a lot older than Cotterell as well, and wary of putting very much trust in what this boy had to say. Thomas, being young and very naïve had no idea what to think but knew that he wanted to be on the good side of his master.

145

At first the work to clear the land and build dwellings for Cotterell and themselves was back breaking and demoralising in the harsh climate, but somehow before they all knew it, they had put up a reasonable three-room house for Cotterell, fenced off paddocks for the numerous sheep that Cotterell kept acquiring and built decent accommodation for themselves. The men took turns at night on shepherd duties to make sure that the natives, or bushrangers, or even other settlers, didn't steal the sheep.

"Right," said Cotterell, in his usually brash but friendly manner "If you can build a small dwelling with two rooms and a kitchen, I'm going to get us a servant girl or two." This news was accompanied by woops from the men and slapping of legs and backs. It was no secret that the men were not so happy with the current meal arrangements, where they shared the task and cooked over an open fire. The food ranged from not too bad to inedible. Having someone who knew how to cook proper food would make them all incredibly happy.

"And," said Cotterell "One of you might be lucky enough to not just get a cook, but a wife out of it," more woops and leg slapping. Men outnumbered women by seven to one in Van Diemen's Land, and many settlers and convicts took native women as partners, some coming by choice and others sadly by force. Cotterrell had banned his men from interacting with the natives for just that reason. To score the attentions of a British woman, even a convict, was a special prize.

That night the men sat around the fire and Cotterell allowed them some cider, which was normally banned, Cotterell having seen the demise of many farms due to the settlers and their labourers becoming addled with liquor.

 **1825**

A date was finally set in 1825 for the family to move to Thomas Brennan's farm at Morven that he'd named 'The Springs'. Thomas had been preparing for the past year to ensure that the house which he had left, that was barely a bachelors shack back then, had been remodelled into a large dwelling suitable for the now seven family members. There were also three sturdy houses for the convict families, a good-sized kitchen detached from the house (which was quite common to mitigate fire risks), stables and the beginnings of a home garden. The family all moved in, along with two convict couples, including Catherine and her husband and three of the single convict labourers. Martha's husband had been appointed as overseer of the McKenzie farm, so they stayed on and moved into the big house, much to their delight, now that they had three young ones of their own.

Ann was also much closer to Elizabeth Porter who now had John aged two and baby Mary Ann born in November 1824. Mary, William, and Margaret still attended school, but John was now working full time on the farm with his stepfather. Thomas at 59 was still able to do most of the work but knew it was time to train someone new to run the place in case he became unable to. Although he still enjoyed working with the cattle and sheep and even the brick making, John could not bring himself to go tree felling. Every time he went, he had terrible flash backs of the night that Sandy died, and he could not shift the nightmares for weeks afterwards. Thomas understood about the nightmares, having his own about his time as a convict, and didn't push the boy. Ann only had little Elizabeth at home during the days, so was free to go visiting, tend to her garden, cook and to indulge in her favourite hobby, dress making; and with three little girls, two boys and a husband to keep dressed she was kept extremely busy.

After the Sunday service in Launceston, John McKenzie watched with much interest as The Cornwall Hotel was being built in Cameron Street by John Pascoe Fawkner who had arrived in 1822 as a builder. John had a fascination with the hotel and, along with his friend John Jordan, would hang around after church and ask Mr Fawkner lots of questions.

Lieutenant Colonel Cameron was replaced by Lieutenant Colonel William Balfour of the 40th Regiment who was appointed Commandant of Port Dalrymple on 6 April 1825. His arrival set off a calendar of events which added some gaiety and celebration into the lives of the mainly farming community. Not long afterwards though, it was with great sadness that the community learned of the death of Balfour's wife Charlotte, who died at Government House on 22 August following a short but fatal dose of the fevers. Charlotte was buried at St John's Church which was undergoing constructions works, to turn it from a blacksmith's shed/ schoolhouse into a beautiful church worthy of the new town. Much of the community turned out to mourn and show their respects for their new Commandant. Among the mourners were Thomas and Mary Brennan who felt the sadness of the losses of Sandy and baby Thomas being at their burial site again.

 **1826**

Lieutenant Colonel Balfour didn't stay for long after his tragic loss, and was replaced in 1826 by Edward Abbott, the first civil Commandant of Launceston, in January. Abbott was a former Army Major and had served as Commandant at Norfolk Island.

Thomas Beswick and his master Anthony Cotterell had developed a strong friendship since they had been working together. Much of the hard labouring work had now been done on the farm and Thomas felt able to talk to Cotterell about his real interest, which was shoemaking, the trade that he had started to learn on the hulk after his arrest. He wondered to Cotterell if there would be much need for such a trade such as that, and how he might go about following what he felt was his calling.

"Thomas, man" said Cotterell "why didn't you mention this before. Of course, all kinds of trades and crafts are needed here in the colony. I'll ask around and see what we can find out."

Cotterell had recently been appointed as the Constable and Poundkeeper (stock controller) at Gordon Plains just south of Morven and spent less and less time at his farm, feeling comfortable enough to leave the running of it to his labourers, which now included an excellent cook who had partnered with the man Cotterell had appointed as foreman. A second woman also worked at the farm as a housemaid and helped to tend the gardens, although being much older than the men, and not of a pleasant disposition, she neither sought their company nor was offered.

The law at the time was managed by the military and the appointed civilian constables, with the senior military (taking the place of gentry) officiating as magistrates. Cotterell's move away from simple farming and into public service duties had already started to bring about many opportunities for him that farming would not have.

Although Thomas was still years away from getting a Ticket-of-Leave, Cotterell advocated for him, and he was granted a small parcel of land which already had a building suitable for a workshop for Thomas' shoemaking.

"The land is in my name until your Ticket-of-leave comes through, and you will need to pay me 70% of any profit that you make

Thomas, as with you away from the farm I will be missing one labourer. But after talking around the town, I think that if you can make a success of this, we will both be better off than sending you out watching sheep all night."

Thomas spent months getting the workshop ready, purchasing tools and leather, and travelling to Launceston to learn more about his trade from one of the working shoemakers, Joseph Craven, who had come to an agreement with Cotterell to mentor young Thomas.

Thomas was at Craven's one afternoon when Cotterell burst in full of energy and excitement. He had a big story to tell them he said. The men poured tea as Cotterell told them his amazing story. It was no secret that for years the settlers in Port Dalrymple and the hilly area of Ben Lomond in particular, had been subject to multiple raids by a bushranger gang run by Matthew Brady. Brady was a convict who constantly rebelled against authority in Sydney and was eventually moved to Sarah Island near Port Macquarie. In 1824, along with fifteen other convicts, he escaped from Sarah Island and ended up in Van Diemen's Land, where for the next two years they wreaked havoc on the poor settlers. Their gang, as well as several other less problematic bushrangers, were the last straw for the settlers, who were also being subjected to regular attacks from the natives, now called The Blacks. This violence had increased in frequency with at least one or two settlers being killed almost every week, often women and children. And while they had previously kept to the hills and mountains and the more remote settlements, they had now started to encroach on the larger settlements near Paterson's Plains and Morven.

Cotterell excitedly told Thomas and Craven that two days before, he had been at the farm taking tea with some friends. One was his neighbour, James Cox, who had the biggest landholding in the area and a magnificent homestead and whom Cox's Creek was named for. Also, at Cotterell's house was John Batman from Ben Lomond (who had styled himself as a bounty hunter) and one of John's native men, William 'Black Bill' Ponsonby, who Batman had brought over from Sydney; when, just after sunset, they saw two men coming towards the house with their hands tied, and an armed man behind them.

"They stopped at a tree at the corner of the garden about 100 yards away, and on seeing that I was not alone but had several armed men visiting, as well as my labourers, he abandoned his captives and ran off into the bushes. The captive men told us an extraordinarily horrific tale, that the armed man Thomas Jefferies had taken them from a farm up near Ben Lomond and intended to use them as meat!" he paused for effect, and it worked as both men almost spat their tea out in shock.

"I noticed that the men were decidedly skeletal, and they explained this was because the third man who was captured with them, Russell, had been Jeffries meals for the past two weeks as he cooked him up piece by piece while they stayed in an abandoned hut owned by a farmer named Miller. Not only that, but when he captured them, Jeffries had pieces of the body of an infant stashed in his saddle bags."

Thomas and Craven stared in horror as Cotterell weaved his awful tale.

"The other men could not bring themselves to eat human flesh so apart from some berries and a rabbit they had caught, they had not eaten since Jeffries had caught them. Three of Cox's men arrived, and we searched for hours. As dawn broke, being totally exhausted, we set up a watch and tried to get some sleep. Bill was on watch and quietly alerted us to a man coming across a far hill. As he approached, we soon saw it was Jeffries, who surprisingly threw down his guns and gave himself up to us, begging for mercy."

"My God Man, what a night you had," said Craven.

"On the way back to Launceston," said Cotterell "he told me that he had killed seven men, and intended to kill many more because the energy and excitement that he gained from eating human flesh made him feel unstoppable."

The men all agreed that the colony was much better off now that this cannibal was in custody, and they were proud that their friend Anthony Cotterrel was partially responsible for such a catch.

Within a week there was more excitement in the area when Matthew Brady was caught by John Batman near his farm at Ben Lomond. However, the capture of Brady did not elicit as much wrath from the community as the capture of the cannibal had. Brady had gained a reputation as a 'gentleman bushranger', taking only what he and his gang needed to survive and treating women and children with respect and kindness.

After his arrest, Brady was taken to Hobart where his cell was filled with gifts of fruit and sweets, letters, and flowers from admiring women. While in Launceston he complained violently about being forced to share a cell with Thomas Jeffries. He ranted to Cotterell, who had been vested with guarding the prisoners, that if he was not relocated, he would cut Jeffries' head off. When Cotterell and the guards searched Brady, they found two large knives on him and promptly relocated him to another cell. The prisoners were soon moved to Hobart where once again Brady expressed disgust at having to be hanged with Jeffries, which occurred on 4 May 1826.

It was with much sadness that year that the Brennan household heard of the death of their friend David Rose. Since his nephew had arrived, David had left the running of his farm to Alexander, as he fell deeper and deeper in depression and drink. His death in July was precipitated by a bite from a dog and the ensuing infection, given David's poor health, took his life very quickly.

In September there was joy again when Elizabeth Porter gave birth to her third child, a son William. Ann had busied herself after David's death by making a full layette for the new baby and concentrating on the garden at The Springs, which was now producing sufficient food for all the farm inhabitants and more to give away to the needy.

 **1828**

Little William was followed by a baby girl almost two years later in September 1828, and this baby was named after her mother, so both Ann and Elizabeth had little Elizabeths. It was wonderful when all the children were together. John at almost 18 was dark and stocky; Mary 15, was the image of her mother with big blue eyes and long chestnut hair, but tall like her father; William 10 and Margaret 9 both had golden curls that bounced around their heads like beautiful clouds; and Elizabeth aged 5 was just like her mother but with a touch more red in her chestnut hair. Elizabeth's children Mary Ann 4, William 2 and baby Elizabeth all had dark hair and blue eyes like their parents.

Mary McKenzie, at 15, was catching the eye of many of the local men, young and old. When they went to Launceston for church or other activities, big brother John kept a close eye on her, and stepfather Thomas kept a beady eye on the men eyeing her off. There was one young man who seemed to have caught Mary's eye and the feeling seemed to be mutual, but he would always make his interactions in a gentlemanly manner; offering to hold her hand as she crossed a muddy puddle, talking to her in a kind friendly manner with no leering, which Thomas and John were looking out for.

Eventually the young man introduced himself to the two men he had realised held the key to romancing Mary. Jeremiah Peck told them that he had recently been granted land down on the Nile at Cox's Creek. He also had an interest in being an innkeeper and a publican but had to prove his worth in the area first. As John also had an interest in that trade he was immediately pleased with Mary's choice. Jeremiah asked if he might 'step out' with Mary to which Thomas visibly bristled, which made him look more troll like and ominous. John had a feeling that this man was good, so he stepped in and said that he would be happy to be their chaperone if Jeremiah wished to get to know his sister Mary better.

Jeremiah's parents, Joshua Peck and Mary Frost, arrived as convicts; Joshua on the First Fleet in 1788 and Mary on the Second Fleet in 1789 and both ended up at Norfolk Island, where Governor Arthur Phillip hoped to establish farms to help supply Sydney with food and other supplies. After serving their time on Norfolk Island, Joshua Peck received land grants at Toongabbie in New South Wales in 1794 and 1797. They sold that land in 1803 and went back to Norfolk Island where Jeremiah was born in 1805. Jeremiah had older siblings: John, Elizabeth, Mary Ann, William and twins Joshua junior and Thomas. He also had three younger siblings: Charles, James, and Sarah.

The family left Norfolk Island on the *Porpoise*, on Christmas Day in 1807 and arrived at Hobart on 17 January 1808, after Governor William Bligh decided to abandon the island as it was not producing sufficient food as it was originally hoped. The Governor was keen to start settlement in the new Van Diemen's Land that held more promise for success. By 1819 the family were living in Northern Tasmania.

Sadly, they did not have the same success as many of the farmers in the area and in 1821 Joshua Peck along with his sons William, Joshua and Thomas were convicted of stealing and killing ten sheep owned by the government stores. There were many witnesses who claimed that they had been stealing sheep for quite some time. They were found guilty and sentenced to be transported to Newcastle for 14 years. Luckily for Jeremiah, he was not with his father and brothers when they were caught stealing. Joshua senior died in Newcastle in 1825.

Jeremiah's brother William also had a prior conviction. He had been deported to Newcastle in 1817 for being a bushranger. He returned in 1820. After his second deportation he escaped from Newcastle in 1822 and after he was caught, he was sent to Macquarie Harbour, the toughest prison in Van Diemen's Land, on an island off the western coast. Brother John was also charged in 1824 for receiving stolen sheep and was acquitted, but he was convicted of a similar charge a few months later and sentenced to 14 years at Macquarie Harbour where he joined his brother William.

Life went on at Paterson's Plains and for the most part things were joyful and bountiful. At the end of 1828 the farms and the children were all flourishing, and the community was getting bigger and better every year. Ann was expecting another baby and Mary and Jeremiah were falling in love.

Their lives, however, were continuously overshadowed by the fear of attack my natives, which along with the bushrangers, ruined the peace and serenity of the burgeoning community.

One afternoon Thomas' foreman from the McKenzie farm arrived to tell him a story of one of the labourers who had found himself alone in one of the workers huts towards the back of the property. He looked out and saw a black man dodge behind a tree. He looked about and saw another, and more on the other side of the hut.

155

Realizing that he was surrounded, and that being alone he would have little chance of making an effective defence, he hit upon a plan of deception. He put on his hat and went outside, came back in, took off his hat and changed his coat, went out again and walked around, came in again and repeated the procedure several times, changing his clothes to simulate the appearance of different men, until he saw the natives quietly go away. It was nine years since Sandy McKenzie who had befriended the natives, had died, and those now near the farm were not from the same tribes, but probably from the Ben Lomond area where there was constant fighting. Everyone needed to be on their guard.

Chapter 16

Launceston, 1829

*J*ohn McKenzie and his friend John Jordan had been eagerly

watching John Pascoe Fawkner, who had built The Cornwall Hotel in
1825, and on 9 February 1829 launched the first newspaper, the
Launceston Advertiser. Along with Jeremiah Peck, the boys all had
an interest in the hotel business and all three pleaded with Fawkner
to give them some work at the hotel so that they could learn the
trade and learn from Fawkner, who they saw as the biggest success
in Launceston. While there were other hotels, the Black Swan on
Brisbane Street and The Launceston on the corner of Brisbane and
St John's Street, the new Cornwall was by far the fanciest.

Jeremiah, 24 and the two John's, both 19, started working at the
hotel after church on Sundays, counting stock and learning the
bookwork that went with running such a business. This enabled
them all to maintain their farm duties as well, but they were all
becoming less and less interested in farm work and more interested
in the business world. Fawkner was glad of the extra hands as his
businesses were now spread out over several different areas. After
a few months he started to pay the boys a small wage for their work
and continued to mentor them.

Fawkner had a chequered background. His father was transported
as a convict, and John with his mother and siblings was approved to
travel with him to the colony in 1803. In 1829 he was the same age
as John McKenzie's mother Ann, 37, and had tried many businesses

in Hobart before moving to Launceston. He had tried farming, having helped his father for many years as a shepherd, and he had several bakery businesses. His success, however, was hampered by several instances of criminal activity. In 1814 he was convicted of aiding and abetting a group of convicts in an escape mission. He received 500 lashes and three days imprisonment for that but was later also convicted of other crimes and sent to Newcastle where he was engaged cutting timber. More business adventures and misadventures happened on his return to Hobart and several arrests for misappropriation and other misdeeds led him to move to Launceston for a new life in 1822. Starting as a builder he finally found success and soon went on to build his two storey 13 room hotel and gained a publican's licence. As well as the hotel, and now the newspaper, Fawkner's business interests included a horticultural supplies business, a coach service between Launceston and Longford, and he was starting to do research about the shipping trade.

One Sunday afternoon he called Jeremiah and the two Johns into his office at The Cornwall.

"Men I have a bit of a problem you might be able to help me with." The three men nodded with intrigue. "The scurvy fools have refused to renew my publican licence," the three men drew breath in surprise.

"But why John? You've successfully run the hotel for almost four years now." said Jeremiah.

"Yes, I know lad, but apparently, I am considered 'not a proper person to keep an hotel'. Don't worry all our friends in the town and the local settlers attested to the orderliness of the hotel, even Black Dick down the road. I'll not let this rest; I intend to fight until my licence is restored. But in the meantime, I need someone else to hold a licence so we can keep the hotel open." He smiled at the three men. "Jeremiah, I believe that the reputation of your father and brothers may cause you issues similar to mine, however you two John's are clean as whistles and just who we need to get us through this mess."

The two John's started to grin when they realised what Fawkner meant. "And for you Peck, I think Hotel Manager would be an appropriate title. All three of you can run the hotel until I am able to get that darn licence back. As it is though, I have so many other interests, handing over the hotel to you all for a while will be a blessing."

They then sat down to organise the business details and remuneration. There would then be the task for the two John's to tell their father, and stepfather, that they had chosen a different path and could no longer help them with their farms. Jeremiah had got little fulfilment from his own farm but still had convicts helping to run it. With this new job he could afford to leave them to the farming work while he got to follow his passion His mother and younger siblings had moved into his eldest sister Elizabeth's substantial home near the McKenzie farm in 1825 after Jeremiah's father had died at Newcastle, so he no longer had to worry about them.

That evening the three men took some time out from their usual duties to go and visit an old friend and tell him the news. Richard White, or 'Black Dick' as he was known, had started the very first hotel in Launceston way back in 1816. A black American man, he had moved from New York to London and became a highwayman, where he was captured in 1797 when he was 24 and sentenced to death, which was then commuted to transportation for life. After spending time on Norfolk Island, where he was pardoned and made a police constable, he came to Launceston in 1813 as part of the second evacuation, as a free settler. Within two years he was a wealthy man, having made a fortune selling beef to the government. It was not long afterwards that he built his hotel which he called simply, The Launceston.

Black Dick was noticeable around the town as he always wore highly polished boots, white buckskin breeches, a frock coat and top hat, and as now he was in his 60's, a monocle, and an ornate walking stick. He had been friends with John Pascoe Fawkner since Fawkner's arrival in Launceston and took an interest in his three young protégé's as well. He was looking for one or two for himself.

Black Dick was very happy for the three young men, and promised to help in any way that he could to make their new career's a success. Just knowing that there were other successful men in the industry made Jeremiah and the two John's more confident that they had chosen their path wisely. And Black Dick was so colourful and a joy to be around, the men all told him that they would call on him often for advice and for company.

The Springs, 1829

It had been six years since Ann's last childbirth with little Elizabeth, and at 37 she was worried that this birth might be difficult, like little Thomas' was. For the first time Ann sought advice from one of the local physicians in Launceston, who declared her to be in excellent health and not to expect any problems during the birth.

As it happened Ann should not have been worried, her first daughter named after herself came bursting into the world in April no sooner than Ann had started to feel the pains. There was not even time to call any of her friends who had been ready to attend the birth, or even the women from the farm. Thomas and Mary were the only witnesses to little Ann's birth, and she came out kicking and screaming, with a head of bright red hair. "Aye, we have a tiny screaming leprechaun my girl," said Thomas with glee as he jiggled the screaming mass. Luckily by then Mary had seen enough births to know how to cut the baby's umbilical cord and help her mother to expel the afterbirth, as Thomas looked on in awe and horror, this being the first birth he had witnessed. Thomas hopped and jiggled around the house directing John and the others with chores to be done. The farm women arrived after hearing the baby's screams and did a lot of explaining to William, Margaret and Elizabeth who were all a little shocked by the happenings in the house. Margaret had only been four when Elizabeth was born and had been kept away from the birthing, so this was something very mysterious and interesting.

William, Margaret, and now six-year-old Elizabeth were all now at school full time, and Mary, having finished her schooling, was at home with her mother. Ann still enjoyed dressmaking and always had a project on the go. There were several formal dresses in the making that had been commissioned by merchant's wives, as well as the continuous job of keeping her own family clothed. Margaret in Sydney, now a very successful merchant's wife who mixed with the Governor himself, regularly sent Ann copies of the lady's magazines with the latest fashions, *La Belle Assemblée* was her favourite from England and *Le Journal des Dames et des Modes* was published in Paris. However, everything else took second place when Mary and Jeremiah announced that they would be wed in the spring. Now began the preparations for Ann's first daughter's wedding, and Thomas was equally excited, as Mary was his daughter-of-the-heart.

It was decided that the wedding would be at St John's followed by a lavish wedding breakfast to be held at the McKenzie farm at Paterson's Plains which had a large undercover barn that could seat at least 100 guests. Jeremiah intended to make their home on his land at Cox's Creek on the Nile River, further south from both The

Springs at Morven and Paterson's Plains. With the money he had been making at the hotel his labourers had built a decent home on the block for the Peck family to eventually move into. But, considering that Jeremiah spent most of his time, including a lot of overnights, in Launceston, Ann and Thomas were a bit sceptical about this arrangement, but decided to leave it up to the young ones to figure out. In the meantime, Ann revelled in having her daughter at home with her to teach her what she needed to know about running a house and of course taking care of a young baby. Little Ann could not have come at a better time.

As the winter chill finally started to lift from the air Ann took the young ones, William, Margaret, Elizabeth, and baby Ann to Elizabeth Porter's home one Sunday afternoon. The children played happily with Elizabeth's three, Richard who had just turned seven, Mary almost five, William almost three, and one-year old Elizabeth.

Ann and Elizabeth mused over the past 13 years that they had known each other. They both had a good laugh about Sandy and what a good man that he was and how proud he would be of how they had both turned out. How excited and proud he would be about his daughter Mary getting married and what a shame it was that he wouldn't be there to see it.

"Oh, I'm sure that he will be there to see it Lizzie," said Ann. "Sometimes when I go to kiss Margaret and William at night, I swear that I can feel and even sometimes smell James leaning over with me."

Elizabeth gave her a funny look. "And sometimes," said Ann "I can feel little Thomas snuggling against me except he's not there, it's at times when I am feeling melancholy, like he is helping me to feel better." Elizabeth smiled indulgently. She didn't believe in ghosts. "He would have been eight now, little Thomas," said Ann with a sadness that Elizabeth could feel for real.

Suddenly the children burst out from around the side of the house to the porch where the women were sitting.

"Mumma, mumma, come quickly, William is hurt and he's bleeding, a lot."

The women jumped up and ran as fast as they could to the barn behind the house. There lay little William crying his eyes out with a big cut down his leg.

"He fell Mumma, he fell from the steps and landed on that rusty bucket there." The children had been playing hide and seek and William had climbed up the steps to the loft and slipped as he was coming down. His little leg had gone right through a rusty hole in an old bucket and the jagged sides had torn his leg.

Elizabeth took him inside and cleaned the wound as best she could and wrapped his leg in boiled bandages. The next day the wound seemed to be healing well and William was allowed to go out and play with his brother and sister again, limping along with them.

Ten days later Ann was busy in the garden when she saw Elizabeth's gig driving up the path from the road. Excellent, she thought, she can help me with the lace on Mary's dress. But it was not Elizabeth in the gig, but one of their farm women and she was crying. Poor little William had seemed to be well recovered, the wound almost healed when he suddenly started having seizures and the lockjaw set in until his little body was contorted out of shape. He then got the fevers and then he just died. Three days before he would have turned three years old.

September was a horrible month. Not only was everyone devastated by little William's death, but there had also been a horrible massacre not far from Launceston, quite close to Paterson's Plains in the mountains.

Over the past few years there had been more and more news of terrible killings by both the natives who were now called 'The Blacks' and the settlers. As David Rose had once told them, it was impossible to know who had started 'the wars' but the skirmishes began during the period when the 600 settlers arrived from Norfolk Island between 1807 and 1813. They were allocated convicts and the ratio of men to women was more than 7 to 1. It was said that white men first captured black women and children to satisfy their lust, which of course enraged the native men who reciprocated by attacking the white population. At first attacks were targeted at the men who had committed the crimes but as time went on the white population simply became the enemy as the black population became the enemy to the settlers and the government. As the settlers increasingly encroached on native hunting grounds there was another reason for the natives to hate the white people who were starving them out of their own lands. In the past few years, news had arrived almost every week of settlers in remote areas being attacked, mutilated, and killed and whole tribes of natives being massacred. Sometimes the attacks would be as close as Ben Lomond. She despaired for both sides.

By 1828 the Government had declared martial law against the natives with rewards for their capture and in some places their killing; and bounty hunters were popping up all over the colony, including John Batman who lived at Ben Lomond and had captured the bushranger Brady in 1826. Batman had been to Sydney and had employed mainland native men for roving parties, hunting Tasmanian natives. In September Batman, aged 28, with the assistance of his Sydney blacks, led an attack on an Aboriginal family group of about 60 to 70 men, women, and children in the Ben Lomond district. Batman later told the police magistrate that they had killed 15 Aboriginal people. He turned up in Launceston with a captured woman named Luggenemenener, her two-year-old son and another young native boy.

The district was rocked by the account of the massacre and shocked to hear that Batman had taken Luggenemenener's son and the other boy into his home to raise as servants, basically kidnapping them. Governor Arthur vehemently protested Batman's roguish behaviour, and the newspapers were full of accounts of the feud between the Governor and Batman. The community were divided by the Black Wars, with many believing it was a good thing to rid the colony of the scourge of the natives, while others who had known the native people as friends were saddened and angry at what was happening.

Paterson's Plains, 1829

On the 2nd day of November 1829, Mary McKenzie married Jeremiah Peck, who officially became the owner of the McKenzie farm as well as his own parcels of land. For Ann it was a truly magical day, seeing her firstborn daughter marry the man she loved. The dress was exquisite, and the barn where the wedding breakfast was served was decorated with swathes of tulle, beautiful pink flowers, and native gum leaves and wattles. Many lovely and useful presents were received by the bride and groom, including a new covered carriage from the Stodges of Sydney that had only arrived three days prior, and was used to transport the bride and groom from the church in Launceston back to Paterson's Plains for the festivities.

All of their friends attended, including Donald and Mary Sutherland, the Porter's (still in mourning clothes), all of the Jordan's, and John Pascoe Fawkner even made a short appearance to give his regards and officially hand the management of his hotel to Jeremiah as a wedding gift, as well as enough barrels of whisky to fill the store attached to the barn that Sandy had first built and which was expanded by Thomas.

The future was looking exciting for the Peck's and Brennan's.

Chapter 17

1830

*E*arly in 1830 Mary arrived at her mother's house at The

Springs in tears. Jeremiah spent most of his time in Launceston managing the hotel and Mary was lonely and unhappy alone on their farm, with only the convict labourers to keep her company. And it seemed that Jeremiah had been unlucky in that regards, his convicts being a lazy and uncivilised bunch. The one female allocated to him spent more time drunk and in the company of the men than she did in the kitchen or garden. As such, Jeremiah's farm had fallen into disarray and was producing very little. Jeremiah did not care too much about this because his heart lay in the town and in the hotel business, the farm was just somewhere to keep a house. And now to keep a wife.

Thomas was now 64, and while he could still ably run both The Springs and the McKenzie farm, he was not up to running another farm further out and with unruly labourers. John McKenzie couldn't help as he was at the hotel with Jeremiah most of the time. William was shaping up to be potentially capable of taking over the farms when Thomas got too old, but he was still only 12 years old and as much as he begged to leave school to work on the farm full time, Ann insisted that he stay for at least another year.

A family meeting was called to figure out what to do, as it was not suitable that Mary had to spend all her time lonely and unhappy. Jeremiah suggested that she move to Launceston and stay in the rooms at the back of the hotel that the two John's and Jeremiah stayed at. Mary burst into louder tears. The rooms Jeremiah was talking about was basically one large dormitory with three single beds and the lad's belongings strewn everywhere.

"Mary," said Ann gently "the farm belongs to you, you know, and it is closer to the town and closer to us. You could move in there. Thomas was going to ask the Bailey's if they would move to Cox's Creek anyway and get that place working properly."

The Bailey's were the latest most trusted convict couple living in the main house at the McKenzie farm. John Bailey came from a business background in England and had been convicted of forgery, and even though he knew little of the mechanisms of farming he had learned very quickly and was a strong and stable foreman who kept the other labourers in line and made sure that the farm made a decent profit.

"But I don't want to be on my own," howled Mary, "And you would still be so far away." She paused and wiped her nose "I want to be with you Mother."

"You mean you want to move back home to The Springs?" asked Thomas, thinking that was not such a silly idea, as she had lived there until a few months ago. But she was a married woman now and needed to start making her own home, which God willing would soon be full of children. And although Thomas loved the little ones, he was getting older and there was already two-year-old Ann running riot around the house.

"I've got it," said Ann "why don't we all move back to the McKenzie farm. The Bailey's can go to Cox's Creek and your men here are quite capable of managing this place, Thomas. Until Mary has her own children she can move into the foreman's home, which is quite substantial as you know Mary," Mary nodded her head. "And the six of us will all move back into the main house, just like old times. And I'm not counting you John McKenzie, you barely grace us with your presence now, you've got a good paying job now, it's time you found your own lodgings."

"But I have Ma," said John "I've got the room at the hotel."

"Yes, well, all well and good that is, but as you can see if you want yourself a wife one day, you're going to need to have more of a home for her than that," with that she gave Jeremiah a sharp side eye.

Although he had little say in the matter and in reality little interest, as his passion was at the hotel, Jeremiah agreed to all of the arrangements. Over the next two months the exchange of houses and jobs went on until everyone was settled in their new abodes and happy.

Mary and Ann joyfully went about decorating Mary's new home that was only a 2-minute walk from the main house, with its own kitchen and garden. Although Mary didn't want a house girl, she did ask Ann if she could take her meals with her mother, Thomas, and the children on the nights when Jeremiah was in town, which was most nights. Ann and Mary spent their days working together in the garden and baking and making preserves in the kitchen with the farm girls, a very necessary task when for six month of the years there was no fresh fruit or vegetables due to the extreme cold.

The women would both entertain little Ann who had proven to be the loudest and most demanding of all of Ann's children, and being the only one at home had no other siblings to entertain her. Ann was very glad of the extra help.

They also spent a lot of time looking at the magazines sent by Margaret Stodges and making patterns and beautiful clothing for the ladies of Launceston. As the area had grown, in size and population, several other seamstresses had opened for business, but there was still plenty of work to go around, and Ann had the advantage of previous 'Sydney' work. In the past year or so she had started to specialise in ladies silk pantaloons and ornate reticules or 'pockets' that ladies used to carry their necessities in when out of the home. Both items were small and could be quickly made but were beautiful and rewarding to produce. Margaret kept Ann well stocked with the latest silk, lace, and fine cotton for those who preferred, or those who couldn't afford silk. The reticules required hours of embroidery in all kinds of patterns to turn them into something unique and amazing for each lady, to be admired by her acquaintances.

Every second week Mary would take the carriage into town to spend some time with Jeremiah at the hotel, which she thought would be a good idea as everything was pointing towards her being a publican's wife. John Pascoe Fawkner had gotten his publicans licence back and was now busy helping Jeremiah to get his own licence. John Jordan already had one now, and John McKenzie was also eager to get one.

While in town, Mary would make deliveries to customers and then fill in her time browsing through the various shops that had opened, selling all kinds of interesting thing. Across from the hotel was a shoemaker's shop, and not only did this shop stock sturdy work-boots and tough leather shoes for the working men and women, but also delicate ladies slippers and children's shoes. Examples of the latest products were displayed on the front counter until their owners picked them up.

Mary enjoyed seeing what the shoemaker could make and had ideas for some of the dresses that she and her mother were currently making. Every time she visited, the owner was very pleasant and friendly and didn't mind that she was just looking and admiring.

One time she decided to take in the magazines from Margaret Stodges, and the owner, who she found out was named Thomas Beswick, was delighted. From then on it became a fortnightly ritual for Thomas and Mary to take tea together and pour over the magazines and the new fashions. Mary told Thomas all about the dresses that her mother was making, and who they were for. Naturally in such a small town they had many customers in common. Thomas would then recommend suitable footwear to the ladies thereby increasing his own business.

Over time, during their conversations, Mary discovered that Thomas was the same age as Jeremiah, 26, and that he would soon get his Ticket-of-leave. Until such time most of the profits from his trade went to his Master, Anthony Cotterell, who he had been with since his arrival in 1823, and who he now counted as a friend. It was on the prison hulk and during the voyage from England that Thomas had mostly learned his trade. Seeing that he had such a talent for it, Cotterell was happy for Thomas to pursue the work, to their mutual advantage, rather than participate in the farm work. The profits that he paid Cotterell were paying off the shop and tools so that when he got his Ticket-of-leave he would own it outright. He had started his business from a workshop on a block of land near Cox's Creek and then Cotterell had purchased this shop for him when the business started to get more popular.

Both Mary and Thomas felt unsettled by some of the divisions in the area. There had always been problems with the exclusives, the people who had come as free settlers and felt themselves socially and morally superior to the emancipists, those who had come as convicts or children of convicts, even if they were now free and successful merchants or farmers. For the most part the emancipists were not welcome at exclusives houses, although there were exceptions. Mary and Thomas laughed at the ridiculousness of the situation.

There was also division in how people felt about what was now known as the Black War. The colony was now in an almost continuous state of war with the remaining blacks who had not already been killed or had died from the white man's diseases. Getting more and more desperate as their traditional hunting lands were overtaken by the settlers and more and more angry as atrocities were committed against them by the white men, the blacks had got bolder and more violent in their attacks.

Under pressure from the settlers, Lieutenant-Governor George Arthur ordered thousands of able-bodied settlers to form what became known as the 'Black Line', a human chain that crossed the settled districts of Tasmania. Every farm was cleared of all available men who were not too young, too old, or too infirm and over a period of weeks the line moved south to intimidate, capture, displace and relocate the remaining black people.

George Augustus Robinson was employed by Governor Arthur as a conciliator to try to establish friendly relations with the natives and convince them to leave their lands voluntarily and travel to Flinders Island near Hobart, which had been set up as an Aboriginal mission. Arthur thought this a better and more humane solution than just indiscriminately killing all the black people they could find, which seemed to be the preference of the settlers. Robinson had come from England to Hobart as a free settler in 1824 and quickly set up a very successful building business. He had become secretary of the Seamen's Friend and Bethel Union Society, joined the committee of the Auxiliary Bible Society, visited prisoners and the condemned in the gaol, and helped found the Mechanics' Institute. He applied for and was given the job of 'Aboriginal protector' by the Governor and oversaw the set up of the mission on Flinders Island. He then travelled the colony overseeing the Black Line. Anthony Cotterell was put in charge of the huge effort by the community to maintain the Black Line and finally rid Port Dalrymple of the black threat.

The government's extreme measures meant that natives were now rarely seen, other than those working for the settlers and merchants and those who had been taken as wives, voluntarily or involuntarily. Both Mary Peck and Thomas Beswick felt it was a shame. They had both known native people and Mary still remembered the love and kindness of her Aunty Mary Rose. They both thought that the white settlers had made a mistake not trying harder to be friendly with the natives as there was no doubt that they knew so much about the land and how to survive, that it would take generations for the settlers to learn and understand, if they ever did.

Mary was very impressed and very happy and charmed to have someone so interesting to discuss fashion and current affairs with. All that her brother and Jeremiah wanted to talk about was brews, and stills and bad customers, boring, boring, boring.

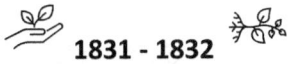

1831 - 1832

Jeremiah was granted his publican's licence in 1831, and promptly started to look for the right area to build his own hotel. Launceston was expanding every day and Fawkner agreed that Jeremiah should open another hotel in the town. That way he would be close to Fawkner's team at the Cornwall, which would still include John Jordan, and the men could collaborate on trade and purchasing. Jeremiah asked John McKenzie, now his brother-in-law, if he would go along with him and help him to start his new hotel, and John was ecstatic. John had big plans to open his own hotels now that he had been granted a licence, thanks to John Pascoe Fawkner's assistance.

The men found suitable land on the corner of Wellington and Canning Streets and hired Fawkner's builders. The hotel was to be a double storey building very similar to the Cornwall and with multiple boarding rooms. By the middle of 1832 it was ready to open. Mary felt that in appeasement to her for never being around, Jeremiah called the hotel The Scottish Chiefs, in honour of Mary's heritage.

The men were also looking closer to home for opportunities as they watched an inn called The New River open at Morven.

Not long after The Scottish Chiefs opened, Mary surprisingly found herself with child. After almost three years of marriage, she was wondering if she would ever become a mother, but Jeremiah's frequent absences left little time for romance. The Brennan household were overjoyed by the news. The baby would be both Ann and Thomas' first grandchild. Little Ann, now four was the most excited of the children, not having her own younger sibling. Elizabeth now nine, Margaret 13 and William 14 were not so overjoyed, having put up with little Ann's personal chaos for the past four years.

In November there was more good news for Mary when she found out that her friend, Thomas Beswick had received his Ticket-of-leave and began his own independent business journey.

Mary also noted that Thomas seemed to be more excited about her pregnancy than Jeremiah did.

1833

Christmas came around with a big celebration at the McKenzie farm, the likes of which they hadn't had since Mary and Jeremiah's wedding at the end of 1829. All their friends and their friends' children, small and grown came along for a delicious feast followed by good old Scottish and Irish singing and dancing, the Scots and Irish trying to out-drink and out-dance each other.

All the farms managed by Thomas were doing well and he had trusted men at each one to make sure that continued. The brick making business was doing exceptionally well, with huge amounts being produced and sold to the government stores and to local builders. Not only did Thomas have assigned convicts at each farm but also paid labourers.

Ann continued with her dressmaking with Mary, Elizabeth Porter and Mary Sutherland working on the embroidery, lace, gloves, reticules, and bonnets, and Thomas Beswick providing a shoe making service for those ladies who wished to have a complete outfit. Mary Sutherland was now also specialising in parasols which were necessary in the heat of summer.

The previous fear of attacks from the natives had almost completely gone. Thomas Beswick told them that he had recently heard from his former master Anthony Cotterell, now Chief Constable of Launceston, that he had been busy in the last two years capturing the remaining aborigines in the Fingal Valley and that he'd brought in the last of the North-East people from near Oyster Bay in January 1832. Cotterell was also in charge of the group of Sydney blacks that John Batman had brought across years earlier to assist in tracking the natives in Van Diemen's Land. When not out and about helping the constables and bounty hunters they lived in a building at the back of the police barracks in Launceston and Cotterell said that he relished the discussions that he had with them about how they had grown up and the interesting customs and traditions that were part of their culture. They were good, strong, brave, and loyal men and Cotterell was glad to have them on his side and not on the opposing side. He greatly wished that the government had been able to find some way to live in harmony with the blacks of Port Dalrymple, they had so much to offer white society that had now been lost.

Cotterell invited Thomas to his Launceston house in early 1833 with several of Cotterell's other friends. He told them about one of the native women who had impressed him in October 1832, after sending some captured aborigines to Flinders Island. George Robinson had gone to Hobart and left Cottrell in charge of his trusted group including a woman named Truganini. Her father was Mangerner, the leader of one of the tribes, and in her adolescence, she lived with her family in the traditional way. Then the European sealers, whalers and timber-getters arrived and by March 1829, when she and her father met George Robinson at Bruny Island, her mother had been killed by sailors, her uncle shot by a soldier, her sister abducted by sealers, and Paraweena, a young man who was to have been her husband, was murdered by timber-getters. At Bruny Island mission in 1829 she married Woorraddy, from Bruny. Truganini told Cotterell that at that time she had decided that she had two options, to fight against the white man and join the rest of her family in death or survive by working with the white man. She, and Woorraddy, decided to survive.

From then on Truganini and Woorraddy became part of Robinson's party and acted as guides and as instructors in their languages and customs, which were recorded by Robinson in his journal.

The native couple had accompanied Cotterell along the West Coast to meet Robinson at Macquarie Harbour.

"She is a most amazing swimmer" he said "who has no fear of the creatures in the sea and can stay underwater for a very long time, always coming up with delicious crayfish for our dinner, after we have all thought her drowned. When we would come across settlers and their families she loved seeing and playing with the children, and on the trail, she would make little dolls and toys to give to them along the way. She and Wooraddy had a most passionate relationship and were not shy for others to see or hear their lovemaking," he paused in memory. "She was the canniest negotiator and could bring even the most fierce and ferocious natives to our side peaceably. I would have her on any of my work teams at any time," he said with passion.

 **Paterson's Plains, 1833**

Mary had some problems with her pregnancy, and it was feared that the baby might come early, however a lot of rest towards the end seemed to settle things and the family were overjoyed when tiny but hearty little Mary Ann Peck arrived early in the morning of 3 June 1833. With little Ann about to start school and her mother very thankful as she was a spirited child, there was now only Elizabeth's three-year-old John and two-year-old Jane to wrangle while they worked. Elizabeth would usually bring one of her farm girls along to care for the toddlers or else she wouldn't get any embroidery done at all.

The following month Jeremiah received two more land grants of 25 and 40 acres at Breadalbane near Thomas Brennan's The Springs. Jeremiah had plans to build a hotel on one of the blocks to service travellers. Thomas diligently sorted out the convict labourers that came with the land and started to organise more farming interests to add to the Peck's portfolio of land and properties. This time, though, he made a point of telling Jeremiah that he was no longer a young man and Jeremiah needed to plan for he and Mary to move into the big house, and arrangements for the farms, so that he and Ann could retire to the house at The Springs again.

However not long afterwards Jeremiah got sick. At first, he had mild stomach cramps and body aches and pains, but it wasn't long before he could no longer lift the barrels and kegs at the hotel, or even work a full day without a rest. Within a month he was forced to stop working and take to his bed back at the McKenzie farm. For once he got to spend extended time with Mary, little Mary Ann, and the family, but for much of the time he was in so much pain he was unable to comprehend who they were. Doctors were called and came and went with different ideas and supposed remedies. Poor Jeremiah was subjected to cupping, various enemas and tonics supposed to heal his illness and was bled with leeches. But the only thing that seemed to help was laudanum which he was taking in huge amounts.

And then, on 25 November, Jeremiah just didn't wake up. He had died sometime in his sleep. By the time he died poor Jeremiah had lost so much weight that he already resembled a skeleton, and his skin was varying shades of yellow and grey. He hadn't known who he was or where he was for weeks.

The whole family and many members of the community had visited him during his illness for business of personal reasons and all were shocked at how quickly his illness had taken hold and taken his life. He had been such an energetic and passionate businessman, always with ideas and plans to expand his hotels and a friend to so many of the townspeople and those from the wider community. His business had been donating lots of money to local charities, particularly to the abandoned mothers fund set up through St John's church. He would be sorely missed by all that knew him. He was only 28 years old.

Sadly, Jeremiah's family had never become friendly with the Brennan's. With Jeremiah so often working and staying in

Launceston there had been few opportunities since the wedding for his family to meet up with Mary's family.

Jeremiah's oldest sister Elizabeth's husband, Peter Lette, had only just died in April and left her a widow with nine children at the age of 40. Although living near the McKenzie farm on a substantial property, Elizabeth had always been too busy and had barely seen her brother or his new family. She had met Peter, who at the time was a soldier with the 46th Regiment, before her parents moved to Van Diemen's Land, and had travelled with him to manage an indigo farm in East Bengal. Finding the climate too harsh the family decided to join Elizabeth's parents in Van Diemen's Land in 1817. Peter became a very successful merchant and farmer and built a substantial home that he called Curramore after his family home in Ireland. After their father Joshua died at Newcastle in 1825, Elizabeth and Jeremiah's mother and their younger siblings James and Sally, who were simple, moved in to live at Curramore. At the time of Jeremiah's death, Elizabeth's eldest son Peter, who had been working as a Constable and pound keeper alongside Anthony Cotterell, had just inherited Curramore.

After serving his time in various prisons, brother John Peck was now married and had just had a son. He was doing well for himself with various farming interests in the area. Joshua, two years older than Jeremiah, and his wife Elizabeth, had just lost their first child not long after birth so were still in mourning. Joshua also had many farming interests in the area.

1833 was another quiet Christmas in mourning for the Brennan family.

Chapter 18

 **1834**

*J*ohn McKenzie took over the running of The Scottish Chiefs,

which was now owned by his sister Mary. John Pascoe Fawkner agreed to have his name listed as the registered publican while he helped John to get his own licence. At nearly 24 and with several years of experience now, it was thought that he would be looked at favourably. The only thing going against him, said Fawkner, was that he was a single man. This was not an unusual thing in Van Diemen's Land, but the government looked more favourably on a man with a wife and family when choosing who to grant a hotel licence to. Having a family lent a stabilising factor to the publican's reputation.

John though, had other ideas. He had no time for a wife and family and although he thought it might be nice to have some company in his bed, he had no need for a wife to take care of him, because the hotel cooks and housemaids took care of that. John was not a saint though and he was lucky that friends such as Fawkner and Black Dick knew of the clean places where he could enjoy an afternoon or evening's entertainment of the female kind. He was also not keen on taking on the responsibility of a family before he had paid off Mary for the hotel. Mary thought that it made sense to 'gift' The Scottish Chiefs to John as allowed for in her Father's Will, but John was having none of that. The hotel remained Mary's until John could pay it off. Sometimes John felt disappointed that Sandy had not left him anything in his will, as he had been John's 'father' for as long, in fact longer, than he was Mary's. He settled with the thought that

Sandy had not thought of dying at age of 48, still being very hale and hearty. And as his mother said, the will that he made in 1815 was made to try and entice Ann to Van Diemen's Land, before his farm had really started to be a success, and probably not well thought out.

Mary went through her period of mourning at home with her mother, but she felt bad that she didn't feel the kind of unhappiness that a wife should for her dead husband. Sadly, she felt that she didn't even really know Jeremiah, having seen so little of him after their wedding and until he died.

She knew so much more about Thomas Beswick, who, if she was honest, she had fallen in love with months before Jeremiah got sick. While trying to maintain an air of mourning, Mary slowly started to come to the big house when Thomas visited her mother with patterns and new shoes, and before they knew it, it was just like before Jeremiah got sick, and Thomas was her 'business friend'.

It wasn't long before neither of them could hide their true feelings for each other. When Mary confided her feelings of shame to her mother, Ann was not surprised by the news.

"Mary. Darling. It is no bad thing to be in love. You have known Thomas now for almost the same time as you knew Jeremiah, and if I might say, I think Tom is a far better match for you. He's certainly a better match for the rest of us here. He's been here often enough in the past few months. And besides, I married my Thomas just six months after your father died."

So, with the Brennan's blessing, the arrangements were made for the marriage of Mary Peck and Thomas Beswick. As Thomas and all the women had business interests together that were conducted from the big house at the McKenzie farm (as it was still known), it was decided that for the time being the newly wed Beswick's would live in Mary's house that she had shared with Jeremiah. This would ensure that there was as little as possible disruption to little Mary Ann who was a fussy baby.

"Well then, we can't be having two Thomas's around here now can we," said Thomas Brennan over dinner as they were discussing the arrangements "And two Thomas B's as well, to be sure. So, you are going to be Tom from now on lad. I'm bigger and older so I get the longer name," he laughed.

And because Jeremiah had hardly been around and Tom Beswick had been, there was little disruption or transition with the new arrangements. The only thing was that poor Thomas now realised that he had again inherited a step-son-in-law who was not going to be up to running any of these farms that were now in his name. Tom was happy sitting with the women discussing fashion and gossip, while Thomas and the men were out doing their hard day's work to make sure that the farms kept going and kept being profitable. But at 68, Thomas was starting to find it hard to do everything that he used to. Certainly, he was no longer able to do the manual labouring jobs, and riding the horses or even driving the gig from farm to farm took too much of a toll on him. He had started getting the foreman to come to see him at the McKenzie farm to report on their work rather than he travel to see them. And with Tom Beswick came another 50 acres at Morven that had to be managed. Tom had already asked but had also assumed that Thomas would take on the management of his farmland as well now that they were all (apart from The Springs and the Peck farms) owned by him thanks to his marriage to Mary. Tom had little appreciation for either the amount of work that farming took, or the amount of money that the farms were bringing in.

While Thomas never said, he knew what his lot in life had become, but he secretly longed to forget all this work and to retire quietly with Ann and the youngsters to his house at The Springs. Ann, however, was not so keen on moving.

Ann considered the McKenzie house to be her real home and during both times that she had lived there she had turned it into exactly what she wanted it to be, homely, cosy, and welcoming for all. She had furnished and decorated it in such a way that it felt like a happy oasis in the middle of the busy hubbub of farm-life. And like her house in Sydney, it had become a meeting place for the local women, and a workplace for Ann and her best friends, young Tom now included. The house at The Springs was still lovely, and Thomas had put a lot of work into it over the years, along with the foremen who he had working there and their wives. But it did not feel like 'home' to Ann. Only the McKenzie house felt that way. And there were still the young ones to think of, Ann, now six and Elizabeth 11, but Margaret aged 15 and William 16 all still lived at home.

Tom's father had died in England in 1826, only three years after Tom had been sent to Van Diemen's Land. The letters he received from his mother were filled with sadness, bad news about health issues and her loneliness. Tom had decided to bring his mother out to live with him the year before, when he could see that his business was going to be a success and he could afford to keep her.

Margaret Beswick, aged 64, arrived in Launceston two weeks before Mary and Tom were married at St John's on 6 May. Margaret was welcomed into the life of the McKenzie home and was fascinated with what her black sheep of a son, who had gotten himself sent to the dreaded colonies, had achieved in the past 11 years. After a while of settling in she had taken to the care of the chicken's and pigs and spent her time tending the garden, all things that she remembered from her childhood, but had been unable to do at Seven Dials. She told Ann that since her husband died and the hotel was sold, she had spent her time moving between her children's houses but had never felt that she belonged or was made to feel as welcomed as she did here at Paterson's Plains.

Ann was glad that Margaret had settled in well and loved that she would also come and sit with the women and Tom as they worked on their latest commissioned garments and discuss what would be most popular for the next season.

Now that it was officially all his, Tom started to take an interest in the farm and along with his shoe-making business, took over the management of the brick making industry that provided an excellent source of income to the family. He employed two apprentices to run his shop in Launceston and travelled from farm to farm making sure that the quality of the bricks was being maintained. Thomas greatly appreciated this effort from Tom as it allowed him to take a small step back and have a bit more time to rest his weary bones.

 **1835**

As 1834 turned to 1835, Tom was invited by his friend Anthony Cotterell to a New Years celebration at John Batman's house at Ben Lomond where he and his friends were going to officially celebrate their recent announcement. Cotterell was a member of the newly formed Port Phillip Association that had the aim of settling Port Phillip on the mainland. They would be the first white settlers there. John Batman had been there several times on his trips to Sydney and declared that it was highly suitable for settlement, and he wanted to be the one to do so. Cotterell had already given up his job as Chief Constable of Launceston and had signed up as one of the members who undertook to share the expenses of the expedition. John Batman and his family, the surveyor Mr Wedge, members of the Association and others including Tom Beswick, made a picnic climb up the mountain to watch from the top as the sun rose on the New Year. Landowner John Glover who had not long arrived in the colony, and was an artist of some note in England, was among the climbers. Large, somewhat overweight, and 67 years of age, all marvelled that he made it, although they took him up on horseback, which considering the rugged terrain was no mean feat. Glover made some sketches there and they named a small lake on the mountain after him. The evening and the morning had an air of adventure and excitement and anticipation of the incredible journey they were all about to undertake.

A few weeks later, towards the end of January Anthony Cotterell married Frances Solomon, the daughter of landowner Joseph Solomon, at the new church at Morven. Frances wore a beautiful cream satin and apricot lace dress made by Ann and her ladies, with a reticule with an exquisitely embroidered scene from Cotterell's farm at Cox's Creek, and satin slippers delicately made by Tom Beswick.

At the wedding breakfast John McKenzie was interested to hear Tom's description of the New Years picnic climb as he divulged to the family that his friend John Pascoe Fawkner was also preparing and intended to go on a separate adventure to settle Port Phillip. John McKenzie had paid off The Scottish Chiefs and had been granted his publicans licence thanks to Fawkner. Ann gave him an extra squeeze when she hugged him goodbye at the end of the breakfast, she was so proud of her eldest son, coming from such a difficult beginning, at age 26 he had already proven to everyone that he was up to running a successful business.

More excitement was brewing for the family when young Margaret who went by the name Brennan, Thomas being the only father she knew, told Ann that William Renton Kerr had proposed to her, but that he intended on asking Thomas for her hand. Margaret just couldn't keep it a secret.

William Renton Kerr owned land near Talisker not far from the McKenzie farm and adjoining the huge 2,000-acre parcel owned and named Talisker by Major Donald MacLeod after his home town on the Isle of Skye in Scotland. 19 years older than Margaret, he was 35 to her 16. He had come out to Van Diemen's Land with his Scottish free settler parents as a young man. He had busied himself making his farm a success and helping his fellow neighbours. He only went into town for church and to purchase supplies. He had met and got to know Margaret on Sundays at church services. Thomas Peck, Jeremiah's brother, owned land next to William Kerr's, and other neighbours were Thomas Brennan's old friend John Jordan and his son Richard. Thomas Peck's twin brother Joshua owned a block next to the one that Thomas Beswick owned in Bathurst Street at Launceston, and another next to the McKenzie farm. As time moved on, the families in the area and their lives became more intertwined.

William Renton Kerr arrived at the McKenzie farm one Sunday afternoon and asked if he could speak to Thomas. The two men disappeared out to the back of the house and returned beaming with Thomas slapping William on the back. He called for Margaret and Ann, who were both inside excitedly waiting for the men's return.

Margaret came rushing outside, her golden curls bouncing, followed by Ann and Mary.

"Well girlie, William here has asked for your hand in marriage. What say you to that?"

"Yes, please father, I would like to marry him very much please." Everyone burst out laughing and Margaret threw herself into a surprised William's arms. Having lived alone for many years he was not used to such exuberance but was starting to realise that he would have to if he was to become part of this large, boisterous family.

"Well then," said Ann with a beaming smile, "I guess we have another wedding to plan," the girls giggled and looked across to see all the farm staff also watching and laughing, and old Margaret Beswick supporting herself on the stair railings as she also made her way to congratulate the newly engaged couple.

William Brennan was now 18, with golden hair like his sister Margaret, broad strong shoulders, and an easy manner about him, that made him irresistible to everyone. He was happiest when he was working on the farm, checking the fences and the shepherds, making sure the lambs were safe, overseeing the brickmaking and checking the crops.

Thomas talked to Ann one night about their handsome son. "Ann love, the boy has the touch for the farming but no land to go with it. I have been thinking that until we are ready to move back there, that we give him The Springs to manage, just so that he's got something of his own to work on. Tom is overseeing the bricks now so that's less that I need to do here."

"I think that is a good idea Thomas," said Ann "But you are 70 years old this year and I want someone here who you can trust to take care of things." It was decided that William would be told that he would have the use of The Springs and the profits from it once Thomas and Ann had no use for it. It was as good as an inheritance and the boy certainly deserved it. In the meantime, everyone was glad of the happiness that just having his good nature and easy smile around the farm brought to everyone.

Mary spent the second half of 1835 pregnant with Tom Beswick's first child. Two-year-old Mary Ann Peck ran rings around everyone at the farm, and like her spirited Aunt Ann before her she kept everyone busy. Little Ann, now seven, rushed home from school every day to play with Mary Ann and the two would be found getting up to all kinds of mischief. Thomas was now too old to get down on the floor to be a troll for the little ones, but he was still able to put on a troll growl and follow them around the house while they squealed with delight.

News arrived in the colony that both Batman's group and Fawkner's group had made it to Port Phillip, Batman beating Fawkner by five months. By all reports they were all doing well.

1836

Mary gave birth to her second daughter, Margaret, on the 9th of February. The babe was named after her grandmother Margaret who was delighted to have the time to cuddle and spend time with her new granddaughter. Mary Ann was indifferent to the red, mewling creature who she was told was her sister, much preferring to run off into the bush with her Aunt Ann.

Sadly, John Porter died in June aged just 33, from a snakebite while on a short expedition with some other men to look for new land near Longford. Elizabeth was left a widow with six children, the youngest Samuel not a year old yet. Ann, Elizabeth's mother Hannah, and the other women all gathered around to support poor Elizabeth at such a difficult time.

Chapter 19

 **1837**

*T*ime rolled on, and the world rolled on around the Brennan's

and their extended family, with the home base being the big house on the McKenzie farm.

Margaret settled well into life as a farmer's wife with William Kerr. Their house wasn't too far from the McKenzie farm, and she would take the gig there several times a week where she had started to do some of the embroidery work with her mother and the others. William and Margaret's first child, a daughter Ann, named after her grandmother, was born on 16 May 1837, and once again the workshop at the big house was full of the sounds of babies cooing and crying, but there was always a lap ready to soothe and entertain them. Elizabeth Brennan, now 14, took great delight in her two baby nieces happily taking them to change their clouts or supervise their meals. Ann was bored with little Mary-Ann now she was four, and poor Mary-Ann was usurped by the babies, Margaret, and Ann.

Elizabeth Porter married William Hughes in a quiet ceremony. William was a sturdy man with good farming experience and quickly settled into running both his own and the Porter farm and being a stepfather to Elizabeth's six children.

 **1838**

Little Ann Kerr was followed by a son, James in October 1838, but the family's joy at having a boy in the family after so many girls was as short lived as poor little James who failed to wake on his fifth morning. The supposedly hale and hearty young lad was found cold and still in his crib at Talisker. Ann swore that she heard her daughter Margaret's wail from Paterson's Plains.

Ann stayed at Talisker with Margaret until just before Christmas. The work went on at the McKenzie farm and sometimes the ladies would come to the Kerr farm to break the sadness with cups of tea and chatter.

 **1839**

Little Thomas Beswick Junior was born the following March, and the family had a new reason to be happy again. That made three little ones now living in what was called the small house at the McKenzie farm. Things were starting to get a bit crowded with six-year-old Mary-Ann, three-year-old Margaret and now baby Thomas, known to all as Tommy Boy.

A family discussion was held one night around the table at the big house.

"Now everyone" said Thomas "we need to start thinking about the living arrangements. The Beswick family is starting to expand, and it no longer seems fair that your mother and I, and of course Elizabeth and Ann, get to live in the big house, with you all cramped up in there."

"But" started Mary "We're never in there anyway Da, we are always here or at the workshop, it's fine for the time being."

Tom cleared his voice "But, um Sir, we thank you for the thought and yes we will need to move before too long."

"Oh, fiddle dee," said Elizabeth, suddenly jumping up but shyly covering her face "I guess I'll just have to tell you then like Margaret did anyway, I'm to marry John Emery."

Everyone stared at Elizabeth.

John Emery was the 21-year-old son of Thomas and Charlotte Emery. Charlotte had been the partner of Benjamin Butcher, a Private on Norfolk Island and came with him to Van Diemen's Land in 1810. After Benjamin died, she married ex-convict and by then free settler, Thomas Emery in 1820 after John had already been born. John's older stepbrother by ten years, William Adams had married one of the Jordan girls, Susannah.

John and his younger brother George, who was the same age as Elizabeth, would often visit the McKenzie farm delivering supplies from town. Thomas Emery had set up a side business to his farming pursuits, delivering orders to the outlying farms, knowing they were too busy to get into Launceston often.

Both Ann and Mary, and astute old Margaret Beswick, had just realised that in the past year they had noticed that when the Emery boys arrived, instead of Elizabeth running off to play with George and Ann while John conducted his business, Elizabeth would hang around to chat with John, and after business was conducted offer him a cool drink, and a walk in the garden.

"And when did this happen?" said Thomas rather aghast.

The women looked at each other knowingly. "Well," croaked old Margaret Beswick "I think it's not just lemon water you've been enjoying with young Emery in the garden then."

Everyone looked shocked, and then Thomas burst out laughing, followed by the others. Elizabeth burst into tears.

"It's alright girl," said Thomas "I think I'm the only one who didn't have a clue about this secret liaison. But do you think we should keep it quiet and allow the lad time to come and do the right thing? I promise to look surprised!"

"John already has land, and he is getting a house and everything ready right now," said Elizabeth.

"That's good then girl," said Thomas "Solves our housing problem. Once you move out, we will move to the little house and the growing Beswick family will move in here. And" he said slowly looking at Ann "we will start making plans to move back to The Springs."

Ann gave a little snort, but for the most part agreed with everything that Thomas had said. It would not be fair for them to stay in the big house while Mary wrangled a tribe of toddlers at the small house. And young Ann, at 11, had recently shown some interest in becoming a governess. She had spent some time with the Porter's down near The Springs, and listened to Elizabeth and her mother talk about how much they had both enjoyed their time teaching children. Maybe it would soon be time to move to The Springs, once all the chicken's had flown the coop.

William had built himself a nice house not far from the big house and had taken over most of the farm management from Thomas who was certainly glad of the rest, and their handshake agreement still stood. The Springs was to belong to William Brennan after Thomas passed. William had also taken to leaving for church early and going to stay with John in Launceston after he finished his work on Saturdays. Not only was John heavily involved now in the hotel industry, but he had also purchased several horses and raced them on the weekends. If William could get there on time, he loved the excitement of the races and the celebrations afterwards. And there were always ladies hanging around the horse races in their finery and they all seemed to enjoy William's company. John tried his best to interest him in the hotel trade, but as much as he tried, William stated that his heart belonged on the land. He wouldn't mind some of those horses though, he thought admiringly.

 **1840**

William Brennan was a witness to the marriage of his sister Elizabeth to John Emery at St John's, Launceston on the 24th of February 1840. Elizabeth's dress was the most outstanding that she had created yet, thought Ann. On a background of cream tulle, pink and cream flowers had been painstakingly embroidered, against a very pale leaf green underskirt and bodice. The bonnet was of the same pale leaf green with multiple ribbons of pink and cream, and of course slippers by brother-in-law Tom.

After the ceremony everyone gathered outside the church to greet the newlywed couple. Ann and Thomas had not known the Emery's very well before, but the first time they met William and Charlotte it was like a warm hug descending on them, and since then the families had been to several gatherings together. Charlotte, six years older than Ann was like the big sister she had never had.

Later, after the wedding breakfast, Ann sat with Charlotte on the wide veranda at the front of the big house, drinking tea with a touch of whisky. Being a beautiful summer day, a long table had been set out in front of the house and under some of the giant wattle trees that surrounded the areas that hadn't been cleared. It was a lovely balmy afternoon, with the trees swaying as a gentle breeze, with just a touch of cool air, wafted through them. The air was filled with the smell of honeysuckle and wattle seed, and the faint, distant squawk of the cockatoos.

I've had a good life, thought Ann. No not just a good life, I have had a very wonderful life.

There stood her still tall and brawny husband Thomas, who had stuck with her through all the good times and the bad times of the past 20 years. Even though he was an old man now, he could still make her giggle and she still liked to snuggle up in bed to his strong, comforting body.

There was John, tall, dark, and sturdy, throwing his arms around as he obviously described one of his horse racing accomplishments, his second passion. No wife yet, but a successful businessman in the town, liked by everyone. She had recently been talked into going to see one of his horse races, and she had to admit it was a lot of fun.

Mary, running around chasing Mary Ann and little Ann, and Tom standing by the table in the best suit of the day, apart from John Emery's of course, jiggling little Tommy Boy on his hip and whispering fascinating thing in his ear, probably about the latest leather he had acquired from Avery Stodges.

William, tall, blonde, and exceedingly handsome was surrounded as usual by a gaggle of girls, daughters, and sisters of wedding attendees. But Ann knew that for now anyway, William's heart belonged to the land and to the farms.

Margaret was there with her golden curls cascading down her back, clutching little look alike Ann, who struggled to get away. Ann worried that Margaret was a bit overprotective of her three-year-old daughter, but it was understandable after her terrible loss the year before. Hopefully she would have another on the way soon to ease the pain. The Kerr farm was doing well, and William was a kind, stable and attentive husband.

Young Ann was the only one of her own children now with dirty shoes and hem, having been playing out the back of the house with George Emery and the youngsters. She still had a few childhood years left in her Ann hoped. The group whooped and squealed as they chased each other down into the paddocks.

Elizabeth, the bride, looked radiant. She stood quietly chatting with her father about very important things, Ann knew, the things that only a father could impart onto his daughter. Ann brushed a tear away as it snuck out and ran down her cheek.

She thought of the friends she had made over the years, some, like Elizabeth Porter who was there at the wedding with her husband and all her children, the oldest Richard now 17. And Margaret Stodges, beautiful Margaret and her brother and his wife, some of the best people she had ever met. How lucky she was to have escaped England and met such wonderful people.

Off to the side of the house under the biggest gum tree, that Thomas had said was now a landmark and could not be removed, Ann caught a glimpse of something in the corner of her eye. Charlotte had just gotten up to stretch her legs and Ann was left alone on the veranda.

She looked, then squinted, then looked again. It was! Oh, my goodness it was! There under the tree in a shadowy mist stood a tall, broad Scotsman, next to a beautiful man with golden hair and a broad, beaming smile, and next to him, her beloved Mary Rose, small and lovely in her possum skin cloak, and David right there behind her. They were all smiling at her, and she smiled back.

Ann blinked her eyes to clear the tears, and in that blink, they all disappeared. But they had been there with her, of that Ann was sure.

She leaned back in her chair, took in a deep breath of the sweet warm air, and smiled to herself, a big warm, happy smile.

This has been a good life, she thought. A very good life.

Epilogue

Ann Brennan

On 29 July 1841 Ann Brennan died aged 48 years old. Records show that she died in a fire however no records can be found of how or when the incident occurred. In those days candles were used for lighting, and food was cooked in ovens and ranges with open flames, and it was quite common for people to die in fires. Women wore long dresses and had long hair that was easy for a flame to catch onto.

After such an amazing life, living through all the hardships and heartbreak that she had to endure, and that she did endure with an astounding resilience, how sad it is that something as common as a fire would take her life. But I like to think that Ann lived a happy life, despite everything that she was handed by fate. She never let anything wear her down, and when she was faced with obstacles, she found a way for herself and her children to survive and thrive. She lived long enough to see all her children, except for Ann who was 13 when her mother died, grown to adulthood, and start a life of their own, and she lived to see seven grandchildren born.

Coming from humble beginnings in Liverpool, we can surmise that Ann's journey to the other side of the world afforded her opportunities that she would have had no hope of living back in England. As with so many of our convict ancestors coming to Australia was the best thing that could have happened to her, even if she was brought there as slave labour to toil for and populate the British Empire. Ann seems to have had a fairly easy life for a convict, but not all of the convict stories are like this. Many women suffered greatly at the hands of sadistic Masters and many turned to alcohol, committed crimes to take them back to The Factory and therefore

197

escape the bad treatment from their Masters, or were driven mad by their forced labours. Ann seems to have been one of the lucky ones, thanks to her Scottish soldier. At a time when the average life expectancy in Britain was 40 years, many of our convict ancestors beat the odds and faired far better in Australia. Ann also arrived at a time when rules and regulations were fluid and the Governor had a lot of power and influence to grant pardons. Later convicts did not enjoy such leniency.

Although she lost two partners early in life and in quick succession, she had over 20 years with Thomas Brennan and it seems that it was a loving and stable relationship, and that they were quite successful farmers for the time and in that area.

David Rose's family

David's nephew Alexander Rose came out from England in 1824 to help him on the farm which he had struggled to maintain since Mary died in 1820. Young John Rose was only 8 years old, and it seems that Alexander took him under his wing.

Lieutenant David Rose
73rd Regiment of Foot
1756-1826

David died in 1826 when John was 14 and Alexander married Isabella Robley in Launceston in 1831. Isabella and Alexander had two sons David and William who were born at Corra Lynn. Isabella had inherited three substantial parcels of land from a wealthy widow, Mary Smith, who was a prominent racehorse owner and breeder. Isabella's mother Elizabeth Riches was a convict, who had arrived on the *Lady Nelson* in 1812, and who Mary Smith had befriended. Sadly, Isabella died on 5th October 1840.

In 1841, John Rose was 25 and capable of running Corra Lynn by himself, so the widowed Alexander sailed to Scotland with his sons on the *Mona* in February 1841. Back in Scotland, Alexander married Madeline McTavish on 17 November 1842 at Kirkhill Inverness. The family then returned to Tasmania where Madeline and Alexander had six children, all born at Corra Lynn, where they would have grown up with John Rose's children. Alexander Rose owned a large amount of land (including 'Glenorchy' at Port Phillip), hotels and racehorses. He went on to become a member of the Tasmanian Parliament. He died in 1870 leaving his estate to his wife Madeline and his son Alexander. When he died the flags on board the steamers Derwent and Tamar, and other vessels in port, were displayed half-mast high, in a token of respect.

Alexander's son, also named Alexander died at Corra Lynn in 1871 aged 26, so it seems that some of the family stayed on at Corra Lynn with John Rose and his family.

It appears that David and Mary's son John (known as John Rose Esquire) ran Corra Lynn sometimes on his own and sometimes with his older cousin Alexander, until his death in 1878 aged 63.

He was 40 years old before he married Ann Caswell in 1855. They had a son who was named John in 1849 and then Mary Ann in 1856 and Elizabeth in 1859.

Daughter Mary Ann married Richard Fahey and had 10 children (their wedding portrait is shown on the left).

John Junior married Eliza Peck, who was Joshua Pecks' granddaughter (Jeremiah's brother).

Donald and Mary Sutherland

In addition to their own children, Donald & Mary (who became known as Marianne) also raised their illegitimate granddaughter, Sarah, who was born to daughter Rosetta in 1836. Sarah later married the son of the neighbouring Lette family at Curramore (Jeremiah Pecks' sister Elizabeth's family), John Maximus Lette, and they became early pioneers of the Monaro region of New South Wales and had a family of 9 children.

Donald died in 1865 aged 79 and he and Marianne are buried in a family grave at St. Andrew's Uniting Church at Evandale, Tasmania. The grave also contains the remains of their youngest daughter, Jane Whittle; their eldest daughter Rosetta Cornish together with her husband, John Cornish and the Cornish's daughter, Janet who died aged 17 years.

Elizabeth Murphy/Porter/Hughes

Elizabeth died on Christmas day in 1847 aged 43, leaving six children, the eldest Richard being 25 and the youngest Samuel just 12.

Thomas Brennan

Thomas was 75 when Ann died, and under his care the many farming interests owned by him, Ann and Mary and the land inherited from Jeremiah Peck and Thomas Beswick, thrived. It is unknown if he ever did get back to his home at The Springs. When Thomas died in 1850 aged 84, he was living with Thomas and Mary Beswick at Paterson's Plains, and Thomas signed as witness on his death certificate. It seems likely that he stayed on with his eldest stepdaughter to look after him in his old age.

Mary Beswick Snr

Thomas' mother was living with Thomas and Mary when she died in 1847 aged 75.

John McKenzie

John was a hotel proprietor in Launceston. He had the Scottish Chiefs hotel on the corner of Wellington and Canning Streets 1836 - 1845, and later the Mason's Arms in Wellington Street, and another at Gravelly Beach. A J. McKenzie also owned a hotel at a tin mining town called Morina, where William Brennan also possibly worked. John married Catherine McKinnon in 1842. No records of children can be found, but in his research, David Beswick (a descendant of Thomas) notes that there are people in the area who claim to be descendants of John McKenzie the publican.

Thomas and Mary Beswick

On 24 May 1840 little Margaret Beswick, the first daughter of Mary McKenzie and Thomas Beswick, died of tonsillitis aged 4 years old. This was a very common thing back in the days before penicillin when any type of infection could kill quickly.

Mary and Thomas Beswick lived at the McKenzie farm for many years. They added more children to their family. When Ann died, they had Mary Peck who was 9 years old, and Thomas who was two. Twins were born in October 1841 (3 months after Mary's mother Ann had died) and they were named Margaret and Martha, but sadly Martha didn't survive. Jane, who is the authors Great Great Grandmother was born in 1843 and Louisa was born in 1845 but died aged just 8 years old. Sarah was born in 1848, Charlotte in 1851 and Samuel was born in 1854.

There was a major Depression in the 1840s, experienced Australia-wide, that put a major halt to economic growth in Van Diemen's Land. The continued low price of wool in the London market after 1837, the 1839 English recession, the collapse of the mainland markets for grain and livestock, and the downturn of Tasmanian capital invested in Port Phillip speculations led to the Depression. Goods piled up in shops as lower earning power led to reduced spending. The influx of British capital ceased. Banks restricted credit. By 1843, bankruptcies no longer involved mainly small retail traders and merchants, but extended to the farm owners.

To add to the problems, transportation of convicts to New South Wales was ceased in 1840 and 1842 saw the biggest influx of convicts to Van Diemen's Land, 5,329. Free immigration was also being encouraged which also served to create a glut in the employment market with free settlers, Ticket-of leave men and others all competing for available employment, of which there was not enough.

By 1845, land sales had ceased, and new taxes were imposed to raise finances. Fortunately rising wool prices brought a return to prosperity after 1845.

Despite the Depression the Beswick's don't seem to have faired too badly, however there are records of various mortgages on their many parcels of land during the 1840's, some for very little money, which shows that they were under some financial strain. They still had Thomas Brennan around until 1850, so perhaps his wise advice saved them until then.

Things seem to have gone very bad for them, however, around 1854. A land trust deed that was registered 1 September 1854 transferred ownership of the farm at Patterson Plains to Samuel Beswick of `Bernard Street, Russell Square, in the county of Middlesex in England, tailor', and William Hill of the District of

Morven, farmer, as trustees, for the benefit of Thomas and Mary and their children. The trustees or others appointed by Thomas Beswick had right of succession to the use of the property after the death of Thomas and Mary in such a way that their children and the heirs of Thomas would all have full rights to benefit from it.

We can only speculate about why all of this came about but it seems that Thomas Beswick did not have the same knack of running farming businesses that Thomas Brennan did and then he was faced with the Depression. It seems that his brother was a successful merchant in England, so Thomas must have reached out to him to try and save his interests. Samuel Beswick, who Thomas had not seen for 30 years arrived in the colony not long afterwards, and settled at Cressy where he became a shopkeeper.

In 1855, Thomas and Mary Beswick, followed Mary's eldest daughter Mary (Peck) and her new husband Martin Hardy to the Quamby/Oaks area and started a farm there. It is unknown if this implies that Thomas' brother took control of the land that he was trustee for, but they left their long-term home for some reason.

The land purchased by Thomas Beswick in 1855 was heavily mortgaged and his original land on the South Esk River was sold and his property in Bathurst Street, Launceston, was mortgaged. There were other mortgages of the new land registered in 1859 and 1861. Five years later he was forced to sell everything and while the sales covered the mortgages there was very little left.

In 1867 he seems also to have mortgaged to Thomas Peck (Jeremiah's older brother), his right to use the trust property at Paterson Plains. While the Beswick's seem to have been reasonably well off in 1855, Thomas had lost practically everything by 1867, and Mary's fine inheritance that had been built up by her father Sandy McKenzie and stepfather, Thomas Brennan, was lost.

When Thomas Beswick died ten years later in 1877 it seems that he was estranged from his family. He died in the Port Sorrell district `on or about' 16 January 1877 when he would have been 72 years old. His death was reported for registration by the Coroner at Torquay (now East Devonport) on 23 January. He was described as a labourer, and it appears that he died alone and was found dead some days later in circumstances that required a coroner's court to record a finding.

The following year Mary Beswick, then aged 64, married Richard Fuller, aged 65. Richard died in Launceston in 1884 and Mary died in 1886 aged 72.

William Wells/McKenzie/Brennan

The only record of William is of his death in 1897 aged 78. There was a William Brennan who was the Manager of the Sarah Ann Tin Mine at Morina in 1883, that may have been him.

Margaret Wells/McKenzie/Brennan/Kerr

Margaret and William Renton Kerr raised a large family at their farm at Talisker. William, who was 19 years older than Margaret died in 1876 aged 76. Margaret died on 14 January 1900 aged 80.

Elizabeth Brennan/Emery

Elizabeth and John Emery had twelve children, three of whom died in childhood. Elizabeth died in 1891 aged 68, and John died in 1895 aged 77.

Ann Brennan/Emery

Ann Brennan ended up marrying George Emery, John's younger brother, in 1846 when she was 16 and he was 21. Their daughter

Sarah Ann was born in May 1847 and then tragically Ann died of tuberculosis in November aged just 18. Little Sarah Ann then died from a chest infection aged only 15 months. George went on to marry again in 1853 and had a large family.

Captain James Wallis and Joseph Lycett

Captain James Wallis, Ann's Commandant at the prison in Newcastle, was an officer with the 46th Regiment. While he was Commandant in Newcastle, he instigated extensive public works in the town in a similar way that Governor Macquarie was turning Sydney from a gaol to a town. He was assisted by convict Joseph Lycett who was born in Staffordshire, England. Lycett was by profession a portrait and miniature painter. He was convicted of forgery and sentenced to transportation for fourteen years. He sailed in the transport *General Hewitt*, in which Captain James Wallis, an amateur artist of considerable ability himself, was coming out for a tour of duty.

Lycett reached Sydney in February 1814 and was soon appointed a clerk in the police office. In May 1815 Sydney was flooded by hundreds of skilfully forged 5s. bills drawn on the postmaster. They were traced to Lycett, who was found in possession of a small copper-plate press. He was convicted of forgery and sent to Newcastle. Whilst there he drew up plans for a new church which impressed Wallis, and the pair seem to have then paired up designing the many public buildings that sprung up under Wallis' tenure.

Lycett was given a conditional pardon, at Wallis' recommendation, and produced many privately commissioned paintings. Wallis left Sydney in 1819 and Lycett in 1822. Wallis went on the serve in the Army in India, retiring in 1826. He lived for a time after his retirement at Douglas, Isle of Man, and thereafter at Prestbury,

Gloucestershire, where he died on 12 July 1858. Lycett published a series of books with paintings of New South Wales and Van Diemen's Land.

There are many authenticated drawings by Lycett in the Mitchell and Dixson Libraries (Sydney), the National Library and Rex Nan Kivell Collection (Canberra), the Tasmanian Museum (Hobart) and in various private collections. Most are landscapes, but the Nan Kivell Collection has a series of thirteen water-colours of Australian flowering shrubs and three of trees, executed with great skill.

Anthony Cotterell

Cotterrell along with John Batman and fellow Tasmanian investors moved to Port Phillip on the Yarra River in 1835 and was one of the original settlers in what was to become Victoria. He later returned to Tasmania. He is officially remembered in the name of a hill in an outer western Melbourne suburb, Mount Cottrell, near Melton.

Cotterrell and his wife Frances had three children who were amongst the first Europeans born in the new settlement of Port Phillip.

The group 'claimed' extraordinarily large areas of land of up to 40,000 acres (160 km^2) or more each. The members of the Association claimed in 1838 to have shipped between 250 and 500 sheep each, and Cottrell is listed with 1,000. The Government of NSW did not allow them to keep this land acquired by treaty with the aborigines, and it is not known what happened to Cottrell's claim or to his sheep. His share in the Association was sold to banker and fellow member Charles Swanston in July 1838 for 411 pounds, which was about one seventeenth of the value of the assessed value of the 10,416 acres (42 km^2) which the Government eventually allowed them to purchase.

By March 1839, Cottrell was working as a stock agent, the first in Geelong, and as an auctioneer in the area West of Melbourne. Cottrell sold a wide range of Batman's possessions under orders from his executors seeking to recover funds to repay Batman's creditors after his death in May 1839. Cottrell's acquisition of his place of business came by virtue of an interesting legal agreement with Batman in January 1839, for which the deed still exists, in which he undertook to pay Eliza Batman, John Batman's wife who was about to leave for England, 60 pounds a year for the rest of her life in exchange for a peppercorn rental on a building in William Street.

In September 1840 he returned to Tasmania where several more children were born. Cottrell's original land on the Nile River passed into other hands in 1839 and he acquired another smaller property of 5 acres (20,000 m2) near Launceston that year. His later years were lived in Hobart where he died at his home on Elphinstone Road on 4 May 1860, aged 54.

John Batman

Before he led his expedition to claim Port Phillip, John Batman sought land grants in the Western Port area, but the New South Wales colonial authorities rejected this. So, in 1835, as a leading member of the Port Phillip Association, and along with Anthony Cotterrell, he sailed for the mainland in the schooner *Rebecca* and explored much of Port Phillip.

When he found the current site of central Melbourne, he noted in his diary of 8 June 1835, "This will be the place for a village." and declared the land "Batmania."

Using legal advice from the former Van Diemen's Land attorney-general, Joseph Gellibrand, and with the support of his Aboriginal companions from New South Wales and Van Diemen's Land, Batman negotiated a treaty (now known as Batman's Treaty but also known as the Dutigulla Treaty, Dutigulla Deed, Melbourne Treaty or Melbourne Deed), with Kulin peoples to rent their land on an annual basis for 40 blankets, 30 axes, 100 knives, 50 scissors, 30 mirrors, 200 handkerchiefs, 100 pounds of flour and 6 shirts. It is unlikely that the Kulin people would have understood this as a transfer of land or agreed to it if they had.

Governor Bourke deemed the treaty invalid and the land was claimed by the Crown rather than the Kulin peoples or any other colonists, including the rival party of John Pascoe Fawkner that arrived at Port Phillip later that year.

Batman and his family settled at what became known as Batman's Hill at the western end of Collins Street. Having sold his property "Kingston" in Tasmania (the property at Ben Lomond in the mountains) and brought his wife, former convict Elizabeth Callaghan, and their seven daughters to Melbourne, he built a house at the base of the hill in April 1836. His son, John, was born in November 1837.

Batman's health quickly declined after 1835 as syphilis had disfigured and crippled him, leaving him in constant pain. By the end of 1837 he was unable to walk and was forced to give up farming and move into trading and investment, but he greatly overstretched his finances and was left vulnerable by his reliance on delegating work to others. As the disease eroded his nose, forcing him to wear a bandage to conceal his ruined face, he became estranged from his wife. In his last months of his life Batman was cared for by his Aboriginal servants, who carried him around in a wicker chair.

Following Batman's death on 6 May 1839 his widow and family moved from the house at Batman's Hill and the house was requisitioned by the government for administrative offices. Batman's will, made in 1837, was out of date at his death as many of the assets bequeathed to his children had already been sold. Years of legal wrangling followed his death, led by Eliza Batman, who had remarried in 1841 to Batman's former clerk, William Willoughby, and had only been left £5 in the will by her embittered first husband. The case dragged on, even after Batman's heir, his son John, drowned in the Yarra River in 1845, aged 8, and its costs absorbed what was left of Batman's estate.

Batman was buried in the Old Melbourne Cemetery but was exhumed and re-buried in the Fawkner Cemetery, a cemetery named after his rival John Pascoe Fawkner. A bluestone obelisk was constructed in 1922 which was later moved to Batman Avenue before being returned to the Queen Victoria Market site in 1992. The obelisk is inscribed with the Latin "circumspice" meaning "look around," the entire city of Melbourne being his legacy. The obelisk also states that Melbourne was "unoccupied" prior to John Batman's arrival in 1835 which is clearly incorrect.

John Pascoe Fawkner

Fawkner was also interested in the reports of the southern coast of the mainland made by sealers, whalers, and bark cutters. In April 1835 he sought a vessel to take an expedition to Western Port. Although a 55-ton schooner was acquired and renamed *Enterprise*, several contracted voyages had to be completed before it changed hands. The day *Rebecca,* hired by John Batman, anchored off Indented Head, Fawkner was arrested and ordered to appear at the next General Session for having assaulted William Bransgrove, and was banned from leaving the colony for two months.

Despairing of receiving the *Enterprise,* Fawkner engaged the *Dolphin* and stores were loaded by 13 July. However, the ship's Master refused to take Fawkner to the area that he wanted to land at Port Phillip and after arguing, his party was told to leave the *Dolphin*.

Two days later *Enterprise* tied up at Launceston wharf, and after two more days of hurried loading left for George Town. While in George Town a sheriff's representative boarded and presented a restraining order to Fawkner because of debt.

Fawkner returned to Launceston to sort things out but was told that he must pay in full or remain. As he had some horses he wished to see loaded, Fawkner entered into a bond to return to Launceston on completing this business, but he didn't tell the ship's Master, John Lancey, until the *Enterprise* was already at sea. After a long argument it was decided that Fawkner should return to port pleading violent sea sickness to deceive the remainder of the expedition members. So, Fawkner was taken back to George Town and the rest of the expedition arrived at Port Phillip Bay on Sunday, 16 August 1835, two months after John Batman's group had arrived. A search was made along the southern shore to the north until, four days later, well-grassed land was discovered some distance up the eastern branch of the Freshwater River. 'Here we made up our minds to settle and share the land in the most satisfactory manner to all parties', wrote John Lancey. A camp was made at the place where the Yarra River flowed over a low rock ledge.

Fawkner himself finally landed at Hobson's Bay in October 1835 and at once began to lay the foundations of a fortune that grew to £20,000 in his first four years on the mainland. In January 1838 he added to his trade of hotel-keeping that of newspaper proprietor, as he had in Launceston. His Melbourne Advertiser was handwritten on four pages of foolscap for nine months until a press and type arrived from Van Diemen's Land, and it was then printed weekly until suppressed because Fawkner had no licence. In February 1839, with a licence, he began the Port Phillip Patriot and Melbourne Advertiser; this later became a daily, and he ran it in conjunction with a bookselling and stationery business. In 1839 Fawkner also added to his already considerable land holdings a 780-acre (316 ha) property known as Pascoe Vale.

Due to the nation-wide Depression Fawkner was forced to sell many of his properties in an attempt to weather the worst of the depression. In 1845 he declared bankruptcy and lost a lot of cash and properties however he had cleverly transferred the Pascoe Vale estate to his wife and the newspaper to his father. Such was his talent though, that within a year he had paid back his debts and had money in the bank again.

Fawkner then entered political life and was the first one of seven market commissioners and, when this work was taken over by the municipality, as a councillor. He represented Talbot in the first Legislative Council in 1851, and on the introduction of responsible government was returned for the Central Province of Victoria holding the seat until his death. During his eighteen years in the Legislative Council Fawkner spoke regularly and often (one member said he made the same speech for fifteen years) on all matters before the House. He was very outspoken about squatter's 'privilege', and when the goldfields opened in Victoria in 1851, Fawkner devoted much of his time to the legislative aspects of gold-mining problems. He was alarmed by the Chinese and American immigrants and saw both groups as potential sources of disorder. In September 1855 he wrote of 'wild Americans—who know no law but the Bowie Knife, the Rifle or Lynch practice'.

With advancing years Fawkner's health declined but he continued to attend every session, always wearing a velvet smoking cap and wrapped in an old-fashioned cloak. He had grown to be regarded as an institution and became more conservative in his views. In his last parliamentary sessions, he opposed manhood suffrage, the secret ballot, and payment for members, yet retained very advanced notions on the rights of married women and deserted wives, and the divorce laws.

Asthma made his voice weak and husky, and he admitted at the end that age and infirmity weighed heavily upon him, but while there was work to be done, he wanted to share in it. Though cantankerous and dogmatic, he was a selfless patriot, honest and, in his way, idealistic. His last words to parliament declared his faith: 'I believe the Colony requires new blood, and that, unless we get more working men here, the work of improvement must stand still, if it does not retrograde'.

In his middle years he had been spoken of as 'half-froth, half-venom', and in many ways was not a very pleasant character, but behind his almost violent aggressiveness lay the pursuit of worthy motives, and a freedom from immorality and corruption that was sufficiently rare in that generation to inspire the confidence of his less fortunate fellows.

His triumph over his early experiences and his struggles with autocracy, convictism, and corruption, demonstrated the strength of his purpose, and his rehabilitation and later career were remarkable. Fawkner died on 4 September 1869 aged 77 at his home in Smith Street, Collingwood, the grand old man of colonial Victoria.

Truganini

Truganini only has a small spot in the story, but I think that it is worth acknowledging her as another important part of Australian and Tasmania history who had contact with the characters in the story. Like Ann, Truganini was just another woman, another human being, caught up in the social experiment by Britain to colonise Australia with slave labour. She and her people got in the way of the British Empire, which was not allowed to happen. But like Ann, Truganini was a survivor and decided to make her own fate rather than have others decide it for her.

It is thought that Truganini was born around 1812 in the area around Bruny Island and her father was the leader of one of the tribes. When most of her family had been killed around her, Truganini made the choice to help the British government and try to help and save her own people, who were being killed off tribe by tribe by the white men. Truganini was instrumental to the success of Robinson's Black Line to round up all the aboriginal people and take them to his mission on Flinders Island. At the time Truganini was shown what was planned for the island and must have thought that it was a better bet for her people than being shot and killed.

However, once Truganini, her husband Woorraddy and the other aborigines who had helped Robinson arrived at Flinders Island in November 1835 it became obvious that the plan had been a failure as one by one the hundred or so displaced aboriginal people succumbed to white men's diseases. Truganini must have been devastated that she had played a part in the annihilation of her people.

She was renamed Lallah Rook by Robinson, but stuck to her traditional ways, shunning the attempts to make her change to the English way of life.

In February 1839, with Woorraddy and fourteen other Aborigines, she accompanied Robinson to Port Phillip. She and four others, without Woorraddy, later joined a party of whalers near Portland Bay. In 1841 all five Aborigines were charged with the murder of two whalers and in January 1842 the two men were hanged. In July Truganini (Lallah) and two other women, Fanny and Matilda, were sent back to Flinders Island with Woorraddy who, sadly died on the journey.

She lived with an aboriginal man called Alphonso for five years and then in October 1847, with forty-six others, she moved to a new establishment at Oyster Cove, in her traditional territory. She resumed much of her earlier lifestyle, diving for shellfish, visiting Bruny Island by catamaran, and hunting in the near-by bush. By 1869 she and William Lanney were the only full blood aboriginals still alive. The mutilation of Lanney's body after his death in March horrified Truganini who expressed her concern to the Reverend Atkinson, 'I know that when I die the Museum wants my body'.

In 1874 she moved to Hobart Town with her guardians, the Dandridge family, and died in Mrs Dandridge's house in Macquarie Street on 8 May 1876, aged 64. She was buried at the old female penitentiary at the Cascades. However, all her fears came to pass when two years later her body was exhumed by the Royal Society of Tasmania, authorized by the government to take possession of her skeleton on condition that it be not exposed to public view but 'decently deposited in a secure resting place accessible by special permission to scientific men for scientific purposes'. But horrifically, it was placed in the Tasmanian Museum where it was on public display from 1904 to 1947.

Truganini was the most famous of the Aboriginal Tasmanian's, but little has been written about her. As the faithful companion of Robinson from 1829-35, she assisted in bringing in her compatriots because she wanted to save them from European guns. The establishment at Flinders Island was a grave disappointment to her. Small in stature, forceful, gifted, and courageous, she held European society in contempt and made her own adjustments on her own terms.

Afterword

The seeds for this story were planted around 2013 when I first purchased Ancestry.com and started to explore and research my family history. For various reasons such as work and raising teenagers my interest and the time available to devote to my research waxed and waned over the years. I discovered Alexander McKenzie about four years later and was fascinated to know that I had a Highlander as a relative, being at the time very absorbed in Diana Gabaldon's Outlander series.

Piece by piece I put the stories of their lives together. But along with my maternal and paternal family trees (Sandy and Ann are from my paternal tree), I was also doing my husband's paternal tree, a little bit on my ex-husband's trees for my kids, and some for friends. By about 2019 I had the skeleton of the family trees on Ancestry for all of them. But what to do from there?

Then along came Covid and suddenly there was a lot of time and not much to do, although I was lucky to still be able to work from home, there were still many hours to fill in when I would otherwise have been out and about doing other things. I'm sure that you can all relate. I then discovered the Mixbooks program which allows you to add text and pictures as well as a huge range of backgrounds and embellishments to your pages. I got to work transferring my Ancestry trees into the books. I did one for each tree. They ended up being over 200 pages long, and for each ancestor, in order to properly tell their story and not just a timeline of events, I discovered Trove and Google was also my friend. From little tidbits that I found about their lives in Trove along with information I found on Google I was able to turn a list of life events into brief, but real-life stories about my ancestors. I was incredibly lucky to find the research of David Beswick who shares Sandy and Ann as his ancestors. David is a retired minister in the Uniting Church in Australia, and Professor Emeritus at the University of Melbourne where he has an honorary appointment as Principal Fellow in the Melbourne Graduate School of Education, and as a Fellow of St. Hilda's College. He had done extensive research into the family and published it online, bless him. It was from his writings that I found out the first intriguing information about Sandy and Ann's lives. However, even with all this information the stories were still only brief outlines.

I got an idea into my mind that maybe, just maybe I could write a book about some of the stories of my ancestors, and that they might be interesting for other people to read as well, not just for my children and grandchildren. It was then that I started reading as many books about convicts and the early settlement of Australia as I could. I read lots of non-fiction, but it was when I started on the fiction books, especially those based on the lives of the authors ancestors, and prominent people of the time, that my interest really piqued.

I started reading the books of Jackie French whose picturesque descriptions of everything she writes about brought colonial Australia to life for me. I adore the amount of detail that she puts into every chapter and have even tried some of the recipes that are usually scattered throughout her books. It was when I read the first book by Jackie, *The Angel of Waterloo*, that I first started to spend my reading time with the Kindle in one hand and my phone in the other googling the details of all the interesting historical facts.

I then found the works of Sara Powter and her late mother Sheila Hunter who weave amazing stories of convict and colonial times. The characters were so adorable I just couldn't stop reading to find out what happened to them. Their descriptions of early life in

Australia were vibrant and fascinating, and their stories powerful and intriguing and just beautifully written.

I just happened to be in a small bookshop in Forbes, NSW in April 2023, not really looking for anything, but I asked the shop keeper if there was anything on colonial Sydney as I was still a bit stumped about the details of Ann's life in Sydney, and what Sydney was exactly like when Ann was there. Again, it was like some force had led me to that shop and I found *Mary Ann and Captain Piper* by Jessica North. Jessica has done some amazing research into these real-life characters who were such a huge part of Sydney in the 1810's and 20's. I could now suddenly picture how Sydney would have looked in my mind, whereas it was a bit of a blur before that. The book is set in Sydney at the same time as Ann and Sandy would have been there, and her second book *Esther*, is also set around the same era. Jessica's detailed description of events of the time, and the town as it evolved, was priceless for me to be able to paint more of a picture of Ann and Sandy's lives.

In 2023 I started to write this book. I chose the story of Private Alexander McKenzie of the 73rd Regiment and his convict common law wife Ann because they both really resonated with me, and the more I learned about them and the more that I thought about them it was like they were compelling me to write their stories. I could see them in my mind, as I would any other family member. To me they became real people with real struggles and real emotions.

The survival instincts and the resilience of Ann, with no family to fall back on, reminded me of times in my own life when I have had to draw from the same well of strength. The adventurous nature of Sandy also reminded me of times in my life when I had done similar things, such as join the Army, and the camaraderie and friendships that I made, that endure today.

As the story started coming together it seriously started to become a bit eerie, but in a good way. I would be thinking about what I needed to write about, and I would start Googling and information specific to what I needed just jumped out at me. These were things that I am sure that I had looked for before but had not found and now it was like, if I needed to know what Ceylon was like in 1815, Bam, up would pop an article or a fully digitalised book with pictures. When I was thinking about where Sandy's land may have been in relation to modern Launceston, up jumped a map with exactly those details. It is hard not to feel that the research was being guided by something other than just me and Google.

So, to Ann and Sandy and the others, if you were there guiding me, thank you so much, and I hope that you approve of this book and that I have done justice to your stories.

Chapter Notes

There are parts of this story that are true according to records and research, and parts where I have had to fill in the gaps to make a realistic and interesting story and paint a picture of life during the early years of Australia.

Chapter 1

Chapter 1 finds Ann making her way from England to 'the colony', onboard the convict ship *Canada*. The dates and the ship are correct, the fact that she was at Newgate Prison first and that she went directly to Parramatta is correct. The midshipman John is made up however it was very common for the younger sons of British gentry to join the Navy or the Army as commissioned officers, many of them having purchased their commissions. It is well documented that convict women and the crew on their ships formed relationships during the 5 or 6-month voyages. We don't know what happened at Newgate or how or why she went to Parramatta Gaol. We do know that she arrived 6 months pregnant, and that her son John was born at Parramatta. It is true that members of The Missionary Society travelled on *Canada*, and on many other convict ships.

We know that Private Alexander McKenzie was stationed at Parramatta and that in 1812 Ann was listed as being a free woman and living with Sandy and little John in Sydney where he had been transferred to. Ann's journey to Parramatta, her work while she was there and how she met Sandy is all imagined.

Chapter 2

In Chapter 2 Ann gives birth to her first child in the Parramatta gaol which is probably true as she was there when John was born. While in the throes of labour she looks back on her life to date. The details of Ann's conviction in Liverpool and her time at Newgate prison are true and records of this are easily found. We know that she came out on the *Canada,* however John, the midshipman is fictitious. We do know the names of her parents and their dates of birth and death. Her sister Mary is mentioned in some but not all records, so it is uncertain if she did have a sister, although it is true that she was caught along with a Mary Clark at her first conviction, and that they spent time together at the new Preston Correction Centre, so it seems likely that they were related. We don't know what occupation her parents followed or what she did in Liverpool before her conviction, but Liverpool was a centre for manufacturing at the time, and in particular clothing manufacture, so it can be assumed that they worked in one of the factories, and there needed to be a way that Ann could easily access the cloth that she stole. Her father's sickness was imagined as a possible way that Ann may have got into thieving, however, the citizens were so poor at that time, many did turn to theft just to survive. Ann's time at Preston is true and her second conviction is recorded. The way Ann and Sandy decided to live together is imagined.

Chapter 3

In Chapter 3 Ann and Sandy move together to Sydney where Sandy takes up a position with the 73rd. The tasks that he was undertaking are assumed but were the common tasks for soldiers in Sydney at the time. We don't know what Ann did in Sydney. Making her a seamstress came from the fact that she was from Liverpool with its large textile trade, and that she stole cloth, which must have been easy for her to find. It is also true that after Sandy left to go to Ceylon (which is true), she was listed as a free woman 'off governments stores', so there must have been a way that she was making a decent living for herself and the children. We know that Sandy named them all as McKenzie in the 1813 muster (Census).

The descriptions of Sydney are accurate for the time. It was a time of great change for the 24-year-old colony, making the transition, under Governor Lachlan Macquarie, from predominantly a prison colony to a New World with so many opportunities for those who wanted it. Construction of government facilities and infrastructure, and commerce and trade were at its peak since the colony began. It would have been an exciting time to live in Sydney. The glamorous stores of the Wills' and Simeon Lord were real.

We know that Mary Taylor (later Sutherland) did travel from England with Ann on the *Canada*, and that she did form a relationship with one of the 73rd Regiment's Sergeants, Donald Sutherland. Mary was at the Parramatta goal with Ann. However, records show that while Donald went to Port Dalrymple in Van Diemen's Land with the 73rd Regiment after he arrived in Sydney he therefore didn't meet Mary at Parramatta. Mary was sent to Van Diemen's Land as a convict, having re-offended while at Parramatta. She is noted as being notorious. It was then that Mary and Donald met. She seems to have calmed down once she was taken under the wing of a strong Scottish Sergeant.

The Smith's, including Ann's best friend Margaret, are fictitious but typical of free settlers who came to Sydney to make a success as merchants, and most did, if they had a talent for it. Ann and Sandy's only child, Mary McKenzie, was born on 26 August 1813, but the details of her baptism are imagined.

Sandy's close friendship with Lieutenant David Rose is supposed, but probable, since they both served together, along with Donald Sutherland, for many years and through many postings and battles in the Army. David did discharge from the Army and moved to Port Dalrymple around the time in the book and his chosen land grant is close to and adjacent to the land later granted to Alexander McKenzie and Donald Sutherland.

The story of Murtagh as a reason why Sandy didn't also take his discharge before Ceylon is imagined, however unless he absolutely had to stay for some reason it is difficult to understand why Sandy didn't transfer to the 46th Regiment that were staying in Sydney, like many 73rd Regiment soldiers did, or take his discharge, when it became obvious that Ann and the children were not going to accompany him. Mary Taylor decided to join Donald Sutherland and went to Ceylon with him, with their young son.

Chapter 4

The time before Sandy left for Ceylon and his time in Ceylon is mostly imagined. We do know that he left with the Advance Party in January 1814 on the *Earl Spencer* with Lieutenant Colonel George Gordon in command. Descriptions of Ceylon at the time he was there can be found in records. The details of Sandy's birth and birthplace and his parents and sibling's dates of birth and death are recorded, as is his date and place of enlistment. The dates that he served in India are correct and there are records of him recruiting for the Dumfries militia, and then transferring to the new 73rd Regiment before they left for the new colony. The story about the soldier John Stevenson being executed for abandoning his post is real, as is the story of how the King of Kandy surrendered and also the story of the loss of the *Arniston* while returning to England.

Chapter 5

The story of Ann's time in Sydney is entirely imagined, we have no idea what she did while Sandy was away, except that letters were received for her several times while he was away. Letters to members of the colony were taken to a central 'post office' and the details were noted in the local newspaper to alert the citizens to go and collect their letters. Before that, and when there were fewer people in the colony, the letters would be handed out to individuals from the ships, but they often went missing or to the wrong people.

The birth of Governor Macquarie's first living son is true, and the celebrations are recorded in historical records. The discrimination by the exclusives against the emancipists is well documented. The story of the explosion of the *Three Bees* is true as is the story of the three fever ships. After the three ships turned up Governor Macquarie consulted with assistant surgeon, William Redfern, and several changes were made to how convicts were treated during their journey, and they started to arrive in much better shape. William Redfern had been a ship's surgeon who had been unwittingly involved in a mutiny and sentenced to death, commuted to transportation to the colony. On arrival he was immediately sent as an assistant surgeon to Norfolk Island, and after working hard there came back to Sydney where he worked as one of the main surgeons for many years.

The story of the Russian ship advising the Governor of Napolean's defeat, and the three-week party that followed was real, as was their finding out later that Napolean had escaped.

Ann's purchase of her own house is imagined as is her life as a seamstress running her business from her home. The story about the Prendergast's is all fiction, meant as a way of explaining how Ann ended up being convicted again for larceny in 1816.

Chapter 6

Sandy and Ann's reunion is imagined, however it seems probable that there were some discussions during this time between Ann and Sandy about her accompanying him to Port Dalrymple, as he stayed in Sydney until after her next conviction. The story of the Grand Ball to celebrate Napolean's final defeat is real and recorded in many historical records. The story about the conflict with the Aboriginal people is true.

Chapter 7

This chapter is all imagined in trying to think of a reason for Ann's next conviction, however the treatment of the exclusives to emancipists was real.

Chapter 8

The details of Ann's conviction, her time at Parramatta Gaol and her transfer to Newcastle on the *Henrietta* with John and Mary is all on record. What she did at Newcastle and her acquaintance with Commandant Wallis is all imagined, however the endeavours that Wallis and the convict Joseph Lycett got up to is all real. James Well's occupation is imagined. All that we know about him is that he was another convict at Newcastle. We know that William Wells was born at Newcastle in August 1818 and that by that time Ann was again a free woman. We have no idea how that came about, and so quickly. We also have no idea what happened to James Wells, I imagined his death as a way of explaining how Ann could, a few months after having his baby, leave Newcastle and turn up at Port Dalrymple to join Sandy. Records show that Ann was sent several letters from Sandy while in Newcastle. And we do know that on November 26, Ann, along with John, eight, Mary five, and 3-month-old William, boarded the *Prince Leopold* bound for Launceston.

Chapter 9

We know that David Rose had been at Port Dalrymple since 1814 and that his land was near a rocky landmark still called Corra Lynn, and that he named his property after the area in Scotland where he grew up. We know that the land grants for Alexander McKenzie and Donald Sutherland were adjacent to David Rose's. We know that David lived with an Aboriginal woman who he called Mary and that their son John was born in August 1815. And we know that Sandy arrived mid-1816. It is on record that Sandy was given government stores and convict labourers to start his farm and that for a while he worked in Launceston as a convict overseer, the same job that he did in Sydney but now as a civilian.

It is true that Sandy married 14-year-old Elizabeth Murphy in August 1818, and that her father had abandoned her mother and siblings. The relationship with Samuel Porter, who was a real settler, is imagined, to later explain her relationship with John Porter, Samuel's son. And we do know that Ann turned up at Launceston around the same time with her three children in tow. David Beswick's account states that Elizabeth was quickly sent back to her father, however this can't be true as her father had disappeared.

https://oa.anu.edu.au/entity/12452?pid=1475 Map of Port Dalrymple, Launceston, with the landowners in 1819, overlaid on a current map of the area.

Chapter 10

While the story of Elizabeth Murphy staying on as a governess and friend to Ann is all imagined, I like to think that it may have happened that way. Ann would certainly have needed some help with her three children and one on the way, in a place where she knew no-one except Sandy, David Rose and the Sutherlands. The friendship between the McKenzie's, Rose's and Sutherland's is imagined but it is more than likely true to some degree. It makes sense that the Scottish settlers and particularly the ex-military ones would stick together; as did the Irish contingent who had come from Norfolk Island that included Thomas Brennan, the Kerr's, and Jordan's. The workers on Sandy's farm are all imagined, but he did have convict workers, and it was very common for female workers to form relationships and marriages with the male workers. And it is true that once the convict workers had served their time well on the settler's farms, they would enjoy the benefit of their own land grants and their own convict labourers to help start their farms.

The story of little Margaret's birth is all imagined, but it is very true that before the relations with the aborigines turned bad, there were great friendships between, and, as in David Rose's case, there were many aboriginal wives in the new colony. There are records of aboriginal people participating in colonial ceremonies and it stands to reason that some of the settlers would have embraced the traditional aboriginal ceremonies as well. What a different country we would be today if everyone had been able to learn to live in harmony and learn from each other.

Chapter 11

There was a government muster In Launceston in 1819 and Sandy did register all of the children under the name McKenzie, but Elizabeth being on the register with them is fictional. The Reverend Youl did carry out a mass wedding and baptism day just before Christmas in 1818. Donald and Mary Sutherland made their relationship official at this ceremony. The Port of Dalrymple had not had a clergyman until then and many civil relationships had formed in the years prior. The Reverend Youl had a lot of catching up to do. It is true that after he performed the ceremony he had to go back to Sydney and wait for his appointment to be made official and his house built. It is also true that during this period there were arguments about where the seat of government for the area should be, with Governor Macquarie arguing for it to be set up at George Town near the coast, while the main population was settling near Launceston which had far better farming land. This went on for years, with large extravagant government buildings being built in the almost desolate George Town, some of which still stand.

The meeting between the Scottish contingent, including Sandy, and the Irish contingent, including Thomas Brennan is imagined, however the story that Thomas tells Sandy about his life is true. He and his partner Mary both came out on the Second Fleet and ended up at Norfolk Island. Mary died just before the second evacuation of the island in 1813, when Thomas came to Port Dalrymple, with others including the Jordans.

We know that Sandy died on 9 December 1819, but the way in which he died has been imagined.

Chapter 12

It is true that Sandy's death is the first entry that the Reverend Youl, newly returned to Launceston, made in the St John's church register. The funeral ceremony by the local aborigines is made up. Ann did marry Thomas Brennan on 28 June 1820, and the records show that the family spent some time at Paterson's Plains and some time at Thomas' property, The Springs. Mary Rose did die in 1820 and records suggest that David Rose had a bad time in the year beforehand, with his, and the Commandant's ethics being called into question over some government purchases. David appears to have fallen into a depression following this incident and Mary's death. It is true that he sent for his brother who had also been a Lieutenant with the 73rd Regiment, but that his nephew Alexander came in his father's place, and that he successfully farmed in the area for many years. John Rose was also noted as a land owner inheriting Corra Lynn and raising his own family there.

Governor and Mrs Macquarie did visit Van Diemen's Land in 1821 and they did visit David Rose at Corra Lynn.

Thomas Brennan Junior was born in May 1821 and did sadly die a few months later.

What Ann did to fill in her days and who she associated with is fictional, she may have been kept busy enough raising her little family and being a farmer's wife.

Elizabeth Murphy did marry John Porter in 1822, but it is unknown if either of them had any ongoing relationship with Ann and her family. They all lived near each other's farms, the Porter farm being not far from The Springs. Elizabeth's ongoing friendship with Ann is imagined.

Chapter 13

The story of Thomas Beswick's background and how he came to Van Diemen's land is all true and is easily found in records. The story of his time on the hulk is imagined, but it is true that convicts were engaged in learning trade skills while staying on the hulks and worked on the docks during the day.

Chapter 14

It is true that Governor Brisbane did overturn the decision to maintain the seat of government at George Town at the recommendation of the new Commandant Cimitierre and from 1823 the move to Launceston started. Elizabeth Brennan was born in April 1823, the first daughter to Ann and Thomas Brennan. The story about James Jordan and the other landowners is true. And it is true that it appears from records that Thomas Brennan was doing very well running the land interests of both himself and his stepdaughter Mary McKenzie.

Chapter 15

The story about Thomas Beswick's march from Hobart to Launceston and his assignment to the young Anthony Cotterrell is all true. Much of the story about the interactions between Thomas and Cotterrell is imagined but it is true that Thomas stayed with Cotterrell for the term of his conviction and that by the time he finished with Cotterrell and got his Ticket-of-leave he had a land grant that included a shoemaker's shop, and also property in Launceston (possibly a shop).

John McKenzie watching the building of John Pascoe Fawkner's hotel is imagined, however John did end up owning several hotels in the area and would have been going to Launceston regularly for church and business when Fawkner was building his business empire in Launceston, in particular his hotel The Cornwall. It's possible that John's interest was sparked by seeing Fawkner's success. The Cornwall hotel still stands in Launceston, and is now called The Cornwall Historic Hotel and is located at 35 – 39 Cameron St.

It is true that the new Commandant, William Balfour's wife died four months after arriving at Port Dalrymple, and that St John's church, where Sandy was buried, was undergoing renovations at the time.

Cotterrell's advancement into public service is all true. The story about Cotterrell and John Batman's involvement in the capture of the bushrangers Matthew Brady and Thomas Jeffries is all true and easy to find.

The death of David Rose in 1826 is true.

Mary McKenzie's meeting with Jeremiah Peck is imagined, but the story about his parents (First and Second Fleet convicts) and siblings is true.

The story of one of the workers at Paterson's Plains deceiving a group of aborigines is a story that was passed down the generations and recorded by David Beswick.

Chapter 16

The relationships between John McKenzie, John Jordan, Jeremiah Peck and John Pascoe Fawkner is imagined. The story about Fawkner's background is all real, as is his losing his publican's licence. Someone had to have taken over the licence so that the hotel could continue trading. Richard 'Black Dick' White was a real person and a very outstanding member of Launceston society. His friendship with the boys is imagined.

Little Ann Brennan was born in 1829. Little William Porter's death just before his third birthday really happened but the reason for his death is unknown, however death by tetanus along with so many other reasons is a very plausible thing to have happened in the days before vaccinations or antibiotics.

The story about what was happening at the time with the Aboriginal people is true and the story of John Batman capturing Luggenemenener and the two boys really happened. John Batman did take one of the boys with him to Port Phillip (Victoria) later on.

The wedding of Mary McKenzie and Jeremiah Peck did happen on 2 November 1829.

Chapter 17

Much of the story of Mary and Jeremiah Peck is imagined, however Jeremiah did get a publican's licence in 1831, so he did have an interest in that area. Accounts from David Beswick note that Mary appears to have lived for much of her life on the McKenzie farm or at The Springs with her mother and stepfather, even after her marriages. Mary's meeting and friendship with Thomas Beswick at this time is imagined, but Thomas did have property in the centre of Launceston at the time and it is probable that it was a shoemaker's shop. The uneasiness between the exclusives and the emancipists has been well written about and was a very real thing at the time, as was the division about the Black Wars, because at the time there were many aboriginal people who had befriended the settlers and many who worked alongside the farm workers or in government service, as well as many partnered with white settlers and with children being raised on the farms and in the towns. There was a lot of sympathy from some of the white people, but a lot of hate from others; and this was reflected by how the aborigines felt about the white people.

The story about The Black Line and Cotterrell's involvement in it is true. The story about Cotterrell, Truganini and Wooraddy is true.

It is true that both Jeremiah Peck and John McKenzie were publicans. How John's first hotel, The Scottish Chiefs, got its name is imagined, but he did own that hotel.

Little Mary Ann Peck was born on 3 Jun 1833. Poor Jeremiah did die aged 28 on 25 Nov 1833 but the reason for his death is unknown. There are records that state that he died after 'a long and painful illness'.

The story of Elizabeth Lette (Jeremiah Peck's sister) and her property Curramore (Curramaugh) is true. There is a portrait of Elizabeth Lette by the artist Robert Dowling in the Launceston Queen Victoria Museum.

Lette was one of the most successful early settlers in the region. He wrote in 1830 that he had acquired eight thousand acres of land by grant and purchase from the government and private individuals. Lette developed and ran his property with the assistance of 18 male and three female convicts and seven free men. Buildings included the house (56 feet square with two feet thick brick walls); three buildings each about 80 feet long (a combined stables, granary and wet store; a penthouse with attic; and a barn), and a well 70 feet deep sunk through rock. He had 90 acres of cleared land, over seven miles of fences, 650 cattle, 4000 sheep and 4 horses.

Chapter 18

The way in which John McKenzie came to own The Scottish Chiefs is imagined. It is just as likely that he bought it himself. The rest of John's story is also imagined as apart from details of his publican's licence, and notes that he may have married, there are no other records of him.

Mary and Thomas Beswick did marry on 6 May 1834, and Thomas' mother Margaret Beswick was living with them at that time.

The New Years celebration at John Batman's house with Anthony Cotterrell and the artist John Glover really did happen and it was there that the final plans for their expedition to Port Phillip (Melbourne) were confirmed. It is imagined that Thomas Beswick was invited by Cotterrell.

John Glover became one of the most prominent landscape artists in Australian history. The John Glover Society was established on 22 August 2001 to honour and promote Glover's memory and his contribution to Australian art. The society commissioned a life-size statue of Glover, unveiled in February 2003 in Evandale, Tasmania. It also runs the annual Glover Prize, which is held in Evandale. John Glover's work features in many prominent art galleries throughout Australia (and the world). His work has been the subject of numerous exhibitions and a symposium in Australia.

From 2004, The John Glover Society has awarded the Glover Prize for depictions of Tasmanian landscapes. It is the richest art prize in Australia for landscape painting. In 2019, the farmhouse once occupied by the Glover family, southeast of Launceston, was restored and 400 ha (990 acres) of surrounding land, which frequently featured in Glover's work, was heritage listed as 'Patterdale and Nile Farm'.

Anthony Cotterrell did marry Frances Solomon, and it is true that John Pascoe Fawkner was planning his own expedition to 'found' Port Phillip at the same time as Batman and his contingent. It's also true that Batman did beat Fawkner by five months.

Little Margaret Beswick was born on 9 Feb 1836 and Elizabeth Porter's husband John did die in June, however the reason for his death is imagined.

Margaret Brennan did marry William Renton Kerr of Talisker.

Chapter 19

The dates of the Kerr baby's births are correct and little James did only live for five days. Elizabeth Porter's marriage to William Hughes is true. Thomas Beswick Junior was born in March 1839. Elizabeth Brennan did marry John Emery and the story about his parents is also true. How they met and their relationships with the Brennan's is imagined. Elizabeth and John Emery were married on 24 February 1840, but the story about their wedding is all imagined.

Acknowledgements

I have already mentioned some of the amazing Australian authors who, without their stories piquing my interest, this book would not have been written.

The most valuable contribution to my interest in this story and the idea that it needed to be made into a book to bring the amazing and interesting characters to life, was the website that I stumbled on (as we family historians do) by David Beswick. David is also a descendant of Thomas Beswick. David has had an illustrious career, a mixture of ministry in the church and academic work in psychology and education. He is a retired minister in the Uniting Church in Australia, and Professor Emeritus at the University of Melbourne where he has an honorary appointment as Principal Fellow in the Melbourne Graduate School of Education, and as a Fellow of St. Hilda's College. David has done extensive research into the Beswick family and thank goodness put it all on a public website where I found this amazing information. Thank you so much David for www.beswick.info, without which I doubt I would have had enough facts to be able to put together such an interesting story.

I'd also like the thank my wonderful Beta (test) readers for their proof-reading and advice about the story. Watch out for the next one, coming soon!

About the Author

Facebook: Lee Boehm – Author

Instagram: Lee_Boehm_Author

Lee Boehm was born in Melbourne and raised near the beach in Adelaide. After leaving school she joined the Army where she served as a clerk until after her three children were born. She then started a career with the Australian Public Service and served in many roles over more than 20 years.

In 2023, Lee has three adult children and three grandchildren, located across Queensland and New South Wales, and travels to new destinations to live every three years with her beloved husband who is still a serving member of the Australian Army.

As well as writing Lee enjoys researching family history, making photo-books, reading, watching movies and series of many genres, and the company of her German shepherd dog and Siamese cat.